MW00477643

SHELTER FOR QUINN

BADGE OF HONOR, BOOK 13

SUSAN STOKER

CHAPTER ONE

*Q*uinn woke up and knew immediately she wasn't at her own house. The sheets she was sleeping on were way nicer than her own. But it was the smell permeating her senses that clinched it. Turning her head into the pillow under her, she inhaled deeply, sighing in ecstasy at the woodsy, masculine scent that filled her nostrils.

Almost scared to look around, she turned her head and opened her eyes, expecting to see John at her side.

The other side of the bed was empty. Which was weird, because now that she was waking up, she definitely heard slight snoring.

Moving her legs, she could feel she was still in the jeans she'd worn the night before. Not only that, but she still had on her blouse as well. She sat up in bed, holding the sheet and blanket to her chest and looked around in confusion. Then she saw him.

John "Driftwood" Trettle was sound asleep on the

floor next to the bed. If she wasn't seeing it with her own eyes, she wouldn't believe it.

Details of the night before came rushing back. The drinks with the girls, finding out Hope and Blythe were pregnant, the guys coming to pick them up, the men at a table nearby making fun of her face...and John losing his shit on them.

But it was his deep, determined words, "We're dating," that were foremost in her thoughts.

The massive crush Quinn had on the man was embarrassing. She knew he liked her back, but she was too gun-shy to do anything about it. Who wouldn't be after living twenty-eight years with a port-wine birthmark on their face and neck?

But apparently John was done tiptoeing around their attraction.

And she'd spent the night in his bed.

And he was asleep on the *floor*.

Not knowing whether or not she should soak in the moment, or try to get up and sneak around him and get the hell out of there before he woke up, Quinn bit her lip in indecision.

John hadn't taken advantage of her drunken state. She was still fully dressed. He'd simply put her to bed and presumably watched over her as she slept to make sure she was all right. A lot of men would've put her on the couch, or at least slept in their own bed next to her, but not John.

Snippets of conversations she'd had with her girlfriends over the last couple months came back. How she'd declared if she ever found a man who treated her like her friends' men treated them, she'd latch on to him and never let go. But she'd been so scared of giving John a chance, of opening herself up to more than friendship.

Watching him immediately go after the men who were making fun of her last night, and watching him sleep now—on the floor by her side—made something inside Quinn snap into place.

Maybe she'd been an idiot. John wasn't the kind of man to lead her on. He wasn't out for a one-night stand.

Settling back down on her side, Quinn propped her head on her hand and kept her eyes on John. She didn't look around. Didn't check out his bedroom. She could only stare at the man below her.

It was probably ten minutes or so later when he began to stir. Quinn didn't move, curious as to what he'd do when he woke up. He sighed, then inhaled deeply through his nose. He stretched, and she saw his forehead wrinkle in what she could only guess was confusion at the hard floor beneath him.

His eyes opened, and the first thing he did was look up at the bed.

Quinn didn't flinch when he met her gaze.

The thing was, when John looked at her, he looked at *her*. His gaze didn't drop to the red birthmark on her face and neck. He didn't look away nervously. He stared into her eyes and held her gaze.

"Morning, Emmy," he said with a deep rumble.

That was another thing. He'd started calling her Emmy because he'd said her eyes twinkled like emeralds. How could she *not* like that? "Morning," she replied.

"Sleep well?" he asked as he sat up slowly.

"Better than you, probably," she said honestly. "The floor couldn't have been comfortable."

"I've slept in worse places," was his nonchalant reply.

"Why didn't you put me on the couch?" she asked. "I would've been perfectly comfortable there."

He stood then. Unfolding from the floor and moving like a sleek panther, he sat on the mattress next to her hip.

Quinn rolled over onto her back to prevent herself from falling into him.

"Because I wanted you here," John said without a trace of guile. "I don't know if you remember what I said last night, but you agreed to be my girlfriend."

Quinn knew he hadn't exactly asked, but went with it anyway. "I remember."

He smiled. "And my girlfriend does *not* sleep on the couch," he said firmly.

"Why didn't you sleep next to me?" she asked.

"I may be an overbearing ass sometimes, and push you to do things you might not be comfortable with, but I'd never do something that intimate without making sure you were okay with it first."

It was a good answer. "I would've been okay with it," she told him.

"Noted." He brushed a lock of her chestnut hair off her forehead. "Hungry?"

Quinn thought about it and, despite all that she'd drank the night before, found that she was. Nodding, she said, "I could eat."

"Great. Feel free to take a shower, although I don't have any fancy shampoo or conditioner that you're probably used to. You can borrow one of my T-shirts, but you'll have to wear your jeans again. Nothing I have here will fit you. Is that okay?"

Sitting up, Quinn tilted her head at him. "And if it's not?"

John shrugged. "Then I'll go over to your apartment and grab something for you. Or I can take you home right now and we can eat breakfast at your apartment, or we can go out. Or you could decide to go back to bed when you get home. It's Saturday and you're not working today, so you might have plans."

It *was* Saturday, but she didn't have plans. Quinn spent most weekends holed up in her apartment. She didn't like going out in public if she didn't have to. Thanks to the stares and comments she'd heard over the years, it was simpler to not put herself in the kinds of situations that would be uncomfortable for everyone around her. "I don't have plans," she told him. "And I'd love to shower here."

John smiled. "Perfect." Then he simply sat there and stared at her for the longest time.

"John?"

"You're the only one who calls me that, you know."

"I know." And she did. Everyone else called him Driftwood. But Quinn had never really liked the nickname. Besides, it felt nice to be different. "Where'd that nickname come from, anyway?"

"It's stupid, really, but it's not like we actually get to pick our own nicknames. I was down in Houston assisting after a huge storm, and I jumped into some water to assist a woman into our boat. I saw what I thought was an alligator. I pretty much freaked out and practically threw her into the boat and scrambled in after her, yelling at my buddies to get their asses in the boat as well. Turns out it wasn't an alligator, merely a huge piece of driftwood that looked a hell of a lot *like* a damn alligator."

Quinn did her best to hide her smile. "Wow, yeah, I guess that sort of thing would stick," she said.

"Unfortunately, yeah." Then, without giving her time to comment further, he got up and went over to a large wooden dresser against a wall. He rummaged through one of the drawers and when he turned back around, had a navy-blue T-shirt in his hand. "Again, it'll be big, but since it's just the two of us here, I don't think it'll matter."

Without getting out of bed, Quinn said, "Thanks."

John walked to the en suite bathroom and disappeared briefly before coming back out and heading for the door. He turned to look at her when he was in the doorway. "I like your hair," he said with a smirk, then closed the door behind him as he left.

Closing her eyes and knowing she didn't want to

see what he was talking about, Quinn took a deep breath before slipping out of bed and heading for the bathroom.

Though, it wasn't really her hair—which looked like she'd been on a weeklong bender and hadn't seen a brush in at least that long—that caught her attention. It was the fact that he'd commented on her hair at all, and not her face.

Not that she'd expected him to, but as she stared at herself in his bathroom mirror, she couldn't remember a time when she was teased about something other than her birthmark.

Her hair really *was* impressive right about now, meaning it was completely out of control. She'd put in more gel than normal the night before, since she was going out, and as usual, after sleeping on it, it was all over the place. There was a snarl on the back of her head and it was sticking out in all directions.

A small smile formed on her face as she stared at herself. A glimmer of hope materialized deep in her heart. It was small, just a microscopic little ball at the moment, but she allowed herself to enjoy the feeling.

Still smiling, she stripped out of her clothes and turned on the shower.

Twenty minutes later, after showering, using a spare toothbrush she'd found in a drawer, and putting on the way-too-big shirt, her jeans, and shoes, Quinn made her way down the hall toward where she heard John puttering around the kitchen.

She hadn't seen any of his house the night before

because she'd been passed out, but she was fascinated by what she saw now. There were two bedrooms besides the master, one of which was set up as an office. That surprised her, probably because she assumed he'd have a workout room or something. She peeked in on her way to the kitchen and saw a big wooden desk with a laptop. A stack of papers was threatening to fall over and there were sticky notes all over the desktop. There were a ton of books on the shelves along one wall and a big comfy couch against the other wall.

Despite all the things she knew about John—he was loyal, in shape, dedicated, strong, bossy, and stubborn —there was obviously a lot more she needed to learn. She hadn't pegged him for a reader, and that made her feel bad...and excited. She couldn't wait to find out more about him.

Quinn had had a crush on him for months, and now she was going to get to know the man behind the one he let the world see. And she couldn't wait.

Wanting to go in and look at the books on his shelves, she forced herself to keep walking down the hall instead. He had a picture of an older couple on the wall, and Quinn assumed they were his parents. She could easily see the family resemblance. There were more pictures in the hall, as well. John when he gradu- ated from the fire academy, posing with his friends from Station 7, and even one of him holding a hose with a huge fire in the background, obviously taken by a photographer on the scene of a house fire.

Quinn quietly stepped into the large great room—and looked around in awe. There was a high ceiling and huge windows letting in the morning light. Dark purple pillows were strategically placed on the couch and the two armchairs nearby. There was a neat stack of magazines on the coffee table and a huge television mounted on the wall.

She again mentally kicked herself for having an image of John living in a place that looked more like a frat house than the neat, uncluttered home she was standing in.

A sound from the kitchen turned her attention from his furniture and lack of clutter to John himself. He was wearing a pair of jeans that molded to his ass, and a T-shirt with the fire station's logo on the back. He was currently bending over, searching for something in the fridge, and Quinn couldn't believe she was truly here.

She stood watching him quietly, enjoying being able to ogle him for a moment without him seeing her. John was a bit older than her at thirty-one, and at six-two, he was almost half a foot taller. His blond hair was in disarray on his head, as if he hadn't bothered to run a brush or comb through it since he'd gotten up. Quinn knew from experience that when he looked at her, his blue eyes would sparkle and he'd give her his entire attention. It had made her uncomfortable at first, but now she liked it. She never had to wonder if he was actually listening to what she was saying.

He had large biceps and a chest that made her want

to cuddle up into him and never let go. She hadn't seen him with his shirt off, but the few times he'd worn a polo, she'd seen a smattering of chest hair peeking through the buttons.

Simply put, there wasn't anything about John that she didn't find attractive.

And that scared the shit out of her.

"Hey," he said, obviously seeing her for the first time. "Are you going to stand there staring at me or are you going to come over and eat?"

Wandering over to the kitchen, Quinn stood by one of the barstools next to the counter. "Can I help with anything?"

John shook his head. "Nope. I got it. Sit."

Quinn immediately sized up the seating choices and took the one on the far left side.

"Don't," John said softly.

Looking up at him in confusion, she frowned and asked, "Don't what?"

"Don't hide from me."

Damn. He'd noticed.

Quinn tried to play it off. "I'm not."

He approached her slowly, not taking his eyes from hers. He walked right up to her and into her personal space. He took her elbow and pulled her gently from the nearest barstool and gestured to the other one. "You think I don't notice that you do whatever you can to always have people sit on your right side? That you wear your hair down all the time, and that you never tuck it behind your ear? I do. You don't have to hide

10

from me." John reached up and curled his fingers behind her ear, taking her hair with them.

She shivered from his gentle touch, but couldn't look him in the eye.

"Look at me, Emmy."

She did…reluctantly.

"You don't have to hide your birthmark from me. I've seen it. And now I've touched it." He ran the backs of his fingers from her cheek to her neck, where she knew the pink birthmark ended. "Don't be self-conscious with me. Not about this."

"It's not that easy," she protested, feeling the urge to shake her hair forward and over the mark. "And don't say something stupid, like you don't even see it or something."

"Of course I see it," he answered. "Just as you see the scar over my eyebrow. Just as you see the freckles on my nose."

"It's not the same," she grumbled, hating this argument.

"I know. All I'm saying is that it's a part of you, and I like you. When you're with me, I want you relaxed. I want you to be yourself. To not worry about what I'm thinking when it comes to this, or if it's too visible. I'm a safe zone for you, Quinn. Period. No hiding, no camouflage. Just you and me, two people getting to know each other better. That's it."

"I'll try," Quinn told him. And she would. It wouldn't be easy, but she understood where he was coming from. Honestly, most of the time when she was around him, she didn't think about her disfigurement. How could she when everything about John was larger than life?

"Good." He stepped away after a second's hesitation. Quinn didn't miss the way his eyes darted to her lips before coming back up to meet her gaze. "The big question is...do you like bacon?"

"Um...doesn't everyone?" she asked.

John chuckled. "You'd be surprised. How do you want your eggs?"

"Over medium."

"Coming right up. How are you feeling? Headache or anything?"

Quinn shook her head and got comfortable on the stool. "No. I'm never hungover. I don't know why. Guess I'm lucky."

"Definitely. But make sure you drink an extra glass of water this morning anyway. Don't want you getting dehydrated."

And that was the beginning of the most surreal breakfast of Quinn's life. John made sure to serve her first, continually asked her if she needed anything, and he went out of his way to make sure she had everything she wanted before he'd even taken one bite. Not once in her entire life had someone doted over Quinn like John did.

Not when she was a kid.

Not with any previous boyfriends.

Not with any of her friends, because they spread out the chores when they were together.

It was weird, and a bit awkward, and very eye opening.

Quinn supposed this was what Sophie was talking about when she said that Chief always made her feel like she was the center of his world.

She could get used to it.

The glimmer of hope in her belly sparked to life, and seemed to grow just a bit.

* * *

Forty minutes later, John was pulling up to Quinn's apartment complex. He pulled into a space right in front of the lobby doors and turned to face her. "Any big plans for the day?"

Quinn shook her head. "You?"

"Nope. I have today and tomorrow off, then I'm working a forty-eight-hour shift."

"Isn't that hard?" she asked.

"Not really. It's a lot of downtime between bursts of adrenaline-inducing action."

"I think it would give me a heart attack," Quinn told him. "Give me my nice and sedate nine-to-five job of sitting on my ass, any day."

John laughed. "Can I call you later?"

Quinn's heartbeat increased, but she tried to be all cool and calm. "Sure. I guess I need to give you my number."

"I have it," John told her.

She stared at him. "You do? How?"

"I asked Chief to get it from Sophie."

Quinn wasn't sure what to say about that. "How long have you had it?"

"About three months."

"Seriously?"

"Yeah. Quinn, it can't be a surprise that I've liked you for quite a while now."

"Well, no, but I didn't know you had my number."

"Does it matter?"

Quinn thought about it. "Not really."

"If it makes you feel better, you can call Sophie and tell her to ask Chief for *my* number," John teased.

"You mean she doesn't already have it?" Quinn asked.

"Of course she does. Chief wanted to make sure she always had someone to call in an emergency if she couldn't get ahold of him. He made her put in the numbers of all of us from Station 7, plus our law enforcement friends too."

Quinn knew that. Sophie had bitched about it, but later admitted that it made her feel cared for. Counting in her head, Quinn knew she had only three true friends' numbers in her phone. Sophie, Tory, and Autumn, all from work. Sad but true.

"Or I could just text you right now," John told her, pulling out his phone.

Before she could answer him, her phone vibrated in her purse.

"There. Now you have mine, and you can't not answer it because you think it's a telemarketer." He grinned, then sobered when she didn't return the smile.

"I'm moving too fast, aren't I?" he asked.

Quinn shook her head. "No. It's just…" Her voice trailed off.

"Just what?" he probed.

"I've liked you for so long, and I'm still having a hard time figuring out how we went from tiptoeing around each other to dating and me having slept at your place."

He chuckled. "Stop thinking so hard and just go with it," he advised. Then asked, "You've liked me for a long time?"

Quinn shyly nodded.

"Me too."

Then, as if it were scripted, John leaned subtly toward her, and Quinn mirrored the move. And suddenly they were kissing.

John's hand wrapped around the side of her neck, the side with her birthmark, but she wasn't thinking about the blemish right now. She couldn't think about anything but the way his lips brushed against hers and how right the moment felt.

John didn't take the kiss too far, didn't shove his tongue down her throat, and didn't move his hand from her neck. Eventually, he pulled back and licked his lips.

Neither said a word for the longest moment, but it wasn't awkward at all.

"I'll call you later," John finally said.

Quinn nodded.

"God, you taste so much better than I ever imagined you would," John said under his breath. Then he kissed her once more, a mere brush of his lips over hers, before sitting back.

In a daze, Quinn opened her door and climbed out. She grabbed the bag he'd given her to put her dirty blouse in and backed away from the truck. Waving once, she smiled shyly at him, then turned and headed for the lobby of her apartment complex.

After she went in, she looked back and saw him still sitting in the same place, making sure she got inside safe and sound. He waved and gave her a chin lift, then backed out of the space and headed home.

The particle of hope deep inside grew a smidge more.

"Please don't hurt me," Quinn whispered, then turned and headed for the elevator.

CHAPTER TWO

*D*riftwood leaned back against his couch cushions and clicked on Quinn's name. He'd waited as long as possible before calling her. He hadn't wanted to drop her off that morning, had wanted to spend the entire day with her, but he also didn't want to freak her out.

He couldn't remember where they were the first time he'd seen her, but he remembered how fascinated he'd been with her eyes. Yes, he'd noticed her birthmark, but it was the deep green of her eyes that had drawn him in.

Her finally agreeing to date him had been a long time coming. Driftwood had been infatuated with her for what seemed like forever, but she was so shy and opposed to a relationship that he'd begun to lose hope she'd ever give him a chance.

The night before, when he'd seen her expression after hearing the strangers' crude comments about her face, he'd snapped. He was sick of people being assholes. Sick of others not having the common decency to treat strangers with respect.

And he was done with Quinn pretending she didn't feel the chemistry between them. She liked him. He loved the way her eyes followed him when she didn't think he was paying attention.

But he'd known she was never going to take the initiative and ask him out. She couldn't even admit that she liked him. After seeing how surprised she'd been when he'd taken the men to task for being rude, he was done pretending they didn't want each other.

And when he'd informed her that they were now dating, she hadn't protested. Hadn't rolled her eyes. She'd simply gazed up at him with a half-confused, half-relieved look on her face.

"Hello?"

Just the sound of her voice was enough to calm him. "Hey, Emmy. How was your day?"

"Mostly uneventful. Just how I like it. Yours?"

"Same. What'd you do?"

"Nothing much. I read for a while, then I put a pork loin in the slow cooker. I had lunch, put in a load of laundry, got stared at by my creepy neighbor when I went to get my mail, cleaned up a bit around here, read some more, ate dinner, and now I'm talking to you."

"Stared at by your creepy neighbor?" Driftwood asked.

"How'd I know you were going to focus on that?" Quinn asked.

"Because. Tell me about him."

She sighed. "There's not much to tell. He lives down the hall and usually when he sees me, he goes the other direction, but this morning we both arrived at the mailboxes at the same time, so he couldn't ignore me. I felt him staring at me while I got my mail."

"Did you ask him what his problem was?" Driftwood asked.

"John, you know how people are. They stare. All the time. They just can't help it. If I went out of my way to tell off every single person that looked at my birthmark, I'd never get anything done."

"But you can't let rude behavior go on without saying something. Otherwise they'll never learn their lesson."

"Did you not hear me?" Quinn asked. "Every single person I pass stares at me. Oh, some at least try to be sneakier about it, but I'm a curiosity. I can't walk from my apartment to my car without one of the residents of the apartment complex staring. Even though I work in a lab connected to a hospital, I get stared at there too. You'd think after a while, people would come to their senses and stop it, but even doctors and nurses I've known for years can't help themselves."

Driftwood hated that. "I'm sorry, Emmy."

"Don't feel sorry for me," she said fiercely.

"I don't feel sorry for *you*," Driftwood told her. "I'm sorry that *they* can't get over their fascination, and that they make you feel uncomfortable."

She sighed once again. "I know. It's just…if you're

going to spend every minute of the time you're with me glaring at other people and telling them off, this isn't going to work between us."

Driftwood sat up straight, his heart hammering. "This will work," he said forcefully, then gentled his tone. "I'm sorry, I just can't stand when people are rude to you. It literally drives me crazy."

"I'm used to it," Quinn told him. "Honestly, most of the time I don't even notice anymore. I can't say I'm not self-conscious about how I look, because you'd know that's a lie, but when I'm with you...I actually forget about it most of the time. And you don't know me well enough yet, but that's a minor miracle. If you're constantly on a quest to educate the world about port-wine birthmarks or to make them realize they're being rude, that comfort I feel around you will go away."

Driftwood thought about her words. She was right. "I get it," he said. "And I'll do my best to ignore the stares as much as I can. But, Emmy, you can't ask me to let the rude comments go. I can't. I know I can't protect you from the whole world, but I can sure as hell try. Do you think Chief lets people get away with making fun of Sophie when she stutters? No way in hell. That's just not the kind of men we are."

She was silent for a long moment, and Driftwood shifted nervously in his seat.

"No one has ever stood up for me the way you have, and we weren't even dating."

He hated hearing the hurt behind her words. The

awe that he would actually go out of his way to try to protect her. It was infuriating and sad at the same time.

Driftwood knew some of Quinn's background from talking with Sophie. How her mother had put her up for adoption right after she was born because of the birthmark—which she'd discovered after overhearing a social worker discussing her case with a potential foster mother. How she'd gone from foster home to foster home. And how some of those homes had been absolutely horrendous. The other kids, and even some of the adults, hadn't wanted to touch her because of the mark on her face.

He hadn't asked for any more details, feeling as if that would be going behind Quinn's back and prying too much into her privacy. But hearing her confirm that no one had ever stuck up for her struck a chord deep within him.

"You've got me on your side now, Quinn," Driftwood told her softly. "You aren't alone anymore."

He heard her swallow hard and take a deep breath before she asked, "How was *your* day? What'd you do today?"

"Well, first off, I took a nap."

"A nap? You don't seem like the nap type," she teased, then groaned. "Oh no, the floor was way too hard, wasn't it? I knew it. You so should've put me on the couch. I feel terrible for taking your bed and making you sleep like crap."

Driftwood chuckled. "I didn't sleep badly because of the floor. I can sleep sitting up on the hard floor in the middle of a firehouse, with people coming and going all around me."

"Really?"

"Really."

"Then why did you take a nap?"

"Two reasons. One, I really was tired, because I got up every hour or so last night to check on you."

"To check on me? I was fine."

"You were drunk, and you were sleeping so deeply you didn't wake up, even when I carried you into my house and put you to bed. I didn't want to take the chance that you'd get sick in the middle of the night and choke. So I set my alarm to vibrate every hour so I could make sure all was well."

"John...you...that was..." Her voice trailed off.

"And the second reason I took a nap was because I wanted to smell you on my sheets."

The words seemed to echo between them, and Driftwood had a feeling if she'd been standing in front of him, she'd be blushing profusely.

She surprised the hell out of him by saying, "I understand that. One of the first things I noticed when I woke up was how good something smelled. It was *your* scent on the sheets."

Driftwood groaned and reached down to adjust his dick in his sweats. He felt as if he'd been hard for months. All it took was remembering the sound of Quinn's laughter, or smelling her shampoo, and he'd get a woody.

He cleared his throat. "Yeah. I can't say that I had the most restful sleep though."

"Why?"

"Because every time I closed my eyes, all I could picture was you lying in my bed. Us there together."

"John, I... This is weird."

"It's not. But I'm sorry. I didn't mean to make you uncomfortable."

"You didn't. Well, okay, maybe a little. But it's weird because when I was watching you sleep this morning, I was disappointed that you weren't lying right next to me."

"Damn," Driftwood said, running a hand over his face. Every word out of her mouth made it that much harder not to get up and immediately head over to her apartment. He'd just left her that morning, but he missed her.

"Too honest?" she asked.

"No!" he said immediately. "I always want you to tell me what you're thinking. I don't ever want you to blow smoke up my ass. You want to do something tomorrow?" he blurted, needing to see her.

"Um...yeah."

Closing his eyes in relief, Driftwood sat back against the cushions once more. Now that he'd finally gotten her to agree to date him, he didn't want another day to go by without spending time with her one-on-one. He knew a lot about her, but he wanted to know more. "You want to come hang over here? Or go out somewhere?"

"Over there," was her immediate response.

Driftwood didn't know what they'd do, but it didn't matter. He'd get to spend time with her, that was what was important. "Perfect. What time do you want me to come pick you up?"

"Oh, I can just meet you there."

"Let me come and get you," Driftwood pleaded.

She sighed, but relented. "Fine. What time?"

"Ten?" he asked. He wanted to come even earlier, but he didn't want to annoy her.

"Sounds good. Should I bring anything?"

"Just you, Emmy."

"John?"

"Yeah?"

"I'm nervous."

"About what? Me?"

"Yes and no. Not you in particular, but I haven't had good luck with dating in the past. I'm afraid I'm going to do something to screw this up. Or you're going to get sick of being gawked at wherever we go. People are going to talk. They're going to wonder what you're doing with me. Some might come right out and ask you."

"I hope they do," Driftwood said vehemently. "Look, I can't tell you I won't get annoyed, because I know I will. But I'll be annoyed that people aren't seeing how pretty you are. That they're being superficial assholes. If anything, they should be wondering why you're with *me*."

"You're kidding, right?" she asked. "You're gorgeous,

John. The kind of handsome that people fantasize over. I bet there are groups on Facebook right now drooling over a random picture of you that was taken at one of the fire scenes you've been on."

He shuddered. "God, that would be awful."

Quinn chuckled, and Driftwood loved hearing it.

"I'm as nervous as you are, Emmy."

"Why?"

"Because I don't want to say or do anything that will turn you off. I don't want you to regret giving me a shot. I'm a guy, I'm going to fuck up sooner or later, and I'm scared to death you won't be able to give me a second chance."

"I'd like to think I'm not like that," she said quietly.

"All I'm saying is that this is new to us both," Driftwood said. "Like any relationship, it'll take some time for us to get comfortable around each other and not worry about saying or doing the wrong thing. But I think the fact that we've known each other for months is going to work in our favor. And we do *know* each other. Maybe not like boyfriend/girlfriend, but as friends. I think that's a pretty darn good foundation to build on."

"I agree."

Driftwood smiled. "Good."

"Are you sure I can't bring anything tomorrow?" she asked.

"Nope. I have no idea what we'll do, but we'll think of something." He didn't mean for his words to sound as sexually suggestive as they did, but he figured

25

drawing attention to them by backpedaling would make things worse.

"I'm looking forward to seeing what books are on your shelves."

A burst of laughter left his lips before he could stop it.

She chuckled along with him. "Wow, that sounded like some really bad pickup line, didn't it?"

"It wasn't any worse than mine," he told her. "I'll be happy to show you my shelves. And I've got some chicken I need to grill up by tomorrow; we can have that for lunch along with some veggie kabobs…if that's okay."

"Sounds perfect. John?"

He'd never get sick of the way his name sounded on her lips. He'd always thought his name was super boring and ordinary, but hearing Quinn say it gave him a whole new perspective. "Yeah?"

"You really don't mind staying in tomorrow? We could go see a movie if you wanted. Or go out to lunch."

He could hear the trepidation in her tone, and figured it wasn't just Quinn reassuring herself that he wanted to spend time with her. "I really don't mind. I spend a lot of time being 'on' while I'm working. No matter how rude people are to me, or if they're out of their mind on drugs or something, we always have to be helpful and nurturing. It's nice to just sit and be me when I'm not at the station or working."

"Okay. I'll see you in the morning."

"Sleep well," he said.

"You too. Night."

"Good night."

Driftwood sat on the couch long after he'd hung up, thinking about everything Quinn had said. He couldn't imagine what life had been like for her. He'd done a lot of research into port-wine birthmarks, and just about everything he'd read said that people who were afflicted always had psychological issues stemming from being so different from their peers.

There was a huge emphasis on beauty in this country, and anyone who didn't fit the norm of the stick-thin, beautiful model was judged unfairly. He hated that for Quinn.

Starting tomorrow, he would make it his mission to be sure not a day went by without her knowing how much he admired her and how pretty she was to him. She wouldn't believe him, not at first, but hopefully if he said it enough, his words would sink in.

CHAPTER THREE

"S-So?" Sophie asked first thing Monday morning when they were all settled in the lab. "How'd the weekend go?"

Pretending she didn't know what her friend was talking about, Quinn said, "Fine. Yours?"

"Oh, don't give m-me that," Sophie protested. "We all know Driftwood took you home Friday night, and then when Chief called him to s-see if he wanted to get together on S-Sunday, he s-said he couldn't, that you were coming over. S-So? How'd it go?"

Quinn looked at Sophie and sighed. "It was perfect."

Sophie squealed in joy and rushed over to hug Quinn. "I told you s-so!"

"Told her what?" Tory asked.

"That when s-she finally let down her guard and let Driftwood in, he'd treat her right."

"And does he?" Autumn asked.

Quinn nodded.

"What'd you do yesterday?" Sophie asked.

"He picked me up around ten and took me back to his house. We hung out and talked for a while, then I got to look around his office and bookshelves. Then we had lunch, talked some more, and played cards. He brought me home around five because I told him I needed to get going."

"And did you?" Autumn asked.

"Did I what?"

"Need to get going?"

Quinn shrugged. "No, but I didn't want to wear out my welcome, and I figured he had stuff he had to do before his shift today."

"And?" Sophie asked impatiently.

"And what?" Quinn asked in confusion.

"Did he kiss you? Did you do m-more than that? I need details, woman!"

Quinn knew she was blushing, but pushed past her embarrassment. "He walked me inside and up to my apartment. I was going to invite him in, but he said something about how he'd had a great day and not wanting to hog all my attention. He was just leaning in to kiss me, but then my creepy neighbor—you know, Willard—walked by."

"What'd that asshole say?" Tory asked.

"Nothing. He never does. And I can't really figure out his looks. Sometimes I think he looks almost friendly, and other times I swear he's trying to tell me telepathically that I'm going to Hell."

"At least he didn't m-make the s-sign of the cross.

What's up with him?" Sophie asked. "It m-makes no s-sense. Do you really think he believes you're going to Hell because you happened to be born with a birthmark?"

Quinn shrugged. "My mom did. You know the notes in my foster paperwork mentioned she refused to touch me after seeing my birthmark."

"Don't even get m-me s-started on her," Sophie huffed.

"Please don't," Autumn said. "I want to get back to Driftwood kissing Quinn."

"Yeah, well, don't get your hopes up too high. Willard walked by and stared at me in that creepy serial-killer way he has, and John immediately got all protective. He pushed me behind him and glared right back at Willard."

"Ooooh, then what?" Tory asked.

"Then nothing. Creepy neighbor looked away and went to his apartment down the hall, and John was pissed. The mood was broken. He said he'd see me later and left…after ordering me to make sure I locked the door behind me. As if I wouldn't."

"I think that's s-so romantic," Sophie sighed.

Autumn rolled her eyes and Tory giggled.

"Romantic? What's so romantic about it?" Quinn asked.

"That he was s-so upset that s-someone dared look at you wrong, the only thing he could think about was getting you s-safely behind a locked door. I bet you a m-million dollars he desperately wanted to lock

tucked it back behind her ear right before he'd kissed her cheek, and she'd been so flustered by his nonchalant affection, she hadn't even thought about re-hiding her birthmark afterward.

Shocked, she immediately brought her hand up and fluffed her hair, bringing it out from behind her ear in the process and making sure it at least covered her neck.

John didn't say anything, but she knew he noticed.

They went through the line and chose their meals and John led them to an empty circular table near the back of the room. He pulled out her chair and waited until she sat before taking the seat next to her.

Quinn immediately felt awkward. She wasn't sure what to say. Talking to him on the phone was so easy compared to this. Even hanging out at his house yesterday was laid-back and comfortable. This? At her workplace? Not so much.

She picked at her mac and cheese and racked her brain trying to come up with a good topic.

"Relax, Emmy," John said softly.

"I can't," she told him honestly. "I feel like everyone's staring at us."

"No one is. They're all either talking medical stuff or looking at their phones."

Quinn took a deep breath and looked around.

John was right. No one cared that she was eating lunch with one of the hottest men she'd ever seen. Which was crazy. If she was sitting by herself eating and John walked in, *she'd* certainly notice him. She relaxed a fraction.

"How's your shift going?" she asked.

"Pretty good, all things considered. We've had one MVA, two patients with heart attack symptoms, two lift assists, and three smoke alarms."

After hanging around with Sophie and the other firefighters for a while now, Quinn knew an MVA was a motor vehicle accident, and a lift assist was when someone fell and couldn't get back up. She also knew better than to comment on how easy his day had been so far. That was akin to telling an emergency room doctor how quiet things were...inevitably, as soon as those words were uttered, things got crazy.

As if he knew what she was thinking, John smiled. "So, what are your plans for the week?"

She let him change the subject. "Nothing exciting. Just normal stuff. Tomorrow night, I'm going with Autumn to a farmers market near her house."

"Hmmm. What about this weekend?"

Quinn's heart sped up. She shrugged. "No plans. Why?"

"I'm working Friday and Saturday, but on Sunday, me and the guys thought we'd head over to The Sloppy Cow for a few hours. Nothing crazy, I know you have to work on Monday, but we haven't all gotten together in a while."

She smiled. Even though she knew they were dating, it felt good to be included. "Sure," she said as nonchalantly as possible. Hanging out at bars wasn't really her thing, but she loved Adeline, Blythe, Beth and, of course, Sophie.

"Cool," John said with a smile of his own. He opened his mouth to say something else, but a man set his tray on the table, across from them, and sat.

Looking up, Quinn saw a doctor she hadn't met before. That wasn't unusual, the hospital was a big place. But the second the man saw her face, he stilled and stared at her.

Looking down, Quinn stiffened.

"Dude. Not cool," John said in a quiet but stern tone.

Quinn felt his hand on her thigh, and when he found hers, he took it in his own and squeezed.

"Sorry," the man apologized immediately. "My name is Doctor Stuart Ballard. I'm visiting from Southern California, and I couldn't help but notice your nevus flammeus."

"What?" John asked.

"My birthmark," Quinn translated.

"Oh."

"I work at the Irvine Laser Institute and Medical Clinic back in California. I specialize in the treatment and management of children and adults with port-wine birthmarks, hemangiomas, and other vascular malformations."

Quinn winced. She'd done a lot of research on the treatment for port-wine birthmarks, and the consequences of not getting those treatments. Before she could cut the man off and tell him she wasn't interested in hearing his pitch, he continued.

"It's remarkable. You don't have any indications that you've had laser therapy, and you don't have any nodules forming yet. It's also still pink, whereas usually they start to turn dark red or purple by now. Interesting." He finally looked into her eyes. "I'd love to talk to you more about your skin regimen, your history, and about the possibility of you flying out to California so I can study you more thoroughly."

"Slow your roll, Ballard," John said with a glare. "She's not a specimen you can just shove under your microscope."

The doctor looked startled, then chagrined. "You're right, I'm sorry. I'm here for a consult and a conference, and I forget to act like a normal human being when I've been in the trenches, so to speak." He leaned across the table and held out his hand. "As I said, I'm Stuart Ballard."

Quinn tentatively held out her hand and shook his. "Quinn Dixon."

"It's good to meet you, Quinn."

She nodded at him.

John held out his hand as well. "I'm John Trettle. Her boyfriend."

Dr. Ballard's lips quirked up but he shook John's hand as well.

"I know I didn't exactly go about this the right way, but I'm serious, your skin is beautiful. You're what... twenty-five?"

"Twenty-eight," Quinn told him.

"Hmm. And older than I thought. Have you considered laser treatment?"

Quinn glanced at John and saw that he was still frowning at the doctor, but she didn't really see anything wrong with his particular question. Yes, he'd startled her by commenting on her birthmark. Most of the time people talked about anything but or said something rude. In many ways, his candor was refreshing. "When I was in college, I did a lot of research about it, but I wasn't in a position to pay for the expensive treatment at the time. Then I just got busy."

"Mmmm," the doctor mused. "And I'm correct that you didn't have any treatment as an infant?"

She shook her head.

"Unfortunate. Baby skin is thinner and the stain is usually smaller, so it's easier to treat."

"My mother took one look at me and refused to touch me," Quinn told the doctor bluntly. "Apparently, she said I had the sign of the devil, and signed the papers to give me up for adoption the day I was born."

The doctor didn't even look shocked. "Sometimes I really hate people," he said softly.

Quinn liked him even more. "Yeah. Well, I went into the system, and I don't think I have to tell you that the state wasn't going to pay for me to have any cosmetic surgery."

"You weren't adopted?"

"No."

"Right. You do know that, as you age, your birthmark is most likely going to get darker? That it will get dark red, then maybe even purple. And nodules will most likely form as well."

Quinn shuddered. She knew. She hadn't lied when she'd told the doctor she'd done research on her affliction. She simply nodded.

The doctor's voice gentled. "I know you don't know me from Adam, and you have no reason to trust what I'm saying, but you *do* have remarkable skin. It's still smooth, and if you were my patient, I'd one hundred percent recommend pulsed dye laser treatments before you get any older. It's an outpatient procedure, and most patients don't even need an anesthetic, other than cooling the skin. You'd need to undergo several treatments over a period of a few months, and it won't ever go away completely, but the lasers can make the stain paler. I'd have to examine you and get a full medical history, but from what I can see, you'd make a perfect candidate."

Quinn stilled. She'd do the treatment today if she could. She wasn't one of those women who refused to alter her body. She wanted the birthmark gone. She hated it. From the second she'd been born, the damn thing had made her life a living hell. Hearing Doctor Ballard's words was akin to someone holding a carrot just out of reach.

As if knowing she was on the verge of tears, John reached out and took the business card the doctor was holding out. "Her job and life is here in Texas. How long do the treatments take?"

"The laser treatments themselves don't take that long. You could fly out and have the treatment on a Friday and go home on Sunday. You'd need to do several treatments, two to four weeks apart. The short intervals have been proven to have more satisfactory results. History shows that because your stain is on the side of your cheek and your neck, the chance of success is even higher. You *would* have bruising after each treatment, however. This isn't an instant miracle cure. But I can guarantee that when everything is said and done, it'll be a lot less noticeable."

"And insurance?" John asked.

Doctor Ballard winced. "That's a crapshoot. Many insurance companies see this as elective treatment."

Quinn looked down at her lunch tray. She knew that. It was why she hadn't had it done before now. She simply didn't have the money it would take to have all the treatments she needed. It was silly to get her hopes up.

"With that said," the doctor went on, "I believe I can get Ms. Dixon a grant. Again, I'd need an in-depth medical history, and she'd have to consent to having a complete physical done at my clinic in California, but from what I'm seeing right now, she's an anomaly. And anomalies are good in my world. If she agreed to let me write an article on her case and treatment—all anonymous, of course—I have a feeling I could easily get a medical grant to pay for the treatment."

And just like that, the carrot was once again within reach.

"I can see I just dropped a huge bombshell on you, and for that, I'm sorry. But, Quinn…you are a beautiful woman. I know you might not feel that way, and you likely aren't treated that way, but trust me when I say that you're one of the lucky ones. I hope you'll be in touch."

And with that, Doctor Ballard got up from the table, his lunch untouched in his hands, and headed for the area where the trays were dropped off. He already had his cell phone out and was talking into it.

Quinn gave John a stunned look.

He didn't smile. "You okay?"

She nodded, but said, "No."

At that, his lips quirked upward. "It looks like you've got some thinking to do. We'll get references, make sure he knows what he's doing and that he has a good reputation. We'll find out more about this study he wants to do too. There's no way I'm going to let you be anyone's guinea pig." He ran his hand over the unblemished side of her face. "All I want is for you to be happy, Emmy. I can't say that I know what you're thinking or what you've been through in your life, but I agree with the doctor on one thing."

"What?"

"That you're beautiful."

Quinn resisted the urge to snort. "Oh, yeah, the beauty magazines are beating down my door to get me to model for them."

John didn't smile. "I know you don't believe me, but you are. Your eyes are amazing. Your skin is soft and smooth. You have a body that I've been doing my best not to gawk at whenever I'm near you. Yeah, you have a birthmark, but, Emmy, beauty is only skin deep. Cliché but true. I wouldn't be head over heels for you if you were a gorgeous bitch."

Quinn blinked back tears. All her life, she'd been called names. Freak, devil worshipper, ugly, hideous, weird...but John was the only person, other than her friends at the lab, who'd ever called her pretty.

His words weren't magic, they didn't take away the hurt she'd experienced throughout her lifetime, they didn't suddenly make her think she could enter a beauty pageant and win...but that little ball of hope deep inside grew just a little more still.

"Thank you."

"You're welcome. I'm guessing you're done?" John asked, gesturing to her tray.

Quinn nodded. She couldn't eat anything else. Not after the conversation with Doctor Ballard.

John held out the business card. "Take it, Emmy. Nothing needs to be decided today. We'll see what info we can find on him, and if you want, I'll ask Beth to look into him as well. If anyone can find dirt on him, it'll be her."

That actually was a great idea. "I'll ask her," Quinn told him. She liked Beth. She'd been through hell in her life, but she'd flourished after being hired as a kind of hacker for the government. There wasn't a computer system she couldn't get into, and she was able to track down information on anyone and anything with a few clicks of her keyboard.

Quinn was glad she was a friend, because having Elizabeth Parkins as an enemy would be frightening.

"Good. Come on, I'll walk you back to the lab before I head out. I'm sure Taco is getting impatient."

Quinn blinked. "Taco's here?"

"Yup."

"You came up here to have lunch with me and he's waiting on you?"

John smiled. "Yup."

"That was so rude!" Quinn informed him.

John merely chuckled.

"John! Seriously! That was rude."

"He doesn't care, Emmy. He's probably been texting the new woman in his life."

"He's dating someone?"

"Yup. Jennifer something or other."

"Is she nice?"

"Don't know. Haven't met her. She'll be at the bar on Sunday though. So everyone will get to meet her."

"Where'd *he* meet her?" Quinn asked.

"I'm not sure. He just told me about her the other day. But my point, beautiful, is that he probably doesn't care that I'm up here eating lunch with you, because he's likely in the truck texting Jen. He's been permanently attached to that phone of his."

"Well, tell him I'm sorry anyway."

"Come on. I'm guessing your lunch break is over, right?"

Quinn looked at her watch and nodded. John stood, then took hold of her chair and pulled it out for her as she stood. They took their trays over to the wall and dumped their trash and put them on the conveyer belt. Then he grabbed hold of her hand and led her out of the cafeteria.

For the first time in a long time, Quinn didn't even notice the stares she got. She was too overwhelmed with the chance meeting with the doctor and still getting used to the fact that John not only wanted to date her, but had no problem with public displays of affection. She wasn't used to anyone touching her.

John held her hand the entire way back to the lab. Outside the doors, he didn't even hesitate; he tugged her into him until they were touching from thighs to chest and leaned down. He covered her lips with his own in an intimate kiss.

Quinn's lips were still tingling when he pulled back and smiled down at her.

"I'm glad I got to see you today," he said softly.

"Me too," she replied.

"I'll call tonight if I can. It depends on what emergencies we get."

"I'd like that," Quinn told him.

"Me too. Okay. I need to go."

"Thanks for eating with me," Quinn said.

"If I could do it every day, I would," John replied. "Talk to you soon."

"Bye."

John ran his hand over her hair once more, then

smiled before turning and walking back down the hall at a fast clip.

Quinn watched until he was gone, then leaned against the wall. Bringing a hand up to her lips, she covered them and sighed in contentment. Why had she been fighting her attraction to John? He wasn't like other men she'd been with in the past. He was...more.

Smiling, knowing she was going to get the third degree from her friends and not even caring, Quinn pushed open the door to the lab.

CHAPTER FOUR

"So, things with you and Quinn are going well?" Sledge asked on Saturday.

Driftwood smiled and nodded.

The entire gang was sitting around the station, shooting the shit and waiting for another call. Crash and Chief had made dinner and it was Moose and Penelope's turn to clean up afterward.

"Good. Glad to hear it. I know you've had your eye on her for a long time," Sledge said.

"Had his eye on her?" Squirrel asked. "Shit, he almost beat the crap out of me for an innocent comment about her birthmark."

"And I still will," Driftwood said. "So watch it."

Squirrel smiled and held up his hands in capitulation. "Not me, man. I learned my lesson."

Everyone laughed.

"We're still on for Sunday afternoon, right?" Taco asked.

"Yup. You bringing Jen?" Crash asked.

"Yeah. She's kinda shy, and I know she'd appreciate getting to know the other women."

"She it for you?" Driftwood asked, honestly curious. He'd seen Taco become obsessed with other women he'd dated in the past, and he couldn't tell if this was a temporary thing or if it was more.

Taco shrugged. "It's too early to know. Jeez."

And that answered that...at least in Driftwood's opinion. He'd known the second he'd met Quinn that she was different. She wasn't like the women he'd met online. He couldn't explain what it was or how he knew; he just did.

Meanwhile, Taco had been dating more and more women lately, as if he was desperate to find what their friends had.

"Does she like animals?" Penelope asked. "Because Adeline will have Coco, and I wanted to bring Smokey."

"You can't bring that donkey to the bar," Moose said calmly.

"Why not?" she asked, turning to the large man with her hands on her hips. "He's as much my service animal as Coco is to Adeline."

"I realize that, but you wanted to drive, remember? Smokey won't fit in your PT Cruiser."

The diminutive woman harrumphed and collapsed on the couch with her arms crossed. "He fits," she said grumpily.

She opened her mouth under his, and he closed his eyes in relief—and ecstasy.

The kiss was the most passionate one they'd shared yet. He'd kissed her before, but every one felt like the first. She relaxed against him, and it made him feel ten feet tall. It had only been a week since she'd agreed to go out with him, and he'd still been afraid she would change her mind, decide she didn't want to date him after all. But with her lips on his now, he could tell she had no intention of backing away.

Moaning in his throat, he pulled away before things could get out of hand. The desire to back her up into her apartment and show her exactly how much he wanted her was strong, but he wanted to bring her to The Sloppy Cow more. He wanted to show her off to his friends. Wanted to see her relaxed and happy with their inner circle.

He knew Quinn was an introvert and didn't mind spending time alone, but he also had a feeling the more time she spent with Beth, Sophie, and the others, the more she'd want to. She'd see that they genuinely liked her and had no agendas. They'd have her back, just as he would, if any idiot felt the need to be a douche about her birthmark. She needed the other women as much as they needed her.

Because as much as he knew the others would stick up for Quinn, he knew she'd do the same right back. If Beth was feeling uneasy because of her agoraphobia, Quinn would be there for her. If someone said anything about Coco, Adeline's service dog, Quinn wouldn't hesitate to set them straight about the laws concerning when and where service pets were allowed. And he already knew she had no problem calling people out who were being dicks to Sophie because of her stutter.

Driftwood licked his lips, but didn't take his hand from the side of Quinn's neck. "You taste good," he told her.

She grinned. "It's my cherry lip gloss," she informed him.

"My new favorite flavor," he said, loving the blush that bloomed on her unblemished cheek. "Come on, let's get going. The others are on their way, and I don't want everyone to beat us there. Gotta get the good seats and all."

"There are bad seats at The Sloppy Cow?" Quinn teased.

He watched as she grabbed her purse then closed her door. She tested the knob, making sure it was locked, then turned to face him.

"Nope. But it's a thing with us. None of us like being last. Just go with it."

She smiled. "Right. Got it. Lead on then."

They chatted about nothing in particular on the way to the bar and Driftwood parked as close to the door as possible. He got around to Quinn's side of the car as soon as she was up and out and laced his fingers with hers as they walked to the bar. He hadn't missed how she relaxed every time he touched her. It made him feel good that he could soothe her in such a

Quinn.

"An unsweetened ice tea. With double lemon," she told him.

Nodding, Driftwood asked the group at large. "Anyone else?" They all declined and Driftwood leaned into Quinn. His lips brushed against her hair as he said softly into her ear, "I'll be right back. You okay?"

She smiled up at him. "Yeah, I think I'll be okay for the two minutes it'll take you to get a drink and come back to the table."

"Smartass," he teased.

As it turned out, it took longer than two minutes. Erin, the part-time bartender who they all knew, and who he hadn't seen since the weekend before when he'd taken Quinn home, had a million questions for him. She'd not only seen the altercation with the dude at the door, but she'd seen Driftwood holding Quinn's hand. She was understandably excited about the fact he was finally with Quinn.

By the time he made it back to the table, Taco had arrived with his date, Jennifer, and Squirrel and Blythe were there too.

There was also an odd tension that hadn't been at the table before he'd left. Immediately, his hackles rose.

He placed Quinn's ice tea on the table and his own soft drink, and put his hand on her thigh as he sat.

"Hey, Driftwood. This is Jen," Taco said, sounding oddly desperate.

"Hi," Driftwood greeted as he eyed the woman at his friend's side. Jennifer was a few inches shorter than

Taco. She had blonde hair and blue eyes. She had on a bit too much makeup for his tastes, but Driftwood couldn't deny that she was pretty.

"It's good to meet you. Hudson talks about you all the time," Jennifer said.

Driftwood saw Taco wince slightly, knew he hated the name Hudson, but no one corrected her.

Conversation continued, but Driftwood was more concerned about why Quinn was sitting stiff and uneasy beside him.

"What happened?" he whispered into her ear.

"Nothing."

"Quinn. What happened?"

She half turned to him, putting her back to Taco and Jen, and said softly, "It's not a big deal. When Jen walked up to the table, she stared at me a little too intensely. It was awkward, so Beth said something. It embarrassed Jen, and things were weird for a second. But she apologized, so...all is well."

Driftwood clenched his teeth. He knew people stared at Quinn. He'd been around her long enough to witness it himself. Every time, he wanted to get in the person's face and ask them what their problem was. But he knew how much she hated it when people drew attention to her birthmark. She'd rather pretend she didn't see the stares or hear the comments.

But to have it happen while with their inner circle was unacceptable. Driftwood was pissed he hadn't been there when the encounter happened, but at least Beth and the others had Quinn's back.

He tried to relax, picking up his soft drink and taking a sip. It was Quinn who ended up comforting *him*, rather than the other way around. She put her hand on his thigh and squeezed gently. Driftwood looked at her, and she smiled at him. He immediately trapped her hand against his leg and did his best to pay attention to the conversation going on around him.

He learned that Jen was taking classes at the local community college to become a nurse. She'd been homeschooled and had taken some time off to work for the family business before deciding to get her nursing degree. As the women talked, Taco had relaxed, and it was obvious how much he wanted her to get along with everyone else.

It was no secret that the women were close. And Driftwood knew as well as Taco did that if any of their girlfriends didn't get along, it would strain their own relationships. The firefighters were extremely loyal, and being able to hang out together and not worry about who liked who or who might be fighting was imperative.

Forcing himself to pay attention, Driftwood did his best to participate in the conversation and get to know the woman Taco was dating.

* * *

An hour later, Quinn was more than ready to leave. She had a headache, and she envied Beth, who'd said she'd had enough and had already left thirty minutes ago. It was exhausting trying to be polite to Jen. It wasn't that the other woman was mean, she was just trying too hard and it was making things increasingly awkward.

Earlier, Sophie had asked Quinn if she needed to use the restroom, and she'd immediately stood, needing a break from the group dynamic for a moment. But Jen had jumped up and said she could use a visit to the little girls' room as well.

With no choice but to go along with it, Quinn followed behind Sophie and Jen. After doing their business, and while they were washing their hands, Jen had turned to her.

"I'm really sorry if I made you uncomfortable when I first got to the table. I just haven't seen anyone with that big of a birthmark on their face before."

"It's okay," Quinn mumbled.

"You do know that you're s-still being rude, right?" Sophie had asked.

Jen looked shocked. "I am? I don't mean to be. I was homeschooled and wasn't around kids a lot growing up, so I think I missed how to pick up all the nuances on that sort of thing. Thank you for pointing out my rudeness. But in all seriousness, and I'm not trying to be rude again, I need to know about these kinds of things, birthmarks and stuff, because I'm sure I'll see them when I'm a nurse. Are you doing anything about it? You know, to get rid of it?"

"Get rid of it? That's not how it works," Quinn had told her. "You probably should go home and google port-wine birthmarks." She usually wasn't this rude herself, but she was tired and not very impressed with the woman.

"You're right. I will. In the meantime, if you want, I could show you how to wear makeup. I noticed you aren't wearing any. It would hide it so you could blend in better."

Quinn had clenched her teeth, but Sophie leaped to her defense. "Quinn doesn't need to wear m-makeup to be beautiful. S-She doesn't need to cover her face with that crap either. S-Society needs to chill out and embrace differences in others instead of judging them."

Silence had greeted her rebuke, and Quinn remembered how Jen had looked like she'd been sucker punched.

"I was just trying to help," she'd said.

"Thanks," Quinn told her, trying to be a peacemaker. "I might just take you up on that. I never really learned how to put on makeup properly, and I know if I tried with this, I'd just look like a clown."

Jen perked back up. "Oh, I'd be happy to show you some things."

Quinn gave her a fake smile. They'd left the bathroom and headed back to the table.

"Anyone want some water?" Jen asked. "I'm going to grab some."

"Sure," Quinn told her.

"No, I'm good," Sophie said.

The second Jen had peeled off to go to the bar for the water, Sophie said, "I can't believe s-she had the nerve to ask you that. Not after the way s-she s-so rudely s-stared at you."

"It's fine," Quinn had said, not wanting to talk about it anymore. "She didn't know any better."

"Well, s-she does now."

"Yup. Thanks for sticking up for me," Quinn had told Sophie.

"Anytime, Quinn. I m-mean that."

And now they were sitting back at the table, listening to the guys talk about some of the calls they'd been on.

"We're going to head out," John said suddenly.

Quinn looked up at him in surprise. He hadn't given her any indication he wanted to leave already. He hadn't asked if *she* was ready to go yet either, which seemed out of character for him. He'd always been very considerate, never making decisions for her, as he was right now.

But since she *was* ready to go, she didn't protest. She stood with him and hugged Sophie, Adeline, and Blythe. She gave Coco some scratches on the head, and said her goodbyes to the guys and Jen.

"You didn't finish your water," Jen said in lieu of a goodbye.

Thinking it weird that the other woman was that concerned about her water intake, Quinn picked up the glass and chugged the rest of it. "There. Now I'm good."

Jen beamed. "Awesome. I hope we get to spend some more time together."

"Me too," Quinn lied, and immediately felt bad. Jen

was trying. Too hard, but she was trying. It couldn't be easy to meet your new boyfriend's friends like she had. And women were notoriously hard on each other. Way harder to please and more judgmental than men.

John looped her hand over his arm and headed for the door after telling his friends he'd see them on Tuesday for their next forty-eight-hour shift.

Sneaking a peek at the man who'd yelled at her when they'd first arrived, she saw that he was still sitting at the same table with his friend. He glared at her, but didn't get up or make any move to harass her.

Belatedly ducking her head, Quinn walked alongside John and waved at Erin before he steered them out the door. Without a word, he headed for his truck. He opened her door and waited until she was settled in the seat before closing it and jogging around to the driver's side.

He put the key in the ignition, but didn't turn the truck on.

"Are you okay?" Quinn asked softly.

"Yeah. But you aren't," he told her, turning to look at her.

"I'm fine," she told him.

"I know we haven't been together very long, but I know you, Quinn. I've been watching you for a while now. I know you have a headache, and I know that you were uncomfortable in there. I can't say that I like Jen all that much myself, and forcing you to be around anyone when you're not feeling good isn't something I want to make a habit of. I have a feeling you want to be home on the couch reading a book, rather than social-izing. Am I right?"

He was. And that really struck Quinn hard. "Just because I'm a homebody doesn't mean that I can't take a few hours and hang out with your friends."

"They're *our* friends—and it does when you aren't feeling it. As our inner circle grows, I'm fully aware how hard it is on Beth to spend long periods of time with us all. It's not that she doesn't like us, it's just that she gets jumpy and uncomfortable. Sledge knows it, and he never forces her to do anything she doesn't want to. For her own happiness and health. That's what I want for you too, Emmy. For us. I want you to be able to feel free to tell me if you've had enough socializing. I can pretty much guarantee that I'll be more than happy to take you home and spend some quality one-on-one time with you."

His words made Quinn's throat close. She'd noticed how Cade watched Beth like a hawk when they were out. She saw the way he constantly monitored her and made sure she was all right. She'd thought it was nice, but knowing John wanted to be that way with *her* was overwhelming.

"I do have a headache," she admitted. She wasn't going to tell him that Jen was irritating, especially not when Taco seemed so enamored with her.

"Right. Do you want to go home? It's still relatively early. I could take you back to my place. I've got some Tylenol and maybe you can find a book to read from my shelves? I could make us some dinner while you're reading."

For what seemed like the first time in her life, going home and being alone didn't seem like the safe haven it always had been in the past. "I'd love to go home with you."

John rewarded her with a big smile. He leaned over and palmed the back of her head before kissing her on the forehead. "Close your eyes, Emmy. I'll have us home in no time."

Trusting him, she did just that.

* * *

Driftwood looked at his wrist. It was late. He was fully aware that Quinn had to get up and go to work in the morning. He had Monday off, but she didn't.

"Emmy?" he said gently, shaking her a little.

He'd done just as he'd suggested when they'd arrived home that afternoon. Had gotten her settled on his couch with a blanket, a book, a large glass of ice water, and some Tylenol.

He left her alone as he puttered around in his kitchen getting a simple meal of stuffed red and green peppers prepared. Every now and then he'd checked on her, getting a smile in return. They hadn't conversed, but somehow he felt more comfortable with her than he had any of the women he'd dated in the past.

Few had been content to just be in his presence. He'd always felt the need to entertain other women in one way or another. Conversation, games, sex...but with Quinn, it was completely different. She was happy to be in her own head space. To be in *his* space as she relaxed.

It was as relaxing for him as it apparently was for her.

By the time the peppers were done, she'd said that her headache was gone and they'd sat at his small dining room table for an hour and a half, talking and laughing together. Long after they'd finished eating, they talked about everything from politics, her view on orcas (that they were truly killers who were just waiting in the oceans to attack and eat people), to his parents. The conversation was easy, as if they'd been friends forever. It felt right.

She helped him put the dishes into the dishwasher, and then they'd settled onto his couch and started watching last night's episode of *Live PD* that he'd recorded.

Quinn had fallen asleep an hour into the show. She was on her back next to him with her legs draped across his lap. It felt good. Intimate.

"Hmmm?" she mumbled as he shook her.

"It's ten. I need to take you home," Driftwood said softly. "You've got work in the morning."

She sighed and, without opening her eyes, said, "I'm too comfortable to move."

He smiled. God, how he wished he could merely carry her to his bed. "I know, me too."

After a few minutes went by and she didn't move, Driftwood tried again. "Quinn?"

"I know. I know. I'm going."

He huffed out a laugh when she didn't move. "How about some incentive?"

She cracked one eye open. "What kind of incentive?"

"A kiss?"

She closed her eye. "Hmmm."

He smirked. "Chocolate?"

She didn't respond.

"I could make a batch of that caramel dipping sauce we had tonight and bring it over tomorrow after you get off work."

That did it.

Quinn sighed and swung her legs off his lap. She sat up and looked at him. "You don't play fair."

He laughed. "I'm not sure if I should be offended or impressed that caramel won out over a kiss."

She smiled at him. "Well, I would've gone for the kiss, but I had a feeling if I held out, I'd get the really good stuff."

"The good stuff, huh?" he teased, then swiftly reached for her.

Quinn screeched but didn't try to get away from him. Driftwood had her on her back in seconds. He hovered over her mock menacingly. "*I'm* not the good stuff, woman?"

The smile left her face as she stared up at him. "You're the best stuff, John."

As Driftwood looked at her, he realized that not once tonight had he thought about the mark on her face. Oh, he saw it, but it was as much a part of her as a beard would be on a man, or a freckle or mole. Quinn was a remarkable person. And she was *his*.

He slowly dropped his head, giving her time to protest. But she didn't. Her arms wound around his neck and she pulled him the last inches down to her mouth. Driftwood felt the heat from her chest against his own, and he wanted nothing more than to straddle her hips and lay himself down on her.

But instead, he simply enjoyed making out with her. She was as passionate as he was. Their tongues dueled, and eventually he reached up and held her head gently so he could get the angle he wanted to kiss her.

How long they lay there kissing, he had no idea, but eventually, he sat up.

He noticed that she was breathing just as hard as he was. He'd never been the kind of man to rush into the bedroom, preferring to get to know the women he dated before going there. But he had a feeling he and Quinn were going to end up tangled in his sheets sooner rather than later. Maybe it was because he already knew her. Because of her friendship with Sophie, she'd been around a lot. They'd already gotten to know the basics.

The foundation for a friendship had already been laid. Now they were filling in the cracks. Getting to know each other on a more intimate level. And he liked what he was finding out about her.

"Come on, Emmy. Let's get you home before I kidnap you and refuse to let you leave my house."

"If you feed me that caramel sauce every day, I won't *want* to leave."

"I'm going to go to the store tomorrow to stock up on supplies to make it," he said, only half kidding. If all it took was some caramel sauce to get her to stay, he'd make sure it was always available.

Taking her hand in his, he helped her stand. They found her shoes under the coffee table and she put them on. They left his house and soon they were on their way back to her apartment complex.

"Working on anything new at work?" he asked as they drove.

After hearing all about what her week had in store, Driftwood pulled into the parking lot and shut off the engine.

"What's that on my car?" Quinn asked.

Driftwood looked over to her Toyota Corolla and saw a pamphlet under her windshield wiper. Then he looked at the Jeep next to her car, and saw the same thing. Every car in the lot had one of the pink sheets of paper tucked under their wipers.

"Just an advertising flier," he said as he got out of the car.

"That's illegal in our lot," Quinn mumbled, but didn't seem too concerned.

Driftwood walked her to the lobby and, after

looking around to make sure it was clear, he said, "Drive safe going to work tomorrow."

"I will. What are you going to do on your day off?"

"Probably meet up with the guys and work out or something."

"On your day off, you're going to meet up with the guys?" she asked. "Aren't you sick of them?"

Driftwood shrugged. "Not really. I'm around them so much, they're like brothers. They annoy me sometimes, but they're family. It would seem weird if I *didn't* see them."

"Do you…want to come to the hospital for lunch?" she asked.

Driftwood nodded immediately. "Yes. But I'll bring us something."

"You don't have to. The cafeteria is fine."

He shook his head. "Nope. If you don't mind, I can bring leftovers from tonight."

"Including the caramel sauce?" she asked with a grin.

"Wouldn't dream of forgetting it," Driftwood said. Then he leaned down and gave her a brief but deep kiss. "I had a good time today, Quinn. Thank you for spending the day with me."

"Thanks for not minding just sitting around doing nothing."

"Doing nothing with you is a hundred times better than watching you being miserable. Sleep well."

He backed away and watched her head up the stairs to the second floor.

On his way back to his truck, Driftwood detoured to take the flier off of Quinn's car. He glanced at it... and frowned. It was a doom-and-gloom advertisement declaring God's wrath was coming and evil was everywhere.

Crumpling it into a ball, Driftwood threw it onto the floor of his backseat before climbing in and starting his engine.

His thoughts were on Quinn all the way home. Right before he headed to bed, he sent her a quick text.

Driftwood: Good night, Emmy. Sleep well.

Not expecting a reply, as he figured she was probably already fast asleep, he grinned when he saw what she wrote.

Quinn: I'll be dreaming of caramel...and you.

CHAPTER FIVE

a week later, Quinn was at the grocery store trying to get everything she needed to make John a nice dinner. Every night he had off, he went out of his way to make her a delicious home-cooked meal. She wasn't that good of a cook but she still wanted to let him know she appreciated him.

Her plan was to make something and bring it over to Station 7. John was working tonight, but she'd hoped to get there before he'd had a chance to eat. She'd left work early so she'd have enough time to get to the grocery store and pick up what she needed, get home, cook, and get to the fire station before dinnertime.

Sophie had spoken to Chief, and he was going to do his best to keep John busy so he didn't eat before she got there.

In a hurry, and not paying attention to her surroundings, Quinn turned a corner down another aisle while looking at her phone and the grocery list she'd made, and crashed into someone else's cart.

Looking up, an apology was on the tip of her tongue—when she met the eyes of a very angry man. A familiar one.

It was Alaric. The man from The Sloppy Cow.

"I'm sorry," she said quickly, not wanting things to escalate out of hand.

"*You.*" Alaric said with a sneer. "Are you following me?"

"What? No!" Quinn said in surprise.

"I think you are," he said, but instead of getting in her face, he took a step backward. "Stay away from me, witch."

Witch. It had been a long time since she'd been called that.

Before she could respond, Alaric went on. "You've got the devil's mark." He gestured to her face. "You're bad luck! A pox on decent society."

Quinn had heard it all before. "You're welcome to believe what you want, but that's a load of crap."

"You're a bad seed who should be eliminated before you can infect the rest of us."

Quinn supposed she should be alarmed—she'd basically been threatened—but she was mostly just annoyed. So much so, she couldn't help egging this jerk on.

She reached toward Alaric—and smirked when he backed away from her even more.

"Don't touch me, witch!"

"Then get out of my way," she told him as she took another step toward him. Her grocery cart was between them, and she had no intention of *really* touching him. She was seriously irritated that he thought *she* was the problem with society.

Without another word, Alaric quickly backed farther away before turning his cart and hurrying down the next aisle.

Quinn chuckled. She really shouldn't take such pleasure in scaring people like that, but they brought it on themselves. And if they were that ignorant, then they deserved to be scared.

A noise behind her startled Quinn.

And she turned to see her neighbor, Willard, standing there. As usual, he didn't say a word, just stared at her in that disturbing way he had.

She guessed he was in his mid-forties, about her height, but he outweighed her by at least a hundred pounds. He had brown hair that was thinning in spots, and his belly stuck out over his pants. He usually wore sweatpants and old T-shirts with the necks stretched out, and today was no exception.

Now it was Quinn's turn to beat feet down the aisle. She supposed her neighbor being there was karma for taunting Alaric the way she had.

She finished up her shopping in record time, and luckily, she didn't see either Alaric or Willard when she went to check out. A woman waiting behind her in line surprised her by bringing up the incident.

"I heard what that guy said to you," she said.

Embarrassed, Quinn shrugged. "I'm kinda used to it."

"Well, *that* sucks. I don't understand people sometimes. I mean, his attitude makes him the ugly one, not you."

Quinn smiled a genuine smile at the woman. "Thanks."

"It's true. I work with the public all the time, and I swear, sometime between nineteen ninety-five and now, people have forgotten their manners."

"What do you do?" Quinn asked.

"Oh, sorry. Here I am, talking about manners, and I apparently don't have any myself." She held out her hand. "I'm Koren. Koren Garner. I work at a travel agency. I know, I know," she said, rolling her eyes after Quinn had shaken her hand. "With all the websites and stuff that are out there now, why does anyone need a travel agent?"

Quinn laughed. "I wasn't going to ask."

Koren smiled. "Yeah, well, you'd be surprised at the number of people who still think it's just easier for someone else to do all the research and booking of hotels and airlines for them. And we can sometimes get really good deals on cruises. But those same people who are so happy after we make all the arrangements can get pretty brutal if anything goes wrong. I once had someone call me a 'fucking bitch' for not refunding their money when their cruise ship left without them in San Juan. They'd been shopping and drinking and lost track of time. I tried to explain that *wasn't* my fault, but they still bitched me out."

"Ugh. That's ridiculous. I think I'm glad I work in a lab all day and only have to talk to my coworkers, who are all very nice."

"I'm jealous," Koren said.

"I'm Quinn," she told her, smiling warmly.

"Hi."

"I love your name. It's very unusual."

She chuckled. "My mom claims my dad misspelled 'Karen' on my birth certificate. She was super pissed when she realized it, but then decided she liked Koren better."

They moved forward in line, and it was Quinn's turn to check out. "Thanks for making a crappy shopping trip better."

Koren shrugged. "My pleasure. Don't take anything that guy said to heart. You're beautiful."

Quinn couldn't think of anything to say to that. She couldn't exactly say that she wasn't, and she'd never been good at accepting compliments, especially about her looks.

"Maybe I'll see you around," Koren went on. "I shop here all the time."

Quinn smiled. "Hopefully."

She paid the cashier and hurried out to her car. As she raced home, she forgot all about the encounters with Alaric and Willard at the store as she mentally planned her surprise for John.

* * *

"What is *up* with you, man?" Driftwood asked Chief as he put off starting dinner for the tenth time. "I'm starving. Get off your ass and get to the grill."

"I will. In a second."

"You've been saying that for the last half hour," Driftwood bitched.

"Hi," a feminine voice said from nearby.

Driftwood turned so fast he almost fell over. "Quinn!" he exclaimed, all thoughts of being hungry dissipating at his concern for the woman looking uneasily at everyone in the room. "Are you okay?"

"Of course."

"What are you doing here?"

She turned and picked up a bag from the floor. "I made you dinner."

Driftwood could only stare at her.

"And because I'm not cruel, I brought tacos for everyone else."

Cheers went up around him, but Driftwood only had eyes for Quinn. He walked up to her and asked, "What's this all about?"

"You're always doing nice things for me. You've cooked for me a million times and never complain when you have to make more caramel." She grinned cheekily. "I just thought maybe I could do something nice for you for once."

"Emmy, simply being with you is doing something nice for me."

She blushed. "I wanted to."

He caught a waft of whatever it was she'd made coming up from the bag she was holding, and his stomach growled. "Far be it from me to complain about someone feeding me," Driftwood relented. "I've been begging Chief here to start dinner for the last thirty minutes."

"Sorry I was late," Quinn told Chief, looking across the room at him. "Traffic."

"It's okay. Tacos make up for just about any inconvenience. I hope you brought enough...you *do* know how Taco got his nickname, right?"

"Yeah. I brought a dozen just for him." She gave Taco a shy smile.

Hamming it up, Taco got down on one knee and put his hands to his heart, saying dramatically, "Will you marry me?"

"Shut it, Taco. You've got your own woman, leave mine alone."

Taco got up from the floor and mumbled, "But *my* woman told me she doesn't like tacos."

Everyone laughed raucously.

"You better go feed your boyfriend," Chief told Quinn. "I thought he was about ready to chew his arm off."

"You set this up with Chief?" Driftwood asked.

Quinn nodded.

He swallowed hard. It meant a lot that she'd gone out of her way to surprise him. Turning his head to his friends, he said, "We'll be out back." Then he reached for the bag she held, so she didn't have to carry it. He headed to a door off to the side that led to the back of the fire station. There was a picnic table back there under a canopy to keep the sun off the area.

It was late enough that the heat of the day was waning and it was a comfortable temperature. But more than that, Driftwood wanted some time alone with Quinn.

He put the bag on the table, then pulled her to him. As if it was the most natural thing in the world, he bent and kissed her. Talking to her on the phone just wasn't the same as seeing her. With their schedules, it wasn't as if they could see each other every day, but with every one that passed without seeing her, he seemed to miss her more. "I missed you." The words were heartfelt and honest.

"I missed you too," she immediately returned.

"Thanks for coming by," Driftwood said.

She shrugged. "I *did* want to do something nice for you, but I admit to being a little reluctant since I wasn't sure what you'd think of me invading your space."

"You aren't invading my space."

"You know what I mean."

He shook his head. "No, I don't."

Quinn waved her hand in the air. "Your fire station. Your work thing."

"Emmy, it's a building. Yes, I spend a fair amount of time here, but in the end, it's work. Hanging out with you at my house...that's what I consider 'my' space."

The smile on her face was absolutely beautiful. "How do you always know the perfect thing to say?"

"Believe me, I don't. I'm just telling you what I feel. I'm sure there will be plenty of times in the future when I fuck up and say something that's taken wrong. So far things have been great with us, but I hope you aren't the kind of person who runs at the slightest provocation."

She frowned and tried to take a step away from him.

Driftwood tightened his arms around her. "Oh, no, you don't. Talk to me."

She braced her hands on his chest and pushed until there was a bit of room between them. Driftwood wouldn't let her go any farther.

"Why do you assume I'm the type to run if something goes wrong?" she asked with a huff.

"I don't. I just said that I hoped you *weren't*."

"It sounded like you expect me to bail," Quinn said, looking at his chest and not into his eyes.

"Look at me, Emmy."

She slowly raised her gaze to his.

"We're gonna fight. All couples do. But believe me when I tell you that I've never felt about another person the way I feel about you. Even if you try to pull away, I won't let you go without a fight. I'm a guy, I'm going to fuck up, it's inevitable, but if you know from the start that you're more than just a casual girlfriend, maybe you'll cut me some slack. And on the same token, don't sit back and take my crap. Call me out on it. If I'm rude, let me know. If I hurt your feelings, for the love of God, tell me so I don't do it again. I don't ever want to hurt you. You've had enough of that in your life. I want to protect you from assholes who think just because you have a birthmark, you don't have any feelings."

He ignored the way her eyes filled with tears and hurried to finish what he wanted to say. "I know you're uncomfortable when people say stuff about your birthmark, and that you'd rather just ignore them than call them on their idiocy. But I'm not that guy. Anyone that hurts you is fair game as far as I'm concerned. I'm not talking about fighting them, but if I hear that crap, more often than not, I'm going to set them straight."

"I hate that you feel like you have to do that," Quinn told him.

"I know you do. But what if the roles were reversed? What if I got hurt in a fire and was in a wheelchair? Would you stand by and say nothing if you heard someone making fun of the fact that I couldn't walk?"

"You know I wouldn't."

"Exactly," Driftwood said seriously. "I care about you too much to let that shit go. *But*," he said quickly, seeing her discomfort, "I'm not going to start getting into fistfights every time we go out in public over it."

"It happens a lot," she warned him. "I can tune most of it out, and most people aren't talking about me maliciously, they're just curious."

"Then we'll educate them," Driftwood said immediately. "The Internet has made people think they can do or say anything and not have any consequences. They don't get to see how their words make people feel inside. They don't understand that words have power. If I can't protect you from hearing the shit they say, I can at least try to educate them on how to be a decent person."

Quinn licked her lips. Then nodded.

Driftwood was relieved she didn't argue with him over that. He knew he'd have to tread carefully, but at least he'd given her a head's up. "And one more thing. I'm pretty hard to offend, but if *you* say or do anything that hurts *me*, I'll tell you, just as I expect you to talk to me if I do the same."

She shook her head and brought a hand up and rested it on the side of his cheek. "I don't deserve you."

"Yes, you do," he countered. "And I deserve you." He moved a hand to the side of her neck and gently kissed her. "Thank you for coming over tonight."

"You're welcome."

"And now, if we're done with the touchy-feely stuff, I'm starving. Chief wasn't wrong when he said I was about ready to start chewing on my arm."

Quinn giggled.

"What'd you make?"

"It's nothing fancy," she warned. "I didn't have a ton of time and I'm not half the cook you are."

"I don't need fancy," Driftwood said, not taking his eyes from her, willing her to understand what he was saying. "You made it, so it'll be delicious."

"I decided to make something that could be served cold, so I didn't have to worry about trying to keep it hot on my way over here. It's a chicken orzo salad. I noticed that you didn't seem to be very picky, so I took a chance and threw in tomatoes, cucumbers, red onion, a few mushrooms, and olives. It's tossed with olive oil and lemon juice vinaigrette."

Driftwood stared at her in disbelief. "Seriously?"

Quinn bit her lip and nodded. "Is it okay?"

"Is it okay?" he echoed. "Quinn, it sounds amazing. Chief was going to make burgers for the millionth time tonight. I've hit the jackpot."

She blushed. "I wasn't sure if you'd like a pasta salad for dinner."

"It sounds delicious. Now, are we going to stand here talking about it or are we gonna eat?"

Quinn laughed and reached for the bag. She unpacked a glass container full of the pasta and rice. She'd packed plates and silverware as well. She quickly had two plates filled with the savory food, and Driftwood could only stare at the spread in disbelief.

"You made this *today*?" he asked.

She nodded. "Yeah, I left work early and ran to the store to pick up some last-minute stuff. Then I rushed home and made it and headed over here. I picked it because it only takes around thirty minutes to make. I chilled it in the fridge while I took a shower and got ready. And...here I am."

"Thank you, Emmy," Driftwood said, feeling more emotional than the situation probably warranted. He couldn't remember when someone had gone to so much trouble as Quinn had simply to feed him. And it was more than that, she'd talked to Chief and organized it so he didn't eat dinner before she'd arrived. It took planning. Anyone could drop by with a bagful of fast food to share, but she'd put forth a lot of effort for her surprise.

"Don't thank me until you've tried it," she quipped.

The next fifteen minutes or so, they spoke only intermittently as the food was consumed. Driftwood thought the lemon juice vinaigrette perfectly complemented the chicken and vegetables. He was already mentally planning on making the same thing for the others at the station. He could use whatever vegetables they had on hand, he'd just have to get the orzo.

"So, I take it your empty plate means you liked it?" Quinn asked with a smirk.

"Come here," Driftwood said. He threw one leg over the seat and patted the space in front of him.

Copying him, Quinn shifted on the seat and scooted until she was resting against his back. Driftwood laced his fingers together on her stomach and they sat like that for a couple minutes, satiated and relaxed.

"Anything interesting happen today?" Driftwood finally asked.

Quinn shrugged. "I ran into that guy we saw at the bar the other day."

Driftwood tensed. "And?"

"Nothing. He said some shit, and I scared him off by pretending I was going to touch him."

"Explain," Driftwood ordered.

She sighed. "He called me a witch. I haven't heard that one in a few years. Anyway, he accused me of being a witch and a blight on society. So I pretended I was going to touch him and he backed away as if I had cooties."

"Probably not smart," Driftwood said, trying not to let his irritation show. He wanted Quinn to stand up for herself, but not like that.

She sighed. "I know. But I was in a hurry and needed to get back home and start dinner. Besides, it worked. He backed up as if I were carrying the plague and I didn't see him again."

"That's something," Driftwood said under his breath.

"Or him leaving might've been because my neighbor showed up around the same time."

"Willard?"

"The one and the same. Once again, he didn't say anything, just stared at me in that weird way he has. I backed away from him the same way Alaric did to me." She chuckled nervously.

"What is it with that guy?" Driftwood asked.

Quinn shrugged. "I have no idea. But he always seems to be around. He's never actually said or done anything to me. But he's always watching."

"I don't like it."

"Neither do I," Quinn said. "But what can I do? He lives in my building. It's not like I can just move."

No, that wasn't practical...but why did he already want to suggest that she move in with *him*? He'd never had the urge to live with another woman. Not once. Even when he'd been in serious relationships in the past, he'd never come close to wanting to live with anyone twenty-four/seven. Why was Quinn so different?

"Anyway," she went on, "that's about it. We're starting a new research protocol at work for dealing with burns on people's hands. The skin on the palm of your hand doesn't respond to treatments the same way as other parts of the body. Sophie is working on trying to find some patients to be a baseline."

Driftwood was only partially listening. He was still processing the fact that he'd almost asked Quinn to move in with him. But the more he thought about it, the more he warmed to the idea. It would get her away from her creepy neighbor, and they wouldn't have to say goodbye at the end of the night.

He would work his way into asking her to stay though, maybe suggest she bring over a sweatshirt or two, so when she got cold, she could put her own on instead of one of his. Or maybe she could bring over an extra set of clothes...just in case.

As he worked through different scenarios in his head, Driftwood was still only half listening to what Quinn was saying.

"Am I boring you?" she asked after a moment.

"What? No!" Driftwood exclaimed.

"You're quiet," she observed.

"I'm still thinking about your creepy neighbor," he admitted.

Before she could reply, and before he could blurt out an invitation to move in with him, the tones indicating a call rang out from inside the firehouse.

"Shit," Driftwood said, immediately standing. He listened for a second as the dispatcher explained they were being sent to a multi-car accident. Knowing that meant they'd most likely be taking all three trucks, he turned to Quinn.

But she was already standing next to him. "Go," she ordered. "I'll clean this up. Unless…am I allowed to be here when you guys aren't?"

"Of course. I'd ask you to wait, but I don't know how long I'll be," he told her with regret.

"I know. It's fine. You're working. Go. Someone needs you."

Relieved that she understood—he'd dated a couple women who'd never grasped that when the tones went off, it meant he had to go and didn't have a timetable on when he'd be home—Driftwood gave her a hard, swift kiss. "Text me when you get home."

"I will. Go."

He nodded and turned to hurry back inside to put on his bunker gear and roll out.

* * *

Quinn took her time washing the glass dish their dinner had been in. After she'd done that, she cleaned the other dishes in the sink as well. She wiped off the counters, then she picked up the shoes around the room and lined them up against the wall. She folded the blanket that was lying in a heap on the floor next to the chair Penelope had been sitting in when she'd arrived. She tidied up other odds and ends in the large room until she had nothing else to do. She'd stalled in the hopes that John and the others would be back before she had to leave.

Admitting that it was time for her to go, Quinn reluctantly picked up the bag with the dishes from their meal and headed for the door. She knew protocol was to keep the door unlocked, but it felt weird to leave it that way. Anyone could just waltz on in and help themselves to whatever they wanted.

The fire station wasn't in a bad area, but still.

Quinn headed to her car—and was surprised to see a flier stuck under the wipers of her Corolla. It was the same pink color that had been on all the cars at her apartment when she'd been with John. Before she got in, she picked up the paper and saw that it was a religious flier. *REPENT*, it proclaimed, with a picture of Jesus pointing his finger toward the reader.

Rolling her eyes, Quinn crumpled the pamphlet and threw it into the passenger seat of her car. She'd throw it away when she got home.

The trip back to her apartment complex didn't take

long since there wasn't a lot of traffic. Quinn parked in her assigned spot and climbed out.

She walked quickly to the lobby and breathed a sigh of relief when the door closed behind her. She'd definitely been watching too many crime shows, because lately, she felt as if she was being watched all the time.

Shaking her head, Quinn headed for the stairs—only to stop short when she saw Willard coming down. She considered taking the elevator instead, but that would be way too obvious. She refused to show weakness. Lifting her head, and trying to look braver than she felt, Quinn looked Willard in the eye as she approached.

As usual, he didn't say anything, simply stared back at her.

Suddenly sick of him scaring her all the time, Quinn said, "Leave me alone, Willard. I've never done anything to you. You have no right to stare at me all the time."

Her words seemed to bounce right off him. He didn't respond...and actually stopped walking down the stairs.

That wasn't the reaction she was looking for. She'd been hoping he'd tell her he wasn't staring at her. That he meant her no harm. That he didn't mean to make her nervous. But instead, he just looked at her without saying a word.

Jogging up the stairs past him, Quinn pushed hard on the stairwell door and practically speed-walked down the hall to her apartment. She unlocked her door in record time and slammed it shut behind her. After locking it, she felt better...and a little silly.

It wasn't as if Willard had made any move toward her whatsoever. He'd simply been going down the stairs.

But then she recalled what he was wearing. He had on a black T-shirt with orange and yellow flames on the front.

Was it a coincidence that the flames reminded her of Hell?

Shivering as if she'd just had a brush with death, Quinn rushed into her bedroom and shut the door behind her. Locking that one as well, she collapsed on her bed. She'd planned on watching some television, but her mood for that had waned.

She quickly changed into her pajamas and climbed under her covers. She grabbed her iPad and pulled up the messaging program. She shot off a quick text to John, letting him know she was home, then clicked on a solitaire app. It was mindless, and always did a good job of helping her turn off her brain.

CHAPTER SIX

The next weekend, Driftwood knew Quinn would rather be sitting at home relaxing, but she was making an effort to be more outgoing for him. A part of him was concerned that she felt like she needed to, but another part was flattered that she was doing what she could to make friends with the other women and *his* friends.

"If you don't want to go, I can take you home," he told her for what seemed like the hundredth time.

"I want to go," she told him. "It's just a softball game. I've heard about this battle for a while now. I need to see it with my own eyes."

Driftwood wanted to protest that it wasn't *just* a softball game. It was firefighters against law enforcement personnel. It was a "thing." Bragging rights were at stake. It was a huge fucking deal. But he knew she'd think he was crazy if he said that. So he simply smiled at her. "I hate that you feel uncomfortable."

"John, every time I step out of my apartment, I feel uncomfortable. When I'm at a red light and notice someone looking at me from the car next to me, I'm uncomfortable. When I go to the grocery store, walk around the hospital, or do just about anything that puts me in contact with others, I'm uncomfortable."

Driftwood's stomach clenched.

"But I'm trying harder not to let it rule my decisions. Being with you is teaching me that I've been letting my life pass me by. I'm trying to get better at not letting what others do or say affect me. All my life, I've been made fun of and teased. Even if I decide to get the laser treatments, I'm always going to have this mark on my face. It stinks, and I hate it, but if I want to be with you—and I definitely want to be with you—I'm going to have to suck it up and deal with it."

"Wrong," Driftwood said, reaching for her hand. "All you have to do to be with me, is *be* with me. I don't give a shit what close-minded people say or think. I know you, Quinn. You're a remarkable woman who had a horrible mother and a not-so-great childhood, which makes the person you've turned out to be all the more mind-boggling."

She gave him a small smile. "Thanks. I want to be the person you see. And the more I'm around Sophie, Adeline, Blythe, and the others, the more I realize that my life hasn't been so bad. We all have demons, it's how we deal with them that lets us really live. This game is important to you, so it's important to me too. I want to cheer on my boyfriend and watch him kick some cop ass."

He burst out laughing. "No one is kicking anyone's ass, Emmy."

"You know what I mean," she grumbled, but with a twinkle in her eye.

"Come here," Driftwood ordered, squeezing her hand as they stopped at a red light. She leaned toward him eagerly.

He gave her an all-too-brief kiss before saying, "No more of that. I have a game to play."

"How about some incentive?"

"What're we talking?" he asked.

"Hmmmm. For every hit you get, you get a kiss."

"I like that. What about a double?"

"Is that if you make it to two bases with one hit?"

He chuckled. "Yeah."

"If you get a double, then I think it's only fair you get to second base with me."

Driftwood felt his cock stir. He forced himself not to shift in his seat. "And if I get a home run?" He divided his time between looking at the road and glancing over at Quinn.

She was blushing, but she said almost nonchalantly, "Then I'll have to see about letting you round the bases at home too."

He almost drove off the road. They'd fooled around a bit when they'd snuggled on his couch or hers, but nothing too hot and heavy. The thought of getting to see her perfect tits without her bra on or getting to see what she looked like when she came was almost over-whelming.

"I have a feeling I'm going to have the best game of my life today," he said. "With that kind of incentive, how could I not?"

Quinn giggled and Driftwood loved the sound. It was times like this, when she forgot all about her birth-mark and was simply being who she was, that he loved the best. She forgot to be self-conscious. Forgot that she didn't look like everyone else. She was just Quinn Dixon. An incredible and beautiful human being.

He pulled into the packed parking lot and they both climbed out. Driftwood slung his bag over his shoulder and put his hand on the small of Quinn's back as they walked toward the field they'd been assigned for the morning. There were three other games going on at the same time as theirs. Three other fire stations were playing today against various branches of law enforce-ment. There were no tickets necessary to watch, but all proceeds from the sale of snacks would go toward charity, and donations were always accepted as well.

They walked toward the bleachers and it was easy to pick out exactly who he was looking for. Adeline's black lab and Penelope's donkey were hard to miss. He steered Quinn in their direction and was happy when she was greeted warmly and loudly by not only the firefighters' women, but most of the police officers' women as well.

"You good?" Driftwood asked in Quinn's ear.

She smiled and nodded up at him.

"Damn, all I'm going to be able to think about is getting a fucking home run," Driftwood grumbled as he felt Quinn's hands rest on his hips.

She giggled once more. "Then get to it," she told him.

"You're killing me," Driftwood complained good-naturedly. Then he kissed her and turned to head to the dugout.

A hard smack on his ass made him whip around and stare at Quinn in surprise.

"Knock 'em dead, stud. And get a home run, would ya?"

All the women laughed raucously and cheered her on. There was a blush on Quinn's unblemished cheek, and Driftwood didn't think he could like her more than he did at that moment.

Dropping his bag, he went back to her in a rush. The expression on her face turned from smugness to surprise. She shrieked when he caught her around the waist and dipped her backward. She held onto his biceps for balance and he kissed her even as she was laughing.

He didn't do anything to hide his growing feelings for her. He took her lips as if they were lying in bed about to make love. Passionately and without holding back.

By the time he stood upright, they were both out of breath. He barely heard the catcalls from their audience. He brushed a lock of hair behind Quinn's ear and kissed her marked cheek. Then, without a word, he turned and picked up his bag and headed for the dugout once more.

* * *

"Giiiiirl!" Sophie said as she fanned her face. "That was hot."

Quinn knew she was blushing, but didn't really care. Smacking John's butt had been spontaneous, but if she'd known what kind of reaction he'd have, she might've done it before now.

Sophie patted a space on the bleacher next to her and Quinn climbed up. She recognized most everyone there, and said hi to Adeline, Blythe, and Jen.

"As you can s-see, Beth isn't here," Sophie said. "Cade s-said s-she's having a rough day, but he brought a camera and s-set it up over there."

Quinn glanced over and saw what looked like a go-pro zip-tied to the fence.

"S-She's watching from home. And I think you've m-met everyone else here at one time or another. M-Mackenzie, M-Mickie, Corrie, Laine, Erin from The Sloppy Cow, M-Milena, and Hope and her s-son, Billy," Sophie pointed out each person as she said their name.

It was a lot of people, but luckily Quinn *had* met most of them before. "Hey, everyone," she said with a little wave.

"It's great to see you again, Quinn," Mackenzie said enthusiastically. "I just love these games. Not only do we get to watch a bunch of hot men running around getting sweaty, we get to hang out together. I don't see enough of you guys. Oh, and I should say that *most* of the time I love these things, but Adeline, if you please, no passing out this time, okay?"

Everyone chuckled. Quinn knew the last time the men had played a softball game, Adeline had an epileptic seizure and had to be taken to the hospital.

Smokey, Penelope's donkey, chose that moment to start braying.

Jen wrinkled her nose and asked, "What's his problem?"

"Nothing," Sophie said. "His m-mama's up at bat!"

Quinn looked and, sure enough, Penelope was stepping up to the plate.

"Show those boys who's boss!" Laine yelled.

"Hey, whose side are you on?" Mackenzie asked her best friend.

Laine smiled. "I'm all about supporting women, especially when they're outnumbered like she is. So that means I cheer really loud when Penelope and Hayden are at bat. I don't care who wins the stupid game. I'm here for the hot guys...and to watch our women kick some ass."

Quinn turned her attention back to the game just in time to see Penelope hit the ball hard enough to make it to first base.

She stood up and cheered along with the rest of their group.

Maybe being out and social wouldn't be so bad...

especially when she was surrounded by some of the most interesting and strong women she'd ever met.

An hour later, Quinn was rethinking her premature assessment of the outing.

First, it was hot. Which wasn't exactly a surprise, since it was Texas, but Quinn wasn't someone who liked to be hot. She never wore her hair up, in order to help hide her birthmark, and feeling her sweaty hair on the back of her neck was irritating and gross. Secondly, the firefighters were losing. By a lot. And she didn't think John would be in the greatest mood when they left as a result, and that sucked.

Third, she was tired of listening to Jen complain.

Quinn was pretty much miserable, but she was sucking it up and trying to have a good time despite the heat and occasional bugs. Besides, if Blythe wasn't complaining, and she was pregnant and still sitting out here on the hard bleachers, Quinn didn't feel as if *she* had any room to bitch.

But Jen had complained that her butt hurt, she was hot, her back was sore, she was hungry, she didn't understand what the rules were. She bitched about Dax cheating by holding back Taco when he went to steal a base, and lastly, that she was bored.

Finally, Adeline had had enough and said what they were all thinking. "Jen, if you're so miserable, why don't you just go home?"

"Because Hudson needs me," she answered with wide eyes.

"He hates being called Hudson," Sophie said. "His

name is Taco. And he's out there on the field. He doesn't exactly need you."

"He doesn't mind when I call him Hudson. Besides, Taco is a silly name. I'm his moral support," Jen said, her lip trembling.

"Oh Lord," Mickie said under her breath from behind Quinn.

"I think I saw an umbrella in John's truck," Quinn offered.

"That's not going to make this seat any more comfortable," Jen said with a pout.

"It's not, but it might make you cooler," Adeline said. "And it was nice of Quinn to offer."

"Aren't you hot?" Jen asked Quinn.

"Of course I am," she replied.

"But you haven't put your hair up or anything," Jen said.

Quinn couldn't decide if Jen was really that stupid, or if she was purposely trying to make her feel awkward. "I never put my hair up," she told her.

"Why?"

"Because s-she doesn't like it when people s-stare at her," Sophie said. "When her hair is up it exposes her birthmark. And if you'd used your brain, you would've thought about that."

"Oh…I…just thought you weren't hot," Jen stammered.

"I'll go with you if you want to go get a Coke," little Billy offered.

Hope looked down at her son with pride. "You thirsty?"

He shrugged. "Not really. But sometimes walking around makes my back feel better when it hurts. And you always tell me that sitting too long can make your butt numb and walking makes it better."

"That it does, son," Hope said.

"So...you wanna go get a Coke?" Billy asked Jen again.

She heaved a long sigh. "I guess I might as well. This game doesn't look like it's going to end anytime soon, especially with everyone cheating as badly as they are. They shouldn't cheat. It's not right."

"It's just a game," Milena told her. "Lighten up."

"Here's some money," Hope told her son. "You can have a soft drink, but only a small size, okay?"

"Okay, Mom. Do you want anything?"

"I'm good. Thanks for asking."

Billy hopped off the bench and looked at Adeline. "Can Coco come with me?"

"Sure," Adeline told him, handing over her leash. "Just hold on tight."

"I will!" he answered happily.

"Isn't she afraid Coco will run off if Billy drops her leash?" Quinn asked Sophie.

"No. Coco is very well trained. S-She wouldn't run off. No way. If anything, s-she'd just come right back over here to Adeline...or s-she'd go to Crash."

The second Jen was out of earshot, the women let their frustrations fly.

"Is she serious right about now?"

"What in the world does Taco see in her?"

"You've seen her tits, right?"

"She's so annoying."

"The game is for charity...who cares how long it takes?"

"If she sighs in that dramatic way she has one more time, I'm gonna have to hurt her."

Quinn kept her mouth shut. She felt kind of bad for Jen. At least she'd known Sophie for a while, so she'd been semi-part of the group before officially dating John. It had to be hard trying to integrate yourself into an established group of friends. Jen was definitely not fitting in, though.

Instead of joining in the bashing, she turned her attention to Hope. The other woman wasn't watching the game; she had her eyes glued on the concession stand.

Quinn leaned forward. "He'll be okay," she said softly.

"I know," Hope said without taking her eyes off her son. "I'm just making sure."

Quinn admired Hope. She'd had a hell of a time, and her son had been snatched from her not once, but twice. Well, maybe one and a half times, since the last time he'd actually run away from the person who'd tried to kidnap him. If that had happened to Quinn's child, she wasn't sure she'd ever take her eyes off him again.

But Billy had taken everything in stride and, from

what Quinn understood, was actually flourishing now that they were living with Calder and the boy had a more stable life.

Quinn took a deep breath and pulled her hair up into a messy bun at the back of her head for just a second. The air felt good against her nape, and she closed her eyes in momentary relief.

"Holy shit, look at that thing on her face," a voice said from nearby.

Quinn reflexively dropped her hand and let her hair cover her neck and cheek once again. But it was too late.

"Gross," a second teenage boy said.

"If I looked like that, I'd kill myself," the first boy said.

Quinn looked out at the field and pretended she didn't hear their conversation.

But Mackenzie wasn't so reticent. "At least she doesn't have ears that stick out for miles like yours do," she said, glaring at the teenagers.

"Yeah!" Laine agreed. "And if you're so stupid that you can't recognize a birthmark when you see it, and don't realize she's dating one of the men you've had a man-crush on for the last hour—who would squash you like a bug if he heard you talking about his woman like that—then you're going to have a hard time doing anything but working at minimum-wage jobs for the rest of your lives."

Quinn gaped at the duo. "I don't think you're allowed to make fun of kids like that," she whispered.

Mackenzie looked her in the eyes. "If they're old enough to make fun of other people, then they're old enough to take what they dish out."

"You're a bitch," the first teenager called out to Mackenzie.

"Yeah. What do you know?" the second one asked Laine.

Just then, Smokey let out a series of brays and honks that startled everyone. He even lunged on his lead, which was tied to the bottom of the bleachers. The boys looked terrified and scurried away from them, making their way down the steps and going over to another set of bleachers nearby.

"Thank you," Quinn told the other women.

"Whatever. Their parents should've taught them manners. Seriously, I don't understand why people feel like it's okay to be like that."

"I'm used it," Quinn said. "But I appreciate your support all the same."

"You shouldn't *have* to be used to it," Adeline complained. "No one with a disability should. I got made fun of when I'd have seizures too. People have actually *laughed* at how funny I looked when I was in the middle of one. What in the world makes people think they're that much better than everyone else?"

"The same thing that makes people laugh when I run into something," Corrie said softly.

Quinn turned to look at the shy blind woman who hadn't said much up to this point. She'd wondered why she was there, since she couldn't watch the game, but then she'd overheard some of her conversations with Mickie and Mackenzie. Corrie could hear when Quint was up to bat, and she could tell how he'd done by the sound the bat made when it hit the ball, and how loudly the crowd cheered.

Milena spoke up then. "TJ told me a story about how they'd gotten a call about a woman inside a locked car in a parking lot. The person calling said that she was in the backseat with a blanket over her head, and he thought she might have overdosed. They all raced to the scene expecting to find a dead body. When they got there, they found the car but it was empty. When they questioned the caller, he said he'd last seen the woman two days ago. TJ was *pissed*. He was *still* upset when he got home hours later. He couldn't understand why the man hadn't called for help the second he saw the woman in distress. Why he'd waited *two days* to call and tell someone that he thought there was a woman in the car. People are just too busy to care about others anymore. They're so caught up in their own lives and their own issues, that they forget other people have feelings. The anonymity of social media hasn't helped."

"And they're so concerned about taking selfies and putting pictures on Instagram and showing others that they have a perfect life, that they forget their lives are actually flawed and not as perfect as they're trying to portray," Erin chimed in.

"You wouldn't believe the number of people who spit on me when I was homeless," Blythe added. "Not all homeless people panhandling are scammers. Sometimes we just want a buck so we can buy a hamburger."

"Maybe we can't change the world," Mackenzie said. "But we can change the perceptions of the people we come into contact with. We can at least educate them a little bit. And if we can't change their minds, I say we shame them into thinking twice before making fun of someone in the future."

Quinn's throat felt tight and she did her best not to cry. All her life she'd felt like an outcast. She'd never found friends she could trust like she felt she could trust this group of women. They'd had her back automatically. Without hesitation. Taking the job at the Burn Center had been the best thing she'd ever done. She'd met Sophie, and in turn had been embraced into the fold of these amazing women.

Jen came back then, and the first thing she said was, "That line was so slow! I swear I could've run home and gotten a drink and made it back before I made it to the front of the line."

Quinn felt sorry for her. Instead of enjoying the moment, she was too busy complaining about things she couldn't control.

"Here, Quinn," Blythe said, leaning over and holding out her hand. "I have an extra."

Sitting on the other woman's palm was a hair tie. A plain black, elastic hair tie.

An hour earlier, she probably would've insisted that she was fine and didn't need it, even though she definitely did. But after being reminded that the women around her were just as flawed as she was, and they embraced their differences instead of trying to hide them, Quinn took a deep breath and reached for it. "Thanks."

"You're welcome," Blythe said.

Quinn bent her head and gathered her hair up with both hands. She made a sloppy bun at the back of her head and wound the hair tie around it.

"Sunscreen?" Adeline asked, holding out a small tube.

Again, Quinn could've been embarrassed and assumed Adeline was only asking because of the blemish on her face, but she pushed that thought back and accepted the offer. She liberally applied the lotion on her birthmark, making sure to cover it completely.

Feeling eyes on her, Quinn turned to see Jen staring at her from the seat to her left. Deciding not to take offense, she held out the sunscreen to her instead. "Need some?"

Jen leaned back as if Quinn was holding a live spider or something. "No, I'm good, thanks."

Shrugging, Quinn handed the tube back to Adeline. "Thanks."

"You're welcome," the other woman said.

With Jen's reappearance, talk once again turned general and everyone watched the game. At the moment, Taco, Chief, and Moose had surrounded Penelope and were escorting her from one base to the next, making sure no one could get close enough to tag her out. Everyone was laughing, and soon it was a free-for-all on the field. With the law enforcement guys doing what they could to tag the small firefighter, and the firefighters doing what they could to keep everyone away from their teammate.

Quinn smiled as she watched the mayhem on the field.

For the first time in a really long time, she felt as if she belonged somewhere. In this band of misfit women, she was just one of the group. She wasn't the weird one, wasn't the disabled one. They were all weird in their own way, and most of them had their own disabilities they were living with. But the bottom line was that they were all people. Attempting to get through life as best they could…with incredible men at their sides.

CHAPTER SEVEN

"*Y*ou're quiet," Driftwood said. "You okay?"

"I'm good," she said. "Are *you* okay? You guys lost today."

He chuckled. "Emmy, we didn't just lose, we got slaughtered. They beat us twenty-seven to ten."

"And you don't care?"

"Not one bit. We had fun. They had fun. Who cares who won?"

"I thought *you* would," she responded.

"Nope. Truth be told, we all pretty much suck at softball. We all cheat to cover up that fact. Getting money for charity is what it's really about. We get to hang out together, watch our women chat and smile in the stands, and generally forget about the real world for a while."

Quinn smiled at him. "That's awesome."

"Yeah. I like your hair up." He wasn't going to bring it up, but she seemed extraordinarily mellow for some reason. He'd never thought in a million years she'd put her hair up like she had. In all the time he'd known her, she'd never worn it any other way than down around her shoulders.

"Thanks. It was hot today."

"Yeah."

"So…" she began with a coy look under her lashes. "You didn't get a home run today."

He chuckled and winced. "Don't remind me."

"Not even a double," she pouted.

Driftwood laughed out loud. He couldn't help it. She looked so cute with her bottom lip stuck out.

"It's not for lack of trying, Emmy. Believe me. I even tried bribing Conor to let me run to second after that pathetic hit I made, but it was a no-go."

Quinn brought her hand up to his shoulder and massaged it gently. "How's the arm?"

His arm? "Fine. Why?"

"You mean it doesn't hurt? I was thinking maybe a massage would help after your long day of swinging that bat."

Oh! He clued in. "Yeah, it does kind of hurt," he said in as pathetic a tone as he could. He grimaced for good effect. "It's really stiff."

"Stiff huh?" Quinn joked, moving her hand to his leg. "I'll have to see if I can rub it out."

Driftwood about choked. He'd never seen Quinn this playful before. He smiled. "Anytime you want to put your hands on me, I'm all yours."

She cocked her head at him. "Are you?"

"Yeah, Em. Just as you're mine."

She beamed and her fingers tightened on his thigh. "I had a good time today, John. Thanks for forcing me out of my comfort zone. I'm not saying I want to get season tickets to the Missions' games, but today was good."

"How do you know about San Antonio's minor league team?" he asked.

"John, I've lived here for a while now. Why wouldn't I know about them?"

He shrugged. "I don't know. I'm being sexist, aren't I?"

"Yup. But I'll forgive you."

"How was Jen today?" It was an abrupt change of topic, but he'd noticed the way the other woman had spent most of the game sitting a bit away from the group. He hadn't mentioned it to Taco, and didn't think Taco had taken any notice of his girlfriend at all, but he and Chief had talked about it briefly during one of the breaks in the game.

Neither of them thought Jen's relationship with Taco would last. It was obvious they weren't exactly compatible, but it wasn't either of their places to tell Taco that he should dump Jen and look for someone else. Besides, actions spoke louder than words, and the fact that he hadn't once looked over at the stands said a lot for the ultimate outcome of their relationship.

"Fine. Why?" Quinn said.

"She just looked...not as happy as the rest of you," he finished lamely.

"That's because she wasn't," Quinn told him. "She was hot and bored. And before you ask, we tried to engage her in conversation, but she seemed to be a million miles away."

"Wonder if anything is wrong," Driftwood mused.

"I have no idea. I don't think she'd tell us if there was," Quinn said. "Sometimes I think she doesn't like us. We're definitely not her type."

"What's her type?"

Quinn shrugged. "People who like to shop more than they like to sit around on a hard bleacher in the sun watching their boyfriends act like lunatics on a softball field."

Driftwood chuckled.

"But seriously, she's nice, if a bit clueless about when she says the wrong things, but I don't personally have a beef with her."

Deciding he needed to stop thinking about someone else's girlfriend—Jen was Taco's to deal with—Driftwood said, "I thought we could stop by your place so you could grab some things, then we could go over to my house, you could shower while I made something for us to eat, then maybe watch TV."

"Yes."

"Yes?" he asked. "To which part?"

"All of it."

"And…if I said I wouldn't be opposed to you bringing a change of clothes for tomorrow and something to sleep in, you wouldn't freak out?"

She smiled shyly at him. "I did say I'd give you a massage."

"So you did." He squeezed her fingers as he got serious. "I'm not inviting you to spend the night so I can get in your pants, Emmy. I just...I hate when I have to take you home. I like holding you in my arms. I liked seeing you in my bed that first night when I brought you home after your girls' night out."

"There may have been times when I've faked being asleep just so I could stay longer," Quinn admitted.

Driftwood smiled at her. "Yeah?"

"Yeah."

"So, you'll bring some overnight things?"

"I'd love it."

"Good."

"Can I bring my special pillow?"

"Of course."

"And the blanket my great-great-grandmother made for me? It smells a little like mothballs, but I can't sleep without it."

"Anything to make you feel more at home," Driftwood told her.

"And I've got this wedge thing that I put under my feet. It elevates them and helps my circulation."

Driftwood looked over at her, trying to figure out if she was kidding. Her face was completely impassive. "Anything you need, Emmy, you can bring."

"There're three stray chipmunks I've been feeding too, and they'd be devastated if I wasn't there to give them their nightly peanuts. Can they come?"

Now he *knew* she was pulling his leg. "I'm drawing the line at rodents, Quinn. But feel free to bring any toys you might have stashed in the drawer next to your bed, and of course that plant in your living room has to come too."

This time when he looked over at her, she was grinning from ear to ear. It was the first time he'd ever seen her looking incredibly relaxed and happy. Her hair was pulled back, he could see her entire face, and entire birthmark, but she didn't seem to care. He loved it. Loved *her*.

Whoa.

Was that true? Was it even possible so fast?

Fuck yeah, it was.

Driftwood had a feeling he'd been half in love with her before they'd even officially started dating. It wasn't surprising to realize he was madly in love with her now that he'd gotten to know her so much better.

"Of course. And I'll have to bring my books. All of them. I don't know what I might be in the mood to read tonight. Oh, and my slow cooker and my special chair. I'll need those too."

He knew she was kidding, but he wanted to tell her to bring every damn thing. That moving all her shit into his house was fine with him. But things were going so well between them, he didn't want to make her uneasy.

"The only thing I really care about you bringing over is yourself, Quinn. You can bring or not bring anything else you want, as long as *you're* there."

Her smile went from teasing to gentle. "Thanks for being so great. I feel like I can talk to you about anything, that you won't judge me and won't be weird about it."

"You *can* talk to me about anything," he told her. "No matter what it is. I want to hear about your childhood at some point. I want to know your mother's full name so I can have Beth track her down, then I can tell her how much she's missed out on by being a douchecanoe when you were born. I want to know the name of every bully who ever made fun of you so I can have Beth track *them* down and I can tell *them* what assholes they are. I want to know when you're happy and when you're mad. I want to know what frustrates you and what motivates you. In short, Quinn Dixon, I want you to be an open book to me. I want to be your best friend as well as your lover."

"Wow, you don't want much, do you?" she asked shakily.

"I want it all," he confirmed. "Does that freak you out?"

"Surprisingly...no. But maybe we can spread out this knowing-it-all thing a bit?" she asked with a smile.

"Yeah. Tonight, I'll be happy with getting my massage and falling asleep with you in my arms."

"Deal."

Driftwood picked up her hand, kissed the palm, and concentrated on getting them back to her apartment without getting pulled over for speeding.

He walked her into her apartment complex and

followed her to the small mailroom so she could grab her mail.

Driftwood blinked in shock at the mess that greeted them when they opened the door.

There were bright yellow sheets of paper everywhere. Leaning over, he picked one up and saw a Bible verse in bold black letters at the top.

Revelation 2:5

Consider how far you have fallen! Repent and do the things you did at first. If you do not repent, I will come to you and remove your lampstand from its place.

Under that, orange and black flames ran along the bottom of the flier. Driftwood turned it over and saw nothing that indicated which church had placed the pamphlets all over the room.

"What does that even mean?" Quinn asked, reading over his shoulder. "Someone's going to break into our apartments and steal our lights?"

Shaking his head, Driftwood said, "I don't think they mean it literally."

"Whatever," Quinn said, shaking her head. "Someone's really got a bug under their butt."

"A bug under their butt?" Driftwood asked. "I don't think that's a saying."

"Sure it is," she argued. Opening her mailbox, she flipped through her letters, then threw an advertisement into the recycle bin. Looking up at him, she said, "Whatever church this is has really ramped up their campaign to save our souls. There have been a ton of these fliers on our windshields lately. I even had one on my car at the fire station."

"You did? When?"

Quinn bit her lip and thought for a second. "The night I brought dinner for you. You guys all left for a call, and when I took off, there was a flier on my car."

"Weird," Driftwood said. "You see anyone around?"

"No."

"And they weren't on any of *our* vehicles?"

"Not that I noticed. But I didn't take the time to look either."

"Hmmm. Maybe one of the others collected them and threw them away before the rest of us saw them. I think Sledge left early that next morning."

"Probably. It's really not a good way to advertise. I mean, I believe and all, but telling me that God has it out for me isn't very comforting." Quinn wrinkled her nose and looked so cute, Driftwood just wanted to kiss her.

"Come on," he said. "I stink and need a shower."

"I wasn't going to say anything, but..." Quinn teased.

Driftwood looped an arm around her shoulders and pulled her to him. She screeched and tried to push away. He held on tighter and shimmied a little, as if rubbing his stench on her. Quinn was laughing so hard she couldn't talk. All she could say was "no, stop," and "ew!"

The door to the small mailroom opened and Driftwood looked up.

Straight into the eyes of Quinn's neighbor, Willard.

The man stood stock still and stared at Quinn.

No, he stared at her exposed face and neck. Her birthmark was on clear display with her hair pulled back as it was.

Willard stared at her as if transfixed. It was weird... and somehow a little threatening.

Moving quickly, Driftwood pushed Quinn behind him and shuffled to the side, putting as much room as possible between them and Willard. He kept his body between Quinn and the larger man.

Willard shook his head as if trying to get himself under control, then bent down and started to pick up the pamphlets that were scattered around on the floor.

Driftwood pulled open the door and made sure Quinn was safely out of the room before saying, "I don't know what your deal is, but stay away from my girlfriend."

Willard stood up, the yellow fliers in his hand, and stared at them without saying a word, as usual.

Not wanting to stick around, just in case Willard decided to do more than stare menacingly, Driftwood backed out of the room. It wasn't until they were halfway up the stairs that Quinn spoke.

"Do you think it's him?"

"What's him?"

"That he's the one leaving the fliers?"

"I don't know," Driftwood said. And he didn't. But that wasn't what was worrying him. It was the fact that her neighbor was so much bigger and stronger than Quinn. If he was fixated on her, and decided to make a move one night, there wouldn't be much Quinn could do to stop him. "If he ever knocks on your door, don't open it," he ordered her softly.

"I won't."

"I mean it. He might tell you the building's on fire or that he's hurt and needs help. If that happens, you call 9-1-1, don't give him the opportunity to get to you."

"I won't, John."

They'd reached her apartment by this time, and Quinn quickly unlocked her door and led the way inside. Driftwood made sure it was locked behind them and went straight to one of the windows in the living room. Looking out, he saw that there was no fire escape, and there was a small bag sitting below the windowsill.

"It's an emergency ladder," Quinn said from behind him. "I took a safety class for single women at the hospital and they suggested everyone have one of these. Since I'm only on the second floor, it's long enough for me to get out if I have to."

Driftwood nodded. "Good. It's perfect."

She walked up to him and straight into his arms without hesitation. He wrapped them around her and held on tight. Neither cared that they were both a little ripe from being in the sun all day.

After a moment, she said, "I've also got one of those glass-breaker things in my car, and a pointy doohickey I can wear on my knuckles that looks like a cat on my keychain too."

Driftwood shivered thinking about her having to use any of the self-defense gadgets she'd armed herself with. "I'll feel better with you staying at my house tonight," he said.

"Me too," she agreed.

After another minute of simply holding each other, she finally pulled back and gave him a smile. "I'm going to go pack."

"Okay. I'll wait out here."

She nodded and, after giving him an assessing glance, as if wanting to make sure he wasn't going to rush out of the apartment and confront Willard, turned and headed into her bedroom.

Driftwood's hands clenched into fists and he paced, feeling oddly restless. If he could, he'd move Quinn into his house permanently, but he knew that wasn't really an option, not yet. It was too early. But he loathed that she'd obviously captured the attention of the older man who lived on her floor.

Within five minutes, she was back, her hair once again falling around her face and shoulders. She'd changed into a different pair of jeans and had put on a fresh T-shirt. The hair around her temples was wet, as if she'd taken the time to wash her face. She was carrying an extremely bright flowered bag over her shoulder.

Driftwood reached for it and slung it over his own shoulder.

"I can carry that," she told him.

"I know. But I'm here, so you don't have to."

Quinn rolled her eyes at him and Driftwood relaxed slightly. He'd been afraid she'd be weirded out after the odd confrontation with her neighbor.

Driftwood smiled at her. "Need to protect those hands. Can't have you getting tired before I get my massage."

She beamed back at him. "No worries, I'm a professional." She flexed her hands. "I'm good for at *least* a five-minute massage before these babies get tired."

Barking out a laugh, Driftwood realized that seeing her relaxed went a long way toward making him feel the same. "Come on, Emmy. I'm exhausted and could use some quality couch time with you."

"That sounds heavenly," she agreed. "Lead the way."

Driftwood kept his eyes open for Willard as they went back down the stairs and past the mailroom, but he wasn't anywhere to be seen. They hustled to his truck and once they were on their way to his house, Driftwood finally relaxed completely.

They were halfway home when he realized he'd been meaning to stop and get gas for a couple of days now. "Do you mind if we stop at the gas station?" he asked Quinn.

"Am I going to have to walk to your house in this heat if you don't?"

Smirking, Driftwood said, "Maybe."

"Then by all means, please stop."

This was another thing that had been missing in his other relationships. The spontaneity. Everything had always been so planned out. He'd always meticulously scheduled dates and the next steps in their physical relationship, following some pre-determined and socially acceptable timetable for progressing toward actually sleeping together. It was no wonder most of the time, once they'd actually had sex, things usually fizzled out quickly.

But with Quinn, Driftwood was flying by the seat of his pants. He'd laughed more with her than he had with anyone else, other than his firefighter friends, in a long time.

He pulled into a gas station and before he got out to pump gas, asked, "Do you want anything? I can run in after I pump the gas."

She shook her head. "No, I can go in if you want."

"It's fine. I got it," he replied, then pushed open his door.

He wasn't surprised to see Quinn exit the vehicle as well, coming over to his side. "I can go in. It'll save us time." She wiggled her fingers at him. "Thought you wanted my hands on you."

Grabbing one of her hands, Driftwood kissed the palm. "I definitely want your hands on me," he told her.

"Ditto," she said softly.

Dropping her hand and reaching for his wallet in his back pocket, Driftwood pulled out a twenty-dollar bill. "Here you go. Get whatever you want. I've been craving some M&Ms, if you can grab me some."

"Regular, peanut, coconut, peanut butter, crispy, almond, or dark chocolate?"

"What?"

"What kind of M&Ms?"

"Good grief. Just plain, regular ol' classic ones."

She smiled. "You mean the boring ones?"

"Yup. And they aren't boring. They're classic."

"I don't need money, John. I've got some."

"No. I got this."

"John…" she complained.

"Quinn…" he retorted, still holding out the money.

"You're not going to let this go, are you?"

"No."

"Why?"

Looking around, and seeing that no one was waiting to pull in behind them for gas and they weren't holding anyone up, he explained, "I know that you have a job. You're completely competent and you don't need my money. But I don't like you having to pay for things when I'm with you. Call me a Neanderthal. Maybe it's a throwback to the olden times when women stayed home and took care of the kids and the house while men earned the money. I just don't like thinking about you spending your money on me."

"So I'm not ever allowed to buy you presents? Or buy any food?" she asked with a tilt of her head.

"No, that's not what I'm saying."

"John, M&Ms cost like eighty cents. It's not a big deal."

He stared at her for a beat. "You're not going to just give me this, are you?"

"No. Because it's crazy. When I get married, I don't want to have 'my money' and 'my husband's money.' I want it to be 'our money.' I want to have a true partnership. If we start keeping track, and I'm only allowed to use 'my money' when I'm not with you, it won't feel that way."

Driftwood thought about what she was saying, and when her words finally sank in, warmth filled his chest. "Did you just propose?" he teased, as he returned the bill to his wallet and put it back into his pocket, conceding the point with his actions.

Quinn smiled. "If I said yes, would you accept?"

"In a heartbeat," he said softly. "Now, go get me some M&Ms, woman."

Looking shocked but happy, Quinn nodded and turned to head into the convenience store.

Driftwood was still smiling several minutes later when the gas pump clicked off. He put the handle back on the pump and twisted the gas cap on. Since Quinn hadn't returned, he strolled into the store.

He wandered past the candy aisle and found Quinn standing in front of the chips.

"Hey," he said. "Can't make up your mind?"

She shook her head but didn't look up.

He couldn't figure out what was wrong until he glanced over at the counter.

Two twenty-something clerks were staring at Quinn. He had no idea if they'd said something before he'd entered, but their stares were making him uncomfortable. And if *he* was uneasy, he knew Quinn would be too. He bent his head to try to look into Quinn's eyes. She was biting her lip and refused to look at him.

Tucking her hair behind her ear, he said, "Emmy?"

She moved her head away from his fingers and her hair fell back over her cheek once more.

Furious on her behalf, Driftwood turned without a word. He stopped briefly in the candy aisle and grabbed a bag of M&Ms before heading to the front counter.

"Hi," the pretty brunette said with a smile. "Is that all for you today?"

"Actually, no, it's not. What I'd *really* like is to know why you think it's okay to stare at someone. It's rude."

Both women froze as if he'd pulled out a gun and shoved it in their faces.

Driftwood continued, "It's a birthmark. A port-wine birthmark. One out of three hundred babies are born with one. It's a vascular malformation, plain and simple."

"Oh...um...we didn't mean anything by it," the black-haired clerk stuttered.

"John, it's okay," Quinn said softly from behind him. He didn't turn around.

"Here's two bucks. That should cover the cost of my

candy. You can put the change in the tip jar," Driftwood said, wanting to say so much more. But to do so would embarrass Quinn, and he wouldn't do that to her.

He grabbed Quinn's hand and towed her toward the doors, barely noticing when she dropped the candy she'd been holding onto a nearby newspaper stand before they left. He didn't speak as he opened the passenger-side door for her, or as he got into the driver's side and started the engine.

He was still trying to get his anger under control when he heard Quinn make a weird noise next to him.

He turned to her, ready to console her, to try to make her feel better and forget the idiot women in the store—but when he saw her, he blinked in surprise.

She was doing all she could not to burst out laughing.

"Quinn?" he asked.

"Oh my God, John, did you see their faces?"

What in the world? "Um...yes?"

"They were all set to flirt with you, and then you laid into them. I thought they were going to burst into tears right then and there."

She wasn't upset. That was the only thing Driftwood could think.

"Shit, that was *hilarious*," Quinn said absently.

"You're not upset." It wasn't a question.

"I was at first," she told him. "I stood looking at those stupid chips because I didn't want to face them. I was embarrassed and frustrated and even a little mad that, once again, I was being stared at like I was a specimen under a microscope. But I couldn't make my feet move. Then there you were, swooping in like an avenging angel, spreading humiliation and chastising them for being normal human beings."

"That's *not* normal," Driftwood replied. "Being curious is fine, but not being rude like they were."

Quinn was still giggling. "I know. But seriously… that was awesome." Then she leaned over and lightly kissed him on the cheek before sitting back in her seat. "I swear, I wish I could have you follow me around everywhere just so you could put people in their places when they do stuff like that. That would be awesome."

"What would you have done if I hadn't come in?" Driftwood asked, somewhat stunned that she wasn't more upset, not only about him butting in, but about what was said.

"Probably stood there for a minute or two more, then sucked it up and gone up to the counter. I wouldn't have said anything, wouldn't have just left. They probably would've talked about me afterward and speculated about whether my face hurt or if I bleed all over my pillow at night."

"Is that what usually happens?"

She sobered then and nodded. "I'm used to it. I don't like it, but sometimes it's easier to just let it go. It's exhausting trying to educate the world. I'm never going to get everyone to see me as normal. I'm always going to be a freak to some people. Whether because they weren't taught that people are still people no matter what they look like or what their disability, or because of their religion, or because they're just assholes who need to put others down to make themselves feel better. I'm trying to come to the realization that it's *their* problem, not mine."

"You're incredible," Driftwood said and held his hand out to her. She took it immediately, and some of the anger in his soul bled away. "I know you don't exactly like it when I do things like that, but I can't help it."

"It's okay," she said. "I mean, I'm not sure I'd like you as much if you were the kind of man who could hear something like that and just ignore it."

That made him feel better. "I'll do my best to keep it to a minimum. But I can't stand it when you look sad, Emmy. I'll always do whatever I can to keep you happy."

"Thanks," she said softly. Then she chuckled again.

"What now?"

She nodded to the console between them where he'd thrown the pack of M&Ms he'd bought. "Did you even notice that you picked up the dark chocolate ones?"

Looking down, Driftwood saw for the first time that the bag he'd grabbed was dark purple instead of brown. "Damn."

Quinn giggled again. He'd never heard a more beautiful sound in his life.

CHAPTER EIGHT

Quinn sat with her legs curled up next to her and listened to John's heartbeat under her ear. She had her head on his chest and his arm was around her, holding her tightly to him. His feet were bare and resting on the footstool in front of him. They were in the oversized armchair he had in his living room, watching an old James Bond movie.

The day had been long and eventful, but surprisingly, Quinn felt wide awake. She'd been surprised that John had been able to spout statistics of people born with port-wine birthmarks to the clerks today. She'd asked him about it while they were eating dinner and he'd admitted that he'd done some research of his own.

That made her feel good. No one had really done that before, always relying on *her* to tell them what they wanted to know. But John had gone out of his way to educate himself on her birthmark.

Her nervous energy wasn't only because of that

though. It was from spending all day with John and knowing she didn't have to go home. It was from remembering how he'd stood between her and Willard in the mailroom. It was from the way he'd backed down when she'd protested him giving her money to buy a simple bag of candy. It was from thinking about the looks of chagrin on the clerks' faces when the handsome hunk took them down a peg.

It was from the feel of his hand in hers as he drove. The contentment she felt sitting close to him like she was right this moment, simply enjoying each other's company.

In short, John Trettle was everything she'd ever dreamed about in a man. He made her laugh, was protective, and didn't seem to have a problem admitting when he was wrong. Earlier, she'd convinced him to at least try the dark chocolate M&Ms, and even though he'd made a fuss, he had. And had been surprised to find he liked them just as much, or more, than the classic plain ones.

"What are you thinking about so hard over there?" he asked, interrupting her internal musings.

"That I haven't given you that massage I owe you." That hadn't been what she'd been planning on saying, but Quinn couldn't be upset when she looked up and saw the interest flare in his eyes.

"Where do you want me?" he asked.

Carnal images shot to her brain, but she controlled the hussy inside her and said, "You could lie on the floor right here."

"Your wish is my command," he said with a smirk.

She sat up, giving him room to scoot to the edge of the chair. He got down on his knees and looked back at her. "Shirt off or on?"

"Off." The answer was immediate. She'd been trying to figure out how to get him out of his clothes since he'd entered the kitchen after his shower earlier. He smelled delicious, and the teasing glimpses she'd gotten of his chest hair peeking from the V of his polo shirt had been driving her crazy.

Without breaking eye contact, John brought one hand up to the back of his neck and pulled, ducking at the last minute to yank the material over his head.

Quinn got a glimpse of a very defined chest with a sexy smattering of blond chest hair before he turned and lay down on the carpet in front of the chair.

She'd seen his grin as he'd lowered himself, but she couldn't even care that he was enjoying himself a little too much. Two could play at that game.

Once he was settled, Quinn kneeled on the floor and threw one leg over his thighs. She lowered herself down until she was sitting on his ass. And what a firm ass it was.

John groaned and rested his forehead on his hands under his head.

"What was that...?" Quinn asked with a smirk.

"Nothing. Carry on," he said.

Quinn leaned over and placed her hands on his warm shoulders and began to knead. Jesus, he was one big muscle. Digging her fingers into his flesh, she lost herself in the feel of his skin under her fingers.

How long she'd massaged his shoulders and upper back, she had no idea.

It wasn't until she moved down to his lower back and pressed with her thumbs that he groaned again and shifted under her.

"Sorry, too hard?" she asked, pausing in her ministrations.

"No, God no. Your hands are fucking magic," he told her.

"Oh. Good." Quinn shifted down farther, giving herself more room to caress his lower back. She was so focused on what she was doing, she didn't even realize that her hips were moving in tandem with her hands. Up and down. Over and over.

Not able to stop herself, she leaned over and placed a kiss in the middle of John's back. Then her tongue came out, and she licked a small path up his spine.

He shuddered beneath her—and the next thing she knew, she was flat on her back on the floor and John was hovering over her. This time, he was straddling *her*. She looked up in surprise and froze at the look in his eyes.

Lust.

The man was beautiful, and intense, and at that moment, Quinn thought she knew exactly how the heroines felt in the books she liked to read, being conquered by a handsome, marauding knight.

"John?"

"I'm sorry. I couldn't take any more."

"It didn't feel good?" she asked.

"It felt more than good. It felt fucking fantastic. So much so I almost lost it with just the touch of your hands on me. But when I felt your lips on my skin, that was it. Game over."

Quinn couldn't help it. Her eyes went south to his crotch. Sure enough, there was a wet spot on the front of his jeans. Holy shit. He'd come from just her hands on his back?

"I've dreamed about having you touch me for so long but the reality was ten times better than anything I imagined. When you kissed me, all I could think of was what your mouth would feel like on other parts. The final straw was your hot, wet tongue on me."

Quinn smiled. She loved knowing she'd done that for him. To him.

"You like that," he said.

"Yeah," she agreed. Feeling braver than she'd ever felt with anyone, she ran her hands up his lightly furred chest, loving how the springy chest hairs felt on her palms. He was all man, and she didn't think she'd ever get enough of him.

He groaned again when her fingers brushed over his nipples, making them stiffen into little points. Lifting her head, she covered one with her mouth and sucked, hard.

"Enough," John croaked.

She felt his fingers at the hem of her blouse.

"Emmy?" he asked.

Loving that, even after he'd come and she was still teasing him, he paused to make sure she was okay with him taking off her shirt, she nodded.

Ever so slowly, John eased her T-shirt up and over her head. She felt her hair billow out above her head and realized that she hadn't thought about her birthmark once since she'd put her hands on John.

"Holy shit," he exclaimed, and she looked up into his face. His eyes were glued to her chest. Quinn had never thought much about her boobs. They weren't huge or tiny. They were proportionate to her body. But John obviously approved.

His hands hovered over her bra for a second before reverently pulling the cups down, exposing her nipples to his view. The material of her bra got caught under the globes and he used his thumb and forefinger on one nipple as he leaned forward and took the other in his mouth.

The second his lips closed over the sensitive tip, Quinn arched her back and moaned. God, this felt so good. Only one other man had seen her bare breasts, and he'd done some courtesy tugging and sucking on them, but had immediately moved to what he'd called "the good stuff."

But John's mouth on her...holy hell...*that* was the good stuff. With every suck from his mouth, she felt a corresponding twinge deep in her core. She opened her legs as wide as she could with him still straddling her and felt John give her his weight. Tipping her hips up, she felt him shift until his hard cock was right where she needed it.

Neither of them said a word. They communicated with body language. When he sucked a little too hard, Quinn squeaked and he eased off. When she moaned, he increased the speed of his tongue flicking against her nipple. When he switched sides, and his fingers rolled the nipple that had just been in his mouth, she couldn't help but spread her legs even farther apart and press upward with her hips.

As if they'd done this forever, John began to gently thrust against her in time to his sucks on her nipple. Quinn felt overwhelmed with sensation. She could feel the cool air from the AC against her naked chest, all the more chilly on the nipple still wet from his mouth. He made noises in his throat, which reverberated through his mouth, making the sensual torture of her nipple more intense.

But as much as she was enjoying his ministrations, she knew she wouldn't be able to come from them. God, how she wished she was the kind of woman who could come from nipple play alone. But she wasn't.

"John," she moaned desperately.

"What do you need?"

She shook her head. "I don't know."

"Bullshit. What do you need, Quinn?"

Without thought other than to ease the ache inside her, Quinn moved her hand down the front of her body. John immediately gave her room and watched as she unbuttoned the top button of her jeans with one hand, then slipped it under the waistband.

"Fuck, that's sexy," he murmured, then leaned down and captured her nipple with his mouth once more. He alternated between nipping at it and sucking hard. He put one hand under her ass and squeezed while the other kept up its assault on her other nipple.

Quinn knew if she thought too much about what she was doing, she'd be embarrassed, but at the moment, all she could do was feel. As she fingered her clit, she hovered on the edge of an orgasm, desperate for the release, but not knowing what else to do to get there.

The choice was taken from her as John leaned up and put his lips on her neck. He licked and sucked before moving up to nibble at her ear. "You're so fucking beautiful," he murmured, his warm breath wafting gently over her, making her shiver and goose bumps raise on her skin. "So perfect."

His fingers tugged on her nipple relentlessly at the same time the others dug into the fleshy skin of her ass. "Let go, Emmy. I'll catch you. So beautiful." Then he took her earlobe in his mouth and sucked. Hard.

That did it.

Quinn's legs began to shake and her eyes slammed shut. She could feel the copious wetness between her legs and used it to help stimulate her clit. The orgasm welled inside her and she put her feet flat on the floor and pushed upward. She didn't get far, not with John's weight on her, but the move pushed the hand inside her jeans against his hard cock, and the extra pressure, along with the thought of how he'd look right before pushing into her, was all it took.

Arching her back, Quinn came.

She started to pull her hand out of her pants, but John grabbed her wrist, holding it in there as he moved it up and down. The extra stimulation on her already swollen and sensitive clit made her orgasm more intense than she'd ever felt before.

"John!" she called out in surprise and ecstasy.

"That's it, Em. Take it."

She felt his mouth latch onto her nipple one last time, which pushed another tremble through her body. Her heart was beating double time and she felt as if she'd just sprinted a mile. Too self-conscious to open her eyes, Quinn felt John's grip on her wrist relax and she pulled her hand out of her pants.

Before she could do anything else, she felt John's mouth close around her fingers.

Her eyes popped open, and she watched as he licked her fingers clean. The reverence on his face easy to see as he tasted her for the first time. Then he moved until he was on his side and pulled her with him.

They remained on the floor, with John on his back and Quinn half on the floor, half on John. Her bra was still shoved under her boobs and her pants were still undone. John's dick was still hard, and he had to be uncomfortable with his wet jeans. But Quinn couldn't make herself move.

Now she was tired. Exhausted. It was as if the

climax had stolen any energy she'd once had. She didn't even care that she was practically naked from the waist up.

"Mmmm," she mumbled, feeling as if she should say *something*.

"Shhh," John murmured.

She could do that. Quinn shut her eyes and completely relaxed. She knew it wouldn't matter if she fell asleep; John would get her up off the floor and into bed.

That ball of hope in her belly had grown bigger than ever before. And that scared the hell out of her. Quinn had no idea what she'd do if John decided she ultimately wasn't worth the effort.

But for now, she was going to hang on and enjoy the ride.

CHAPTER NINE

"Can you believe those idiots?" Autumn bitched as she entered the lab a week later.

Tory, Quinn, and Sophie were already inside and getting ready to start their morning.

"Right?" Tory said. "I'm glad they aren't allowed on this side of the street. They were kind of scary."

"They were definitely a bit intense, weren't they?" Sophie asked.

Quinn shivered, remembering the things the men and women yelled as she'd walked from the parking garage down the street to the Burn Center Annex. There'd been around ten people, all holding signs portending doom and encouraging people to turn to God to be saved.

It was definitely odd that it seemed every time she turned around, someone was trying to shove religious ideology in her face. From the fliers at her apartment and at the fire station, and now this group at her work?

In her life, she'd had more than her fair share of people telling her to find God because of the mark on her face, but lately it seemed as if everywhere she went, religion was being forced down her throat.

"Can't security do anything about them?" Autumn asked. "They've been here every day this week. Talking about judgement day and telling us we're all going to Hell and babbling about consorting with the devil."

"I know s-someone who's been doing s-some consorting," Sophie quipped, wiggling her eyebrows in Quinn's direction and successfully changing the subject.

Quinn could only laugh. She'd been waiting for this since the first day she came to work after spending the night with John. She was honestly surprised Sophie had controlled herself for this long.

"Happily consorting," she agreed, smiling broadly.

Sophie made a weird squeaking noise in the back of her throat. "S-Spill!" she demanded.

Quinn shrugged. "John's been so great. When he's not working, I've been staying at his place."

"Shut up!" Tory exclaimed. "You've moved in?"

"Well, no. But ever since Willard showed up in the mailroom and stared at me when John was there, he doesn't like me being at my apartment. And honestly, that's okay with me."

"But you s-stay at home when he's working?" Sophie asked.

"Yeah. But once I'm in my apartment, I'm in. And John texts me on and off all evening and first thing in the morning. Other than Willard, I don't feel unsafe there. I think John's blowing things out of proportion. I was perfectly fine before we started dating. I don't know what he thinks...maybe just because we're now dating, I can't take care of myself?"

"But you said yourself that Willard creeps you out," Autumn noted. "Has that changed?"

"Well, no. But it's a little frustrating that John doesn't seem to think I can keep myself safe. I'm always careful to check to see who's at my door before I answer it—not that anyone ever *knocks* on my door. I carry my keys in my hand with that sharp pokey thing around my knuckles. I have that emergency ladder so I can get out if I need to. In other words, I'm completely able to take care of myself."

"Be honest, Quinn, when you s-stay at his place, you s-sleep better, don't you?" Sophie asked.

Sighing, Quinn could only nod. "Yeah."

"I was the s-same way. When Roman works, I'm not afraid to be in our house by m-myself. But there's just s-something about having another person there that's comforting. And the fact that it's Roman m-makes m-me feel even m-more s-safe."

"It's the same with me. Why is that? I mean, we're grown-up, competent adults. I've never been worried about anyone breaking in or someone doing something awful to me before. But late at night, when I'm in my bed and I've just hung up from talking with John, every little noise has me tensing. It's crazy."

"I don't know, but if you figure it out, let m-me know," Sophie said wryly.

"And... No, never mind," Quinn said.

"What?" Sophie asked.

"Nothing."

"Spit it out," Autumn ordered. "You know this is a no-secret zone." She twirled her finger in a circle indicating the space the four of them were sitting in.

"Fine. What happens if we break up? Will I go back to my invincible attitude, or will I be all shaky and scared all the time? Because that would suck."

"Are you thinking about breaking up with him?" Tory asked.

"No!" Quinn exclaimed. "I'm just thinking out loud."

"That's your problem," Sophie said wisely. "You can't predict the future. Don't borrow trouble. You s-said things were good between you guys, right?"

"Right."

"Then why think negatively?"

Quinn sighed. "Everywhere I go, I'm gawked at. Just the other day he had to give two gas station employees a verbal tongue lashing for staring at me. I know how tired *I* am of it, and I've lived with it my entire life. I'm just afraid he's going to wake up one day and wonder what the hell he's doing. Being with someone else would be a hell of a lot easier for him, that's for sure."

"Maybe, maybe not," Autumn said. "Look, I'm not saying I know what you've been through, I don't. But it sounds to me like you're just making excuses now. Like you're giving yourself excuses as to why he'll break up with you even before he does it...if only to protect your heart. Quit it. Honestly, Quinn, this guy has liked you for ages. He's a grown man. It's not like he didn't know what he was getting into before he declared you were dating. You need to let him in. *All* the way in. Trust him."

Quinn bit her lip. Then looked at her three friends. "Everyone in my entire life has let me down...except for you guys. Every time I've decided to fully trust someone, I ended up being disappointed and hurt. And that's gone for families I thought I finally fit in with, friends at school, boys I dated...I'm not sure I know *how* to trust John wholeheartedly."

"Then you need to figure it out," Autumn retorted unsympathetically. "Quinn, I love you, but you're twenty-eight years old. You're not a kid anymore. People are assholes, there's no doubt about it, but John isn't one of them. Think about it this way...what do you think could happen if you *did* open yourself up all the way to him?"

Quinn stared at her friend.

"Did you ever think that maybe everything you'd ever yearned for in life could be right there, yours for the pickin'?"

Quinn blinked. No. She hadn't thought about that. She'd been so busy trying to protect her heart from being hurt again. She'd held a part of herself back from John because she was half waiting for the other shoe to drop. For him to tell her that she was too much effort.

That he didn't like the attention she drew when they went out.

But John hadn't given her any indication that he was that kind of man. Not even before they'd started dating. He'd been nothing but attentive and concerned about her. In all the months she'd known him, he'd never made her feel as if she was a burden or an embarrassment to him.

"You're right," she whispered.

"I know," Autumn said smugly. "Question is, what are you going to do about it?"

"S-She's going to continue to be the m-most awesomest girlfriend Driftwood's ever had," Sophie said. "Right?"

"Right," Quinn agreed, ready to be out of the hot seat, even if Autumn was correct.

The conversation turned to the cases they were working on and how the latest burn victims were healing. As she worked, and the others chatted, Quinn reflected on her life.

Yeah, she'd had a hell of a childhood. Kids were cruel, and not having a stable or loving home life to help her deal with the taunts and teasing had been hard. She'd had no one to rely on but herself for practically her entire life.

But John had been there for her since they'd met. Calling out people who were intentionally or unintentionally being rude. Knowing he was only a text or a call away when she needed to vent, or if she wanted to share with him something good that had happened, was pretty wonderful. But what had she done for *him*?

Quinn realized suddenly that he was giving way more than he got in their relationship.

Oh, she knew he wouldn't look at it that way, but she made a vow right then and there to do her best to let down her shields that she'd always kept in place to protect herself. She didn't need to protect herself from John. He'd continue to treat her with care.

But she needed to treat *him* with care too. Show him that she appreciated him. That she was proud of him. She hadn't done enough of that lately. Starting today, that was going to change.

* * *

Driftwood pulled into his driveway, thrilled to see Quinn's car parked there. He hadn't expected her to already be at his house. He'd given her a key, but to his knowledge, she had yet to use it. There was something so...right...about coming home and knowing she was inside waiting on him.

The day had been hard. They'd been very busy, with hardly any time to stop and eat. From traffic accidents, to downed trees, to medical calls, they'd been going nonstop.

And right before his shift ended, they'd been called to a possible drowning.

A three-year-old little boy had gone outside when the family was busy and not paying attention and had fallen into their pool. By the time his mom had realized he was missing, he'd been in the water over five minutes.

Driftwood and Chief had done their best, though they both knew the child had little to no chance of survival. The paramedics had loaded him up in their ambulance, but things didn't look good for the little boy.

Right before his shift was over, they'd gotten word that the boy had been pronounced dead at the hospital.

It wasn't as if Driftwood hadn't dealt with death before, he had, but for some reason, this case hit him harder than most. Maybe it was because the mom reminded him a little bit of Quinn. She had the same hair and was about the same height and build. The anguish and self-recrimination on her face was hard to witness.

Not bothering to pull his truck into the garage, Driftwood hopped out and headed for his front door.

The second he pushed it open, he smelled something delicious coming from his kitchen. Following the smell, he couldn't help but smile when he saw Quinn leaning over looking into the stove.

"Hey," he said quietly so as not to spook her.

She still jumped and spun around with one hand on her chest. "Oh! You scared me."

"Sorry, Emmy. It smells delicious in here."

She tilted her head and stared at him for a beat before walking toward him with a look he couldn't interpret on her face. Quinn stepped close and put her arms around him. Her head rested on his shoulder and he felt her lips against his neck.

Sighing in contentment, Driftwood pulled her tighter into him and closed his eyes. She smelled like whatever she'd been cooking and her hair tickled his face. This wasn't a sexual hug, it was a comforting hug. And man, did he need it right about now. Needed her.

They stood like that for a long moment. Driftwood eventually pulled back, but only far enough to see her face. "You okay?" he asked.

She nodded. "Yeah, but you looked like you could use a hug."

"It was a tough day," he told her.

"Can you talk about it?"

Driftwood nodded. "But not right now. Later. I'm starving, and whatever you're making smells delicious."

"It's just a pork loin and potatoes. I was having a stare-down contest with the potatoes and losing. I'm not sure they're going to be done in time."

"We can take them out and stick them in the microwave to finish them off," Driftwood told her.

Quinn sighed. "I know, but I didn't want to have to resort to that."

He chuckled. "Trust me, I'm not going to even notice. That's how hungry I am."

"Well, then, by all means, let's get you fed."

It took another thirty minutes for everything to be ready, but as soon as the food was plated, Driftwood dug in. It was one of the best meals he'd had in a long time. Not because of the food itself, which was good...

but because of the company. He'd eaten dinner with Quinn before, but this meal felt different. He couldn't put his finger on why, but something about her was different tonight. She seemed more relaxed or something.

They talked about her day at work and about the religious zealots who were gathered outside. She recounted how, after many complaints, hospital security had tried to get them to move on their way. When that didn't work, the SAPD had to be called to get them to disperse. And then, of course, when she'd gone to her car at the end of the day, there had not only been religious fliers stuck under everyone's windshield wipers, but also handwritten notes about going to Hell and resisting the devil added to the bottom of the one on her car, and a few others.

Driftwood wasn't happy about the harassment, but he felt a little better knowing that the hospital officials weren't thrilled either. They'd arranged for extra security in the garage for employees leaving and were going to be working with the local cops to make sure the protestors, whoever they were, didn't get out of hand.

After they ate, they cleaned the kitchen together and then wandered into the living room. Driftwood sat on the couch and Quinn immediately snuggled into his side.

"Tell me about your day," she said gently.

This was new for Driftwood. He'd never had someone to discuss work with before. Not like this.

And he had absolutely no desire to keep anything from her.

Once he started talking, he couldn't seem to stop. He told her about Penelope and how she'd been acting weird lately. Disconnected and not seeming happy to be at work. He talked about how hard it was to be polite to the guy who'd been completely smashed at one in the afternoon and had crashed into a minivan with a mom and two kids. He was fine, didn't have a scratch on him, but the family had all been sent to the hospital.

He admitted he was having a hard time getting over the scene with the little boy and the pool. That every time he closed his eyes, he saw the anguish on the mother's face. How pissed he was that the gate surrounding the pool hadn't been locked.

"It was a mistake, I get that, but things could've been so different if someone had just noticed he'd snuck out of the house. Or if that gate had been locked. Or if someone had missed him earlier. It was just so stupid. It didn't have to happen. That little boy would be alive right now if a little more care had been taken."

"Shhhh," Quinn said and put her hand on his cheek as she leaned into him. "You did the best you could. It wasn't your fault. It wasn't anyone's fault. Sometimes things just happen. I'm not saying they shouldn't have kept a better eye on him, but kids are curious. They get into things."

Choking back a sob, Driftwood squeezed his eyes closed. He felt Quinn move until she was straddling him. She buried her nose into the side of his neck and forced her hands between his back and the couch. She held on tightly and gave him time to grieve.

Holding her, feeling her touch surrounding him, gave Driftwood the strength to keep the tears at bay. It wasn't that he thought crying wasn't manly or anything, he'd bawled his eyes out more than once after getting home and thinking about a heartbreaking call. It was the fact that she was there, supporting him, letting him talk things out. Feel however he needed to feel.

They sat like that for a long time. So long that Driftwood wondered if Quinn was still awake. He rubbed one hand up and down her back and turned his head just enough to kiss her temple.

"Better?" she asked softly.

"Yeah, Emmy. Thanks."

"I'm sorry I've been taking so much and not giving back. I'm going to work on that."

"What?"

She sat up and looked him in the eyes. "Throughout the entire time I've known you, you've always been the one to back me up. You haven't hesitated to educate little kids when they stare a bit too long and you've never been ashamed or afraid to tell someone off when they say something rude. I haven't even thought about what your job entails, or that you might need someone to stand up for you too…even if it's only in private here in your home. I'm going to try to be better at that."

Driftwood couldn't help it; he burst out laughing.

Her brows drew down in irritation. "What are you laughing at?"

"You, Quinn."

She tried to pull away, but he tightened his hands behind her. "I'm laughing that you think you haven't been giving me anything."

"I haven't. I've been selfish and I'm always relying on you."

"I wish you'd rely on me more," Driftwood told her. "Seriously. You're one of the hardest women to do things for. I know you don't like it when I 'educate people,' as you so eloquently put it, so I've held myself back so many times when I hear someone talking about you. You won't let me pay for an eighty-cent bag of candy and you have no idea how much your fun, breezy texts mean to me."

"You ended up paying for those stupid M&Ms," she mumbled, looking away from him.

Driftwood put a finger under her chin and eased her head back so she was looking at him. "I'm not keeping score, Emmy. This isn't a softball game. When you need me, I want to be there for you. And when I need you, like tonight, I know without a doubt you'll be there for *me*. I was thrilled when I pulled up and saw your car here. You were just what I needed, and I didn't even know it until I realized you were here."

"Really?"

"Yes. I gave you a key to my place for a reason. I want you here. I like you being here. I wish you'd stay when I've got a shift."

"It feels weird."

"What does?"

"Being here without you. I don't like it."

Driftwood smiled and gathered her hair in one hand and held it at the nape of her neck. He gently pulled until her head was tilted to the side, and he leaned forward and licked her neck. Whispering into her ear, he asked, "Why?"

She shivered in his arms and didn't pull away from his touch. "Because I don't like sleeping in your bed without you."

He liked that answer. A lot. But at the same time, it worried him. "I can't change my schedule, Emmy. I hate that I can't sleep by your side every night, but I love my job."

"I know," she said immediately. "I just...I don't live here, so it feels weird to be here when you aren't."

"Then move in."

His words sat between them like a heavy fog.

Quinn sat back, and this time he let her. She stared at him. "Seriously?"

"Yeah, seriously." He hadn't thought about the words before he'd said them, but now that he had, they felt right. He'd already had the thought that he'd be okay with her bringing all her stuff over to his house, and this was why. He wanted her here. All the time. Even when he wasn't. He wanted to know she was sleeping in his bed, eating his food, watching his TV. It may seem fast, but the months he'd been friends with her, getting to know her, made this absolutely feel like the right thing to do.

"We haven't even been dating that long. What if you get sick of me? If I irritate you?"

"Emmy, we've known each other for months. I'm not going to get sick of you. Having you sleep here the last week has been wonderful. If it makes you feel more comfortable, you don't have to get rid of your apartment just yet. But bring over as much stuff as you want. There's plenty of room in the closet and I'll clear a few drawers for you."

She stared at him with wide, shocked eyes, and Driftwood wasn't sure what she was thinking. But it certainly wasn't what came out of her mouth when she finally *did* speak.

"My entire life, no one has *wanted* to live with me."

His heart twisted, and Driftwood wanted to hurt someone on her behalf all over again. "Tell me," he coaxed instead of getting pissed.

"You know about my mom. I was shuttled from one foster home to another. No matter how much I might've liked a place, I always got moved eventually. The older I got, the less welcoming my new 'families' were. No one wanted me there, not the freak with the thing on her face. I was too weird looking. Too different. Even in college, I was assigned a roommate my first year and she certainly didn't like living with the weirdo. I moved into my own place my sophomore year and lived alone until I graduated. Then I got the job here and moved into my apartment. I don't even know if I'm a good roommate. I've lived on my own for so long, I have no idea how to even *be* a roommate."

"Then don't be my roommate," Driftwood told her. "Be my lover. My best friend."

Tears glistened in her eyes as she processed his words.

"If anything, I need to be the one worrying. You haven't had to share a bathroom with anyone before. You've only had to worry about your own messes and doing your own dishes and laundry. If you move in here, you won't have as much privacy as you're used to. You'll have to deal with my moods, and I do get in them, especially after a long shift. Inevitably, I'll want to watch TV when you want quiet to read. You'll be irritated when I want to watch football or basketball and you want to watch something else. We're going to get in each other's way and that's a big adjustment, not only for you, but for me too. But, Emmy, I can tell you this—I've never asked a woman to move in before because I haven't felt the deep-seated need to be with anyone that I feel with you. Keep your apartment. We'll see how things go. Okay?"

She nodded.

"So…you'll move in?"

She nodded again, and gave him a small smile.

Without a word, he suddenly stood, holding Quinn tight.

She screeched and grabbed hold of him around his neck. "Don't drop me!" she exclaimed.

"As if," he scoffed. "I can carry Moose around when

he's wearing all his gear. Compared, you're as light as a feather."

She rolled her eyes. "Where are you taking me?"

"To our bed," he said, moving down the hall.

"But it's only like seven o'clock."

"And?" he asked, raising one eyebrow.

Quinn offered a sly smile then. "You're right. I'm awfully tired. And you have to be exhausted after the day you've had."

Driftwood smirked. "Tired. Yeah. Is that a euphemism for horny?"

She giggled.

He dropped her on the mattress and she laughed even harder.

Driftwood came down over her and caged her in with his arms. He waited until she looked up at him. "Thank you for being here, Quinn. I didn't think anything could shake me from the funk I was in when I left the station. But I was wrong. Just seeing you did wonders. It made me focus on the good things in my life rather than the bad things I'd witnessed."

"I feel the same way," she told him. "When I'm with you, I forget all about this thing on my face."

Driftwood leaned down and kissed her then, showing her without words how he felt about her. How much he was coming to love her. She returned the kiss with the kind of passion he'd seen glimpses of over the last week. They hadn't made love yet, but everything they'd done before now had hinted that

"Ten minutes ago," she responded a little petulantly.

John chuckled, and she was about to reprimand him when she felt the tip of his cock press again her folds. She lifted her leg to try to give him more room. John grasped it and put it over his shoulder as he leaned closer.

Looking up, Quinn saw his head was bent and he was staring at her intently.

"Okay?" he asked quietly.

"Yeah."

He pressed in a bit more, and Quinn couldn't help but wince.

"Shit," he muttered and began to pull out.

Quinn tightened her leg on his shoulder and tugged on his arms. "No! Please. Don't stop."

"I won't hurt you," he said firmly.

"John," she pleaded. "You're not hurting me, not really. It's just been a while. I can take it. I can take you. I *want* you. Please."

With a nod, he pushed into her once more.

Trying to relax her muscles, Quinn did her best to keep her face impassive.

"I'm in," he said softly.

Quinn could feel his balls pressed up against her backside, and she felt full. Really full. When he didn't move after a moment, she asked, "John?"

"I'm giving us both a minute," he said. Then he chuckled and said, "If I moved even an inch right now, I'd blow."

Quinn laughed and he groaned. "Fuck, that felt good."

"What? This?" she asked, and tightened her Kegel muscles around him.

"Oh yeah, that," John agreed. "Do it again."

She did, and he moaned again. Then he pulled out until only the very tip of his cock was inside her and slowly pushed back in. He did that several times before her hips began to move upward to meet his slow and steady thrusts.

"You ready for more?"

"Yes," she told him emphatically.

"Touch yourself," he ordered.

With any other man, Quinn might've balked. Might've told him she was fine, or might've faked an orgasm. But this was John. He'd already gotten her off with his own hand several times, and the last thing she wanted was to fake anything with him.

She took her right hand off of John's arm and moved it between their bodies. Every time he pushed inside her, the back of her hand brushed against his lower belly.

"Faster, Emmy. I want your orgasm to trigger mine."

Well, shit, no pressure there, huh? But she didn't say the thought out loud, she just quickened her fingers against her clit. John leaned over her farther, making it harder for her to finger herself, but she didn't complain and didn't take her eyes from his.

She watched as a blotch of red formed on his upper chest, felt the muscles in his arms tighten.

Seeing for herself how much he was enjoying making love to her did wonders for her self-esteem. His eyes stayed on her face the entire time he was thrusting. He didn't close them, didn't throw his head back. He was fucking *her*. Quinn Dixon. The chick with the weird birthmark.

All her life, she'd prayed for this. For someone to see her. The real her. And here he was. With her, inside her, loving her as she'd never been loved before in her life.

As if that thought was all it took, she detonated. Her thighs shook with the overwhelming ecstasy. She forced herself to keep her eyes open even as her world exploded.

John moved one hand to her ass and lifted her into his last thrust. He planted himself as deep inside her as possible as he plummeted over the edge himself. His jaw tightened, and it wasn't until her own body stopped shaking that he finally closed his eyes and let out a huge exhale.

After he'd recuperated, he gently took her leg off his shoulder and eased out of her. He rolled over onto his side and pulled her with him. They lay like that for several minutes, recovering.

Finally, he said, "I need to get rid of this condom."

"Okay," Quinn mumbled.

He chuckled and eased out of bed, taking the time to throw the comforter over her so she didn't get chilled while he was gone.

Quinn watched him walk butt naked toward the

bathroom, admiring the way his muscles moved under his skin. He entered the bathroom and was gone only a short time before he was coming back to bed. And the view from the front was just as nice as the one from the back.

His cock was semi-hard, and Quinn couldn't help but be impressed. She'd felt it, even seen him when he'd undressed earlier, but watching him stride toward her completely comfortable in his own skin, was glorious.

When he arrived back at the bed, he was smirking. "I'm happy to let you see my cock up close and personal if you want," he quipped as he lifted the comforter and climbed back into bed with her.

Quinn sighed.

"What was that for?" he asked.

"I'm just content," she told him.

"Me too," he said softly. "I didn't think anything could get better than holding you while you slept, but this definitely tops it."

"Having sex?"

"No. Watching you sleep after having made love to you."

"Good answer," Quinn said softly.

"My home is your home," he told her. "You don't have to ask to come over. You don't have to worry about snooping. I've got no secrets. At least not from you. I need to clean out my garage so you can park in there, but I'll get that done soon."

"Your truck is way more expensive than my car," she argued.

"It's not about money," John said. "It's about safety. And both our vehicles can fit in there, I just have to move my shit around."

"Thank you."

"You're welcome. The best day in my life was the day I met you, Emmy. It took us a while to get here, but I think it made us both appreciate what we have in one another."

He was right.

"Go to sleep," he said.

"It's still early."

"I know. But I can tell you're tired by the circles under your eyes. I am too. It was a hell of a shift. I'll set the alarm and make sure you're up in time to get to work. Okay?"

"Okay."

"Good night, Emmy."

"Night, John."

CHAPTER TEN

"*W*hat the *fuck*?" Driftwood exclaimed the next morning when he walked Quinn out to the driveway.

The word *repent* was scratched into the hood of his truck.

"This is why I want to clear out my garage," Driftwood seethed as he fished his phone out of his pocket.

"Who are you calling?"

"Quint Axton. He works for the San Antonio Police Department."

"Do you need to use my car today?" Quinn asked.

It was sweet of her to offer, but he didn't care about his truck. "Thanks, Emmy. I'm good. This isn't an emergency, so it might take a while for someone to get free to come out here to take the report, but I don't have any plans for this morning."

Looking around, Quinn asked, "Was your truck the only one vandalized?"

"Don't know," Driftwood said. "But I'm sure whoever comes out to take the report will check around to make sure."

"I swear I've seen the word repent more in the last few weeks than any other time in my life. What exactly should we repent for? Do you think someone knows what we did last night?"

Driftwood hated the way she looked so worried. What they'd done was beautiful. He didn't want her to feel anything but content when she remembered the night they'd shared.

"This wasn't random," he said quietly. "Especially after everything else that's been going on."

"I'm beginning to think that too," Quinn admitted.

"The fliers, the protesters, and now this? Someone's harassing you for some reason—and it's got to stop."

"But who?"

Driftwood sighed. "I don't know. Willard? He always seems to pop up in the same places you are."

"I hate this," Quinn whispered.

Driftwood opened his mouth to reassure her when someone picked up on the other end of the line.

"Hello?"

"Quint? This is John Trettle. Driftwood. I need some assistance."

"Are you okay?"

"Yeah, fine. But my truck was vandalized last night. It was parked in my driveway and the word *repent* was scratched into the hood sometime between six o'clock last night and now."

"You got something you need to confess?" Quint joked.

"Not funny, man."

"Sorry. You're right. I'll see what I can do about getting out there as soon as I can. You working today?"

"No. Just got off a forty-eight."

"Okay. I'll give you a yell when I'm on my way."

"I'm going to take Quinn to work, will that be all right?"

"Yeah. It'll probably be an hour or so before I can make it out there."

"Perfect. I'll see you later."

"Yup. Oh, and Driftwood?"

"Yeah?"

"I'm assuming you'll be taking her car. Don't touch yours. Just in case."

"Gotcha. Later."

"Later."

Driftwood hung up, put his phone back in his pocket, and turned to face Quinn. She had her hair down, as usual, but unlike over breakfast, when she'd had her head up and was completely relaxed, now her shoulders were hunched and she looked uneasy.

"There is nothing wrong with what we did last night. It was beautiful, and I've got nothing I need to repent for. Neither do you. Got it?"

She let out a huge sigh. "Yeah. You're going to take me to work?"

"If you don't mind."

"Of course not. I told you that you could use my car."

That wasn't why he wanted to take her to work, but he didn't correct her. Driftwood was uneasy. He wasn't a hugely religious man. He believed in God and in Heaven and Hell, but was uncomfortable with the fire-and-brimstone stuff that a lot of people in the south believed and participated in.

But vandalism was going above and beyond when it came to trying to preach the word of God. Fliers and demonstrations were one thing. Carving shit into people's vehicles was something different altogether. Maybe it was kids being kids. Maybe it was nothing more than an overzealous member of a congregation. But for some reason, Driftwood couldn't get the face of Quinn's neighbor, Willard, out of his mind.

The man had a lot going on in his head. He hadn't ever said anything aloud, that Driftwood could remember, but his eyes spoke volumes.

"Have you seen your neighbor lately?" Driftwood asked Quinn.

"No. I've been over here a lot and when I *have* been at my apartment, I've just parked and, after checking my mail, gone straight upstairs."

"And he hasn't been around?"

She shrugged. "Not that I've noticed. Do you really think he did this? How would he know where you live? Oh my God...do you think he followed me? Should we call the police?"

"Shhhh," he soothed her. "I just called them, remember?"

"Oh yeah."

"Try not to worry. I'll talk to Quint and we'll see what we can figure out."

"Do you have cameras? You know, those things you can hook up to your phone that let you know if someone walks by?"

"Unfortunately, no. This is a good neighborhood. I've never felt the need for them."

Quinn raised her eyebrows and stared at him.

He laughed. "Right. I'll order a set today."

"I'm sorry about your truck."

"It's just a vehicle. My insurance will pay for the damages."

"Still."

"Come on, you need to get to work."

"You want to drive?" she asked.

"Sure."

"It'll be easier for you to drop me off if we don't have to switch places when we get there."

"I don't mind if you drive, Quinn," Driftwood told her. "I'm not the kind of man who always has to drive if we're going somewhere."

"I know. But I always feel safe with you behind the wheel."

"Okay, Emmy. Get in. Let's get you to work."

"Okay."

* * *

Two hours later, Driftwood ran a hand through his hair in frustration.

"I found religious fliers at just about all of your neighbors' houses," Quint told him. "I don't think you were targeted specifically."

Driftwood wasn't so sure about that, but he didn't have the expertise that Quint did. But without concrete proof and not wanting to sound paranoid, he decided to keep quiet...for now. He also made a mental note to keep a closer eye on Quinn, just in case.

"Then why was my truck the only one tagged?" Driftwood asked.

Quint hesitated. "Is that your bedroom?" he asked, lifting his chin and indicating a window at the front of the house.

"Yeah, why?"

"Were your curtains open last night?"

Driftwood looked to his bedroom window then back to Quint. "Not wide open, as you can see, but yeah, cracked open just like that."

"Maybe some overzealous parishioner was walking around hanging out their fliers and feeling holier than though and they got a glimpse of...you know...and decided to leave you a special note."

The thought of someone watching him and Quinn making love made Driftwood's blood run cold. "Seriously?"

Quint shrugged. "I don't know. Without cameras or any other kind of evidence, there's no way we'll be able to find out who did this or why. I checked for fingerprints, but there weren't any usable ones. This is basically a dead case before it even goes anywhere. My best advice is to get that garage cleaned out so you can put both your vehicles inside next time. Oh, and…make sure your curtains are shut all the way." He grinned.

"Fuck," Driftwood muttered. "Fine. I can get a copy of the police report to send to my insurance, right?"

"Of course. I'll type it up this afternoon and email you a copy."

"Thanks."

"No problem."

"I appreciate you coming out this morning."

Quint shrugged. "It's my job. And even if it wasn't, I'd drop everything for my friends from Station 7."

Driftwood held out his hand and Quint shook it. "Later."

"Later."

After Quint had driven away, Driftwood turned and studied his house for a moment. He'd been joking when he'd told Quinn about ordering security cameras, but it wasn't a bad idea. He could put one above the garage, one at his front door, one around back, and maybe even one on the side of the house. He wasn't sure if he bought Quint's theory about what had happened, but at this point, they didn't have any proof that anything more sinister was going on.

The other thing he needed to do today was go to the store and buy a new set of curtains. The ones he had now weren't wide enough. He might even buy blackout jobbies. If someone had spied on him and

Quinn in bed together, he would do whatever it took to make sure they didn't get a second chance.

But he wasn't going to tell Quinn about Quint's theory. He wanted her to feel comfortable in his home. He wanted it to be a safe haven for her, and it wasn't going to be so if she thought someone was peeking in through their windows.

Shaking his head and taking a deep breath, Driftwood headed into the garage. He had a lot of work to do before it was time to go pick Quinn up from work.

"What's the surprise?" Quinn asked for the hundredth time as John drove her home that afternoon.

"Wait and see," he said for the hundredth time as well.

"I'm not good at surprises," Quinn grumbled. "Probably because I never had any growing up. Other kids always got fun surprises, but not me."

"Then that just means I need to give you more of them," John said.

"No! I wasn't fishing. I really don't like them," Quinn was quick to say. "I can't stand the suspense."

John chuckled. "This one isn't super exciting. But now that I know I need to train you to like them, I'll see what I can do in the future."

Quinn groaned and put her head in her hand. "I should've kept my mouth shut."

John grabbed her hand, kissed it, then held it in his

own for the rest of the drive to his house. "I know you need to get back to your apartment to pick up more clothes and stuff, but I wanted to show you what I've been busy with all day."

He clicked the garage door opener on the visor she hadn't noticed before now, and Quinn stared in disbelief as both doors rose to reveal a pristine garage.

"What… Where'd all your stuff go?"

"Some is in the attic, some I hauled off to the dump. I also made a few runs to Goodwill. I'd been using my garage as a sort of dumping ground for stuff I didn't want to deal with. But I didn't want to wait even one more day to get your car secured…so if I didn't need it immediately, off it went."

Quinn turned to look at John in shock. "But that was your stuff."

He shrugged. "Junk," he corrected.

"But…it was your *stuff*," she repeated.

He looked over at her and tilted his head. "Talk to me," he ordered.

Quinn took a deep breath and tried to organize her thoughts. She decided to tell him something she'd never told anyone else. "I was in this foster home once. The adults were okay, but I guess knowing what I know now, I'd say they were hoarders. They had a garage, but it was full. There was a shed in the back-yard, also stuffed full of boxes and other odds and ends. My room was small, and I only had a twin bed, but it was okay because it was mine. They had two biological children who had their own rooms too.

"One day, I came home from school and they'd started putting some of the crap that had been in the living room into my bedroom. I tried to complain, but was told I was lucky they even took me in. I knew they were right, so I shut up about it. Every day, more and more stuff got moved into my room, until the night they finally told me that I was going back. That they needed my room for storage."

"Goddamn assholes," John murmured.

"They got rid of me because they needed my space to put their stuff," she said. "Their things were more important than a nine-year-old kid who needed a family to give a damn about her." She looked at him briefly, blinking back tears. "I didn't realize how much that incident affected me until just now. It's stuck with me all these years. That I wasn't important enough to have my own space in their home." Her voice fell to a whisper. "But you just cleaned out your garage so I could park my car in there. So I could be safe."

"Look at me," John said.

Slowly, Quinn brought her eyes back to his.

He brought his hands up to her face and wiped her tears off her cheeks with his thumbs. "You are more important to me than anything else. I would gladly give up every damn thing I own if it means getting to keep you in my life and keeping you safe."

Quinn shook her head. "Do you really mean that?"

"I do. I don't care if my house burns down with everything in it, as long as *you're* not in it. I don't care if someone steals my truck, as long as you're okay. And I definitely had no problem giving away a bunch of shit I never used to make room in my garage for your car, and to make you safer in the process. Okay?"

Quinn nodded. John's words and actions went a long way toward making those long-ago memories of being less important than a bunch of junk lose some of their grip. John wanted her to move in. He'd given away some of his things just to make room for her. It felt good. Very good.

*I*t hadn't been a good day, so when Quinn's phone rang while she was eating lunch and she saw that it was John, she was more than happy to answer. He had today and tomorrow off, and it was great to have him home. She'd found that, over the last two weeks, she really did miss him when he was gone. She'd been so used to being alone for so long, even after only two weeks of living with John, she knew she'd have a hard time going back to her solitary life if things didn't work out between them.

"Hey."

"Hey. How's work going?"

It was shitty, but instead of inflicting her bad mood on her boyfriend, Quinn merely said, "It's going."

"Hey, I was talking to Taco this morning, and he invited us over for dinner."

Quinn's shoulders slumped. "Yeah?"

"Yeah. No occasion really, but he told me that Jen's

feeling left out. I told him it was just because she was new to the group, but she argued that *you* were new, and you weren't being excluded from get-togethers and things."

"Did you tell him that's because I already knew Sophie? That I've basically been hanging out with you guys for months?" she asked a little petulantly.

"Of course. But she's trying, and Taco thinks Jen might be more comfortable hanging out with just a few people at a time rather than everyone all together."

"Just us?" Quinn asked.

"No. Beth and Sledge are coming too."

"So you said yes?" she asked with a bit more heat than she meant to.

"Yeah. I didn't think you'd mind. Is it a problem?"

Sighing, Quinn closed her eyes. She was on the verge of tears. The morning had sucked, plain and simple. She'd stopped to get gas and the card reader on the pump hadn't worked, which was annoying. So she'd gone in to pay and the clerk refused to meet her eye. It was obvious she was uncomfortable with Quinn's birthmark. Then at a stoplight, she'd looked over at the man driving the car next to hers and saw him staring.

When she was passing the entrance to the hospital to get to the Burn Center, she almost ran into a woman coming out. The stranger had taken one look at her and backed up as if Quinn had cooties or something. And to top it all off, the research she'd been doing had been contaminated, and two weeks' worth had to be trashed and she had to start all over.

So John *telling* her they were going over to Taco's apartment to have dinner wasn't sitting well. "I just... I'm tired," she said somewhat lamely.

"Apparently, Jen's already over at his place preparing," John said quietly. "She really is trying, Emmy, and I know if the roles were reversed, Taco would do what he could to make you feel comfortable and to try to help you fit in."

Quinn swallowed hard. She didn't like the guilt trip John was putting on her, but he was right. Having dinner wasn't the end of the world. It wouldn't kill her. "I know. And it's fine. Do we need to bring anything?"

"Probably. You want to pick something up on your way home? It doesn't have to be fancy. Maybe a potato salad or something?"

Resisting the urge to sigh once more, Quinn merely said, "Sure." She didn't know why he couldn't go to the store while she was at work. He was the one with the day off, and *he* was the one who wanted to go have dinner in the first place.

"Cool. You'll be home around five-thirty, right?"

Hating the mood she was in and how resentful she was feeling, Quinn forced herself to lighten her tone and said, "Yeah. I should be as long as there isn't any traffic."

"Great. I told Taco we'd be there around six."

Knowing she needed to get off the phone before she said something she'd regret, Quinn said, "I gotta go."

"Okay. See you later, Emmy."

Usually she loved the nickname, but today it just

irritated her. Then again, just about everything irritated her at the moment. "Bye."

"Bye."

Quinn didn't get to leave work until five-fifteen that afternoon because she had to finish up the project she was working on. Starting over was costing her both time and research money. She had no idea what had happened to the other skin samples she'd been working with, but she'd had to take brand-new samples and start from scratch.

Sophie and the others hadn't blamed her, even though it was obvious they were as irritated as she was about the setback.

And now she was late leaving, which meant she'd be late getting back to John's house, especially since she still had to stop and get the stupid potato salad. And since John had told Taco they'd be there at six, she'd have no time to freshen up before they left. She'd barely have time to change.

She pulled into the grocery store and cursed when it seemed as if everyone and their brother had the bright idea to go shopping after work today. She had to park at the back of the lot and when she was walking to the entrance, she overheard a kid asking his mom what was wrong with "that lady's face."

Ignoring them, she walked quickly into the store and straight to the deli department. She took about two seconds to decide which tub of potato salad to get. She got in line at the twelve-items-or-less checkout and tapped her foot impatiently as the woman in front of her got out her checkbook.

Who in the world still wrote *checks* in today's day and age?

As she was waiting, Quinn happened to look to her right, and she saw two men in line at the register next to hers. They were younger than her, probably twenty-one or twenty-two. They were staring, and not even trying to hide it.

When she accidentally caught one of their eyes, he nudged his friend and whispered something to him.

The other guy laughed and shook his head.

Quinn sighed and turned her head away and prayed the cashier would just hurry up and process the lady's stupid check.

She couldn't hear what they'd originally said, but she *did* hear the next comments.

"Bet she's a virgin."

"Of course she is. Who would be able to stomach looking at *that* while they fucked her?"

Quinn wanted to turn to the guys and tell them that her boyfriend would, thank you very much. And he had no problem with her birthmark, and that he'd made her come twice the night before. But instead, she tried to ignore them.

As sometimes happened, when assholes didn't get the rise they were looking for out of her, they started talking louder and being even more obnoxious.

"It looks like a jellyfish attached itself to her face and neck."

"Maybe it's a herpes outbreak," the other guy quipped.

"Cut it out!" the old lady in front of her ordered as she waited for her check to clear. "You should be ashamed of yourselves," she scolded the men.

Quinn smiled weakly at the woman.

Then she went on. "Don't you know those things are contagious? That if she got irritated enough and reached out and touched you, you could end up looking like her too?"

Quinn could only stare at the woman in disbelief.

"No shit?" one of the men asked.

"Stay away from us," the other one ordered.

It wasn't as if she was doing anything other than just standing there. Just to be annoying, she took a quick step toward the men as if she was going to come near them, but didn't actually step out of her line.

As she could've predicted, the men leaped sideways as if she'd brandished a knife or something at them. Rolling her eyes at the ridiculousness of the situation, Quinn turned her attention back to the woman in front of her.

Luckily, the men in the other line moved forward to pay for their stuff, and the old woman in front of her finally had her check cleared and she grabbed her bags and hurried off as if just being in the same vicinity as Quinn would infect her in some way.

Quinn didn't glance at the cashier, knowing she couldn't stand even one more disapproving look right now.

The lady scanned her potato salad and Quinn handed over a ten-dollar bill.

When the cashier handed back her change, she said softly, "Don't listen to them. They're just idiots. There's nothing wrong with your face that a little makeup couldn't fix."

Quinn nodded. She knew the lady was trying to help, but telling her all she had to do was cover herself with a bunch of makeup wasn't exactly what she wanted to hear.

She took her change and threw it in her purse, not bothering to put it back in her wallet. She grabbed the bag with the potato salad and left the store as if the hounds of Hell were after her. She didn't see the two men who had been staring at her, thank goodness.

By the time she arrived at John's house, Quinn wasn't in the mood to do anything other than put on pajamas, eat junk for dinner, and crawl into bed and read.

She walked into the house and the first thing John said was, "You're late."

Without a word, Quinn dropped the bag with the potato salad on the kitchen counter and went straight to the bedroom. She walked into the bathroom, shut and locked the door, and sat on the toilet with her head in her hands.

She didn't have time to break down. She had to go pretend to be happy and congenial to John's friends. But she was peopled out. She didn't want to see or talk to anyone...John included.

A knock sounded on the door. "Quinn? Are you all right?"

"Yeah," she called out. "Just washing my face."

"Okay. We need to leave as soon as possible. We're already running late. Taco texted and said that Jen had everything planned out to be on the table right at six-fifteen."

Having the uncharitable thought that if Jen had planned everything that rigidly, then maybe she shouldn't be dating a firefighter, Quinn got up off the toilet and bent over the sink. Lord knew John had a lot of really good qualities, but a regular schedule wasn't one of them. He kept a handheld radio on at all times, even when he wasn't on duty, just in case there was a big fire and the station needed backup. There had been a couple of times when they were hanging out that he'd jumped up and left when a call came in.

She knew it was just part of who John was...he wanted to help. She couldn't fault him for it. Well... maybe a little. When she wanted to spend time with him. When she wanted to be the focus of whatever they were doing. Quinn wondered for the first time what would happen if the stupid tones went off when they were in the middle of making love...would he leap up and go even then?

Sighing, knowing she was just feeling bitchy and she really didn't care that he left when he was needed, Quinn quickly washed her face. She leaned forward with her hands on the counter and examined her birthmark. Was it getting darker? Was that one little spot the beginning of a nodule? She'd seen pictures of people with port-wine stains who were covered with the little bubble-like nodules. It was horrifying and scary. She knew the longer she went without getting laser therapy, the better the chance they'd start to form on her own skin.

Shuddering, she took a deep breath and unlocked and opened the bathroom door. She thought John might be standing there, but the room was empty. She quickly took off the shirt she'd worn to work and put on a clean short-sleeve white shirt with a mason jar filled with pink flowers screen-printed on the front.

She took off the scrub pants she usually wore to work and exchanged them for a pair of jeans. Deciding she was as presentable as she was going to get, Quinn made her way back out into the living room.

John was standing by the door with the bag of potato salad in one hand and her purse in the other. "Ready to go?"

She opened her mouth to say no, she wasn't ready, because she didn't want to go, but then John said, "I'll drive. Got my truck back from the shop this afternoon. She's as good as new."

"Great," Quinn mumbled, following behind John.

He either didn't notice that she was being reticent or simply wasn't commenting on it. He opened her door for her, and the ride to Taco's apartment was mostly silent. When they got close, John said, "I know Jen is different from your other friends, but she's trying."

Quinn swallowed the retort on the tip of her tongue. She wanted to ask what John thought she was going to do...spit out the food she'd cooked? Tell her she wasn't fitting in? She may not have clicked with the other woman, but she'd never be rude. Quinn had a lifetime of people being rude to her, she'd never do that to someone else.

John pulled into a visitor parking space and, nodding at a big black truck, said, "Looks like Beth and Sledge are already here."

Quinn had been surprised to learn Beth was coming to the impromptu dinner party, as she wasn't exactly Ms. Social, but since it was just going to be the six of them, she supposed the other woman figured she would be fine.

Quinn admired Beth. She had agoraphobia and sometimes had a hard time leaving her house, but with the right combination of drugs and therapy, she was getting better and better. Of course, having Sledge at her side didn't hurt either.

John took her hand as they walked into the complex and to the elevator. As they were riding up to the fourth floor, he asked, "Are you okay?"

Now was a fine time for him to ask. A little too late. "I'm good."

He squeezed her hand. "If you get too tired, just let me know and we'll go. I know you have to work tomorrow."

His words made her feel a little better. It would've been nice if he'd asked if she wanted to come over in the first place, but at least if she told him she wanted to leave, they could go. The last thing she wanted to think about was working in the morning.

Taco opened the door two seconds after John knocked.

"Hey, you guys. You're late. Come in."

The song "Fuck You" by Lily Allen came to Quinn's mind, but she simply smiled at Taco as she entered. He wasn't trying to be a dick, it was really just that she was in a horrible mood and not sitting at home in her pajamas.

She followed John and Taco into the other room. Beth came over and gave her a hug. "Hey, Quinn."

"Hi." Quinn turned to Jen and wasn't surprised when the other woman didn't come forward for a welcoming hug, but gave her a little wave and a half smile instead.

"Hi, Jen," Quinn said.

"Hi."

"Good to see you!" Sledge said and wrapped Quinn in a big hug. His arms felt comforting around her, and Quinn had to swallow hard to hold back the tears she'd been struggling against all day. If John had hugged her like this, there would've been no way she could've held back.

Taco hugged her next and said, "Thanks for coming over. I know you were working all day and are probably tired. It means a lot to Jen and me though."

"You're welcome," Quinn said. "It's good to see you guys."

185

"Here," Jen said, holding out a glass of water. "You look thirsty."

Quinn *was* a bit thirsty, and she reached for the glass. But instead of handing it to her, Jen put it down on the kitchen counter and scooted it closer to Quinn.

Mentally shrugging, Quinn picked it up and took a long swallow. She forced herself not to grimace. She wasn't a water snob, but something about the taste was off. Maybe it was because it was warm. "Can I get some ice?" she asked Jen.

"Of course." She turned to Taco. "Hudson, will you get Quinn some ice?"

"Sure, babe," he said, and took the glass from Quinn and turned to the freezer.

"Can we do anything to help?" Quinn asked Jen, doing her best to try to be friendly.

"No. I've got it. Go sit. When Hudson told me you and John were running late, I turned the brisket down, so now we have to wait a bit more for it to be done."

"It smells really good," Quinn tried again.

"It should, I've been slaving over it all day."

All right then. Quinn took her water glass back from Taco and sipped it. The ice made it a bit more palatable, but it still tasted funny.

"Come on," Beth said, looping her arm with Quinn's. "We're just in the way here. Let's go into the living room."

Letting the other woman tow her out of the kitchen area, Quinn sat on the couch next to Beth. The guys headed into a back room to look at the new workout machine that Taco had apparently just purchased.

"What's wrong?" Beth asked in a low voice the second they sat.

Her question made the tears she'd been holding back spring into Quinn's eyes. She squeezed them shut and willed herself not to cry.

Beth didn't push, she simply put her hand on Quinn's leg and waited.

When Quinn felt as if she had herself under control, she opened her eyes and smiled weakly at Beth. "I'm sorry. It's just been a long day."

"And now here you are, instead of snuggling with Driftwood at home. I'm sorry."

"What are *you* sorry for?" Quinn asked.

Beth shrugged and chuckled. "I don't know. I just feel bad."

"I'll be okay. It's just been one of those days. The idiots are out in full force."

"If you ever want to talk, I'm here, okay?"

"Thanks. It's just some days are harder than others. You'd think in today's day and age, people wouldn't be so ignorant when it comes to my birthmark, but I'm still surprised at the level of stupidness that's out there."

"Is stupidness even a word?"

"If it's not, it should be," Quinn retorted.

"Hey, I've been meaning to call you," Beth told her.

"Yeah?"

"Yeah. I checked up on that doctor Cade told me

about. I guess Driftwood talked to him about it. The vascular guy? Doctor Ballard?"

"Oh yeah! I forgot I was going to see if you would look into his background before I decided on whether or not to go see him."

"Right. Well, I did, and he's completely legit. He and his colleagues actually developed the 'dynamic cooling device' that everyone now uses in conjunction with the pulsed dye lasers to treat port-wine birthmarks. I guess it was super revolutionary, and now it's what everyone does. He's been invited to all sorts of different countries to talk about how he treats patients like you, and he's published over three hundred articles in various scientific journals."

"But what do his patients say about him? What are his results?" Quinn asked. She couldn't care less how many papers he'd written. She wanted to know how successful he was in reducing birthmarks like hers.

"I could only find one person who was disgruntled with his results," Beth said. "And from what I found out —and don't ask me *how* I found out—he didn't do what he was supposed to do. His appointments were too far apart and erratic. He went on a Caribbean cruise between one of the treatments and one of the things Doctor Ballard recommends is that his patients stay out of the pool and the sun. And I can see by the pictures this guy posted on his social media pages, he definitely didn't follow that advice."

"Ass," Quinn muttered.

"Exactly. Most of his clients are babies, which is

normal. It's been proven that there's a higher chance of the stain fading, and staying faded, the earlier treatment is started. But the before and after pictures of his adult patients are remarkable."

"That's good," Quinn said.

"Yeah. I even looked into your insurance. Yes, this is cosmetic, but if the grants he told you about don't work out, I think you can ask your insurance company for an exception based on your mental health and other factors. I can help you fill out the form if you want."

Quinn knew she should probably be upset that Beth had pried into her insurance, but she couldn't be, not when she was helping her. And honestly, hearing that Beth approved of the doctor was pretty much the only thing she needed to know. "I'll call and make an appointment soon."

"Good. And Quinn?"

"Yeah?"

"If Driftwood can't go with you, I will."

Quinn blinked in surprise. "You will?"

"Yeah. I'm not saying it'll be easy for me, but I know what it's like to travel away from home for something that you know is going to be scary and could change your life. Even if it's changing it for the better, it's still hard."

Quinn pressed her lips together to try to keep herself from bursting into tears. Out of all the women who were dating the firefighters John worked with, Sophie was the one she'd say she was closest to. But knowing about Beth's agoraphobia, and how difficult leaving the house was for her sometimes, made her offer to go with her to California huge.

"Thank you. You have no idea how much that means to me."

"Yeah, I think I do."

"I'll talk to John and see what his schedule is. If he can't go, I'll definitely call you."

"Good." Then Beth looked up toward the kitchen and lowered her voice. "Do you think she'd flip if I said I was a vegetarian?"

A burst of laughter escaped before Quinn could control it. "I'd pay you to say it."

Beth smiled and rolled her eyes. "I'm not sure I could deal with the drama."

"True."

"Dinner's ready!" Jen called from the kitchen.

"Ready for this?" Beth whispered as she stood.

"No," Quinn said.

Something was up with Quinn, but Driftwood didn't know what. She was smiling and saying all the right things on the surface, but he could definitely feel the tension in the air.

It had started when she'd asked what else was available to drink. Jen tensed and asked if something was wrong with the water. Quinn had said no, but that she wouldn't mind a glass of wine or something.

Taco hadn't had any wine, but he had some beer. Jen had frowned when Quinn said that would be fine.

Driftwood had tried to smooth over the awkwardness by taking a beer himself, but Jen just frowned at him too.

The brisket was delicious and cooked to perfection. The rolls, asparagus, and salad Jen had made were also flawless. In short, there had been nothing to complain about with the food. But conversation still seemed stilted.

Beth talked a little about the job she was currently working on, tracking down suspicious shipments in and out of the country, and Quinn shared that she'd had to start over on a case she'd spent two weeks on because it had somehow become compromised overnight.

He hadn't known that, and figured that was part of the reason why she seemed off.

But it was also obvious that things between Jen and the other women weren't actually going well either. He wasn't an expert on women's behavior, but even he could see that Jen spent most of the dinner talking to Taco, Sledge, and himself, and not Beth or Quinn.

The ladies even offered to help with the dishes afterward, and Jen insisted that she and Taco could take care of them.

They finally all settled down in the living room after the dishes had been done.

Driftwood was next to Quinn on the loveseat, Jen

and Taco were on the couch, and Beth was sitting in Sledge's lap in an oversized chair.

"So, what do you do for a living, Jen?" Sledge asked. Somehow in all the talk at the dinner table about Beth and Quinn's jobs, Jen's never came up.

"I help my brother with his business. It's only part-time though, so I have time to do things like cook dinner for Hudson."

"And you're going to school for nursing too, right?" Quinn asked.

Jen looked at her blankly for a moment, then nodded. "Of course. That too."

Taco gave her a small smile.

"What does your brother do?" Beth asked.

"He owns his own company," Jen said.

"And what's that?" Beth asked once more, obviously prying for more information.

"He's a spiritual advisor."

Driftwood blinked. Wow, he wasn't expecting that.

"Really?" Beth asked. "I'm not sure I've ever met a spiritual advisor. What exactly does he do?"

Jen looked annoyed now. "He's like a mentor. He meets with people and helps them with life choices from a spiritual perspective."

"What people?" Beth pressed.

"Why are you so concerned about my brother and what he does?" Jen asked, more than a little belligerently.

"I'm just curious," Beth said without raising her voice.

"He meets with homeless teens and families and tries to help get them back on their feet. He runs a website as well, and answers questions that people ask there."

Driftwood could see Beth's mind spinning. A website meant she could hack into it and find out more information. Sledge obviously realized the same thing, because Driftwood saw him put his hand on Beth's leg and squeeze in warning.

"Hey, did you guys hear about the call the guys got today?" Driftwood asked, wanting to change the subject.

"No, what?" Taco asked. "I was helping Jen most of the day."

"And I was...um...*helping* Beth. What's up?" Sledge asked.

Driftwood knew how Sledge had been "helping" Beth was probably very different than how Taco was helping Jen. He tried not to smirk at his friend's sexual innuendo.

"They were called to a grass fire. Which isn't that unusual around here, but when they got there, they found a DB at the origination point."

"A DB?" Jen asked.

"Dead body," Taco interpreted.

"Gross," Jen said.

"Anyway, it was burned to a crisp. They couldn't even tell if it was a female or a male."

"Holy cow, what happened?" Quinn asked.

"Not sure," Driftwood said. "They're still investigating, but it looks like it was a homicide."

"That's terrible," Beth said.

"Yeah, and unusual. The ME will have to tell us if the person was already dead before they were set on fire." Driftwood felt Quinn shiver next to him.

"Disgusting. Can we talk about something else?" Jen asked. "Quinn, I talked to one of my friends who's a makeup artist, and she said that she wouldn't mind seeing if she could do anything about your...thing."

Quinn stiffened. "My *thing*? You mean my birthmark?" she asked quietly.

"Yeah. I told her all about it, and she's willing to give you a deal. She works out of her home. She said that she could see you next Saturday. I'll give you her number."

Driftwood felt Quinn looking at him, and he turned toward her. She had a weird look on her face. He lifted his eyebrows, silently asking what was wrong.

She shook her head and turned to look at Jen.

"Thanks, but I'm okay."

"But she could make you look pretty. No one would be able to see it. She could even teach you how to apply the makeup so you could do it yourself. Don't you want to look like everyone else?"

It was Driftwood's turn to stiffen. He didn't like what Jen was implying. But if Quinn wanted to do it, he wouldn't stop her.

"Here, look. I have her card for you." Jen leaned forward and fished a business card out of her pocket and handed it to Taco, who was sitting closer to Quinn.

"I don't think she has to look like everyone else. Quinn's pretty exactly the way she is already," Taco said, his brows furrowed as he looked at Jen before leaning forward and handing the card to Quinn.

"Thanks," she said softly.

"So you'll call and set it up?" Jen asked, ignoring her boyfriend's words.

"I'll think about it," Quinn said.

"Great. Maybe I could come over at the same time. I mean, that kind of thing is always more fun with friends, right?"

"Sure." It was the right thing to say, but Driftwood didn't hear much emotion in Quinn's tone. He dipped his head to look at her, but she looked at Beth. "How's your brother?"

"David? He's great. He got a new job, and he's now in charge of the online marketing for Campbell's Soup. They're based out of Philly, and over the years they've seen their revenue fall. In nineteen ninety-six, they were ranked one hundred and seventeen on the *Fortune* 500 list, but this year they were three hundred and forty-second. So he's got an uphill climb ahead of him, but he's super smart and I know he'll be able to work wonders for them."

"Wait...Campbell's Soup? Didn't someone post on their Facebook page that their commercial made her sick? The one with two dads enjoying a bowl of soup with their son? I think that post went viral because the company had that great comeback about making sure she enjoyed their soup hot, because it would warm up her cold, dead heart. It was awesome!" Quinn exclaimed.

Beth nodded. "Yeah, that happened, but it wasn't Campbell's that responded. It was an Internet troll pretending to be from the company. It was funny, but of course Campbell's got blamed."

"Oh. People do that?"

"Do what?" Beth asked.

"Make up fake customer service accounts to reply to bigoted comments like that?" Quinn asked.

"Yup. So much of what's posted on social media is a lie. Not everything, of course. And a lot of crazy people will always post their opinions, even if it's misogynistic, bigoted, or discriminatory. It's amazing how many of *those* comments aren't lies. Most people who aren't insane don't share that kind of thing in public, they keep their crazy to themselves," Beth said.

"So are you saying they aren't allowed to have opinions?" Jen asked.

"No, not at all. But if you look at Twitter, Facebook, or even Amazon, you'll see all sorts of off-the-wall posts and reviews. Everyone's allowed to have an opinion, but when it's hurtful against any particular population, it's not cool. I guess having a brother who's gay has made me super sensitive and less tolerant of people's bigotry."

Driftwood agreed. He'd come across quite a few people in his line of work who had extreme beliefs of one type or another. Typically in regard to medical treatment. They were very hard to deal with because they refused to compromise or hear anyone's opinion that differed from their own.

"Well, anyway, congrats to your brother. That's great that he got the job with Campbell's." Quinn smiled at her.

"I'll tell him you said that next time I talk to him," Beth said. Then she yawned. A huge yawn that made Driftwood chuckle.

"On that note, I think we'd better get going. Beth was up late last night doing something I'm sure I don't want to know about," Sledge quipped.

Driftwood turned to Quinn. "You ready?"

"Yes," she said immediately.

"Then I guess we'll be going too," Driftwood told the group.

Everyone stood and Jen disappeared into the kitchen. They were all giving hugs and saying their goodbyes when she returned. "I got you all some water to go," she said with a smile, handing out bottles of water to everyone.

"Uh, thanks," Driftwood said. He wasn't really thirsty, but he didn't want to offend Jen. He had no idea why she kept pushing water on him and Quinn. Maybe it was something to do with her nursing studies or staying healthy.

Taco slapped him on the back and thanked him for coming.

Within minutes, he and Quinn were back in his

truck. He watched as she took a sip of the water, wrinkled her nose, put the cap back on, and placed it in the drink holder between their seats.

"Not good?" he asked.

She shrugged. "I'm sure it's just me."

Driftwood wasn't sure that bottled water actually went bad, but since Quinn was obviously in a weird mood, he didn't say anything. He started the truck and backed out of the space.

"Will you take me home?" Quinn asked.

"What? Why?" Driftwood asked in surprise.

"I don't have what I want to wear tomorrow at your place. It's just easier for me to stay there tonight."

"We can stop by and get what you need, then go home," Driftwood offered.

"No. That's okay."

Now he was getting a little pissed. "What's up with you tonight?" he asked, a little harsher than he'd intended.

"Nothing. It's just been a long day."

"It's not nothing. You've been short all night. Jen went out of her way to make a nice meal, and you and Beth hardly said two words to her at dinner."

He saw Quinn clench her hands together in her lap and turn her head to look out the window on her side, effectively cutting him out.

"Please don't turn away from me when I'm talking to you," he bit out in frustration.

She whipped her head toward him—and Driftwood was shocked to see tears shining in her eyes. He had to alternate paying attention to the road and looking at her. It wasn't ideal. He didn't want to fight with her at all, but definitely not while he was driving.

"Why didn't you say something back there?" Quinn asked.

Driftwood was confused. "About what?"

She sighed. "You always say you'll never let anyone talk shit to me. But you sat there tonight and let Jen do just that. She basically told me I was ugly, and that the only way I'd ever feel normal was if I let her friend cover my birthmark with layers and layers of makeup. And you sat there and didn't say a word as she insulted me."

Driftwood cringed. He hated that he hadn't spoken up. "I'm sorry. I should've said something."

Quinn looked at him for another second before turning her head once again. "You're right. You should've. Instead, Taco had to."

Driftwood was frustrated, and slightly exasperated. "What did you want me to say?"

Quinn shook her head. "If you don't know, then I can't explain it."

"Taco said Jen doesn't have a lot of girlfriends. That she works really hard for her brother's business and doesn't get out much. I'm sure she didn't mean to make you feel that way. She was trying to do something nice."

"Please. Just take me home," Quinn said softly.

Tired of trying to convince her, Driftwood did as she asked.

When he pulled into her apartment complex, he didn't say a word as Quinn got out of the truck, but then again, she didn't speak either. She walked into the lobby of the apartment complex and didn't look back.

Smacking his hand on the steering wheel, Driftwood swore.

He wanted to keep talking this out. Hated to end their night this way. But he had a feeling that anything he'd say right now would be taken the wrong way. That he'd say something he'd regret.

Feeling as if he had no other choice, he pulled out and headed home.

CHAPTER TWELVE

For the first time in a very long time, Quinn called in sick to work the next morning. She wasn't really sick, even though her stomach *was* a bit queasy. She felt bad that Sophie was so worried about her, but she told her friend she just had a headache and would be fine by the next day.

She felt guilty because she knew she had a lot of work to do on the samples she'd had to start over, but she just couldn't bring herself to get out of bed.

Remembering the way Jen had so carelessly shredded her to pieces, and how John had sat there, clueless, hurt.

And Quinn had no doubt that Jen knew exactly what she was saying. She wasn't as clueless as John and Taco believed. Quinn saw the way Jen stared at her when she thought she wasn't looking. Saw the curl of her lip when John kissed her on her blemished cheek.

Hell, she couldn't even bear to touch her. Quinn hadn't missed how she'd gone out of her way to avoid it.

But to have John sit there and not say anything when Jen had declared her friend could make Quinn look "pretty" had been the last straw in her epically bad day.

She just needed some time alone. She didn't want to tell John about all the stares yesterday. Didn't want to explain that when Jen said her friend could make her look "normal," it made her feel even more like a freak.

Quinn knew John was upset with her, but she was mad at him right back. Yes, she should've said something before she'd gotten out of his truck last night, but she couldn't. Now she was stuck at her apartment without her car and John was probably pissed way the hell off. She could take an Uber to his house to get her car, but at the moment, she just wanted to stay curled up into a ball and not talk to anyone—and she definitely didn't want to see anyone. With her luck, she'd call for a ride and the driver would take one look at her and drive off.

She fell back asleep and woke up when her phone chimed with a text. Then it chimed again. And again.

Sighing, Quinn reached out from under her cocoon of covers, which didn't smell nearly as good as John's sheets did, and grabbed it.

. . .

John: Are you all right? Chief told me that Sophie said you called in sick.

John: I'm worried about you.

John: You were right. I should've spoken up. What Jen said definitely wasn't cool.

John: I was thinking too much about trying to be a peace-maker and making Taco feel better about Jen not seeming to fit in that well. I should've been thinking about what she said, and how it was making you feel.

John: I'm sorry. I'm so sorry.

John: Can I come over? I can bring you some soup. :)

How could she stay mad at him when he didn't hesitate to apologize? He'd taken what she'd said to heart and he was sorry. Quinn wasn't sure he really understood how Jen had made her feel though. And he wouldn't... unless she talked to him. *Told* him.

Quinn: Don't bring soup. I need doughnuts. Maple and vanilla iced. The cake kind. With sprinkles.

John: Done. I'll be there soon.

Quinn threw her phone back on the table next to her bed and snuggled down. She knew she should get up. Put on some real clothes. Brush her teeth. But she felt blah. She didn't want to move.

Apparently, she fell back asleep, because the next

thing she knew, she heard knocking on her door. Swearing, she stumbled out of bed and hurried down the hall. She checked the peephole before answering... the last thing she wanted to do was open it to find the same religious people she and John had seen the last time she'd stopped by her apartment. They'd started on the first floor, and when they'd knocked on her door, she and John had tried to control their giggles and keep quiet so they wouldn't know anyone was home.

Seeing it was indeed John, Quinn opened the door and turned away, knowing he'd shut and lock the door before following her. She went to her room and climbed right back into bed.

Seconds later, John stood in the doorway. She watched his eyes take in the bedroom. The clothes from the night before strewn in the middle of the room, the used tissues on the nightstand and those that had fallen on the floor.

With only a slight hesitation, he walked toward her and sat on the bed at her hip. Quinn didn't say anything, but that didn't seem to hold him back.

"I'm sorry," he said immediately. "You were right. I told you that I wouldn't let anyone get away with bad-mouthing you, and when we were in a place where you should've felt safe and content, I let you down. I don't have an excuse. I was thinking about the DB the guys on the other shift had found and wondering what the fuck was up with that, and before I knew it, Jen was talking about someone teaching you how to do your makeup and handing you a business card."

"She said her friend could teach me how to make myself pretty. So I would look normal," Quinn said in a level voice. "Do you know how many nights I used to lay awake praying I would wake up looking *normal*? Too many to count. And makeup doesn't work. My stain is dark enough that by the time enough foundation and cover up is used, it doesn't look natural. And I'm not like some women, I can't just put that stuff on my face. I have to put it on my neck too. And both sides. I can't just use it on my birthmark, because then one side of my face and neck is darker than the other. It takes forever to put on and it always comes off on my clothes. I've tried it, John. *All* of it. You name it, I've done it. I even used bleach on my skin when I was a teenager in the hopes of making it fade. All that did was irritate my skin and make it redder."

"I'm sorry," John said again.

"And Jen should know better than to offer something like that. How old is she, anyway? It doesn't matter…she's old enough. She was staring at me all night, like she was either disgusted or fascinated. It was uncomfortable. But you didn't notice."

"I should've been paying more attention to you. I'm sorry."

"I've told you I'm an introvert, and would rather sit at home than socialize with people."

"You're right, you did."

"Most days I can ignore the looks I get and the way some people react to me, but yesterday wasn't one of those days. There were no less than six people who either physically recoiled when they saw me or had some obnoxious comment. Even an old lady at the store felt the need to make sure I knew how disgusted she was by my birthmark. Then my research at work was contaminated and I had to start two weeks of work over again. On top of all that, you called and *informed* me that we would be eating at Taco's apartment. You didn't ask."

"I'm *sorry*, Emmy."

"I rarely go out on a workday. I'm lame, I admit it. But just because *you* have a day off in the middle of the week, doesn't mean I do. I should've said something, I know, but I didn't, so that's on me. But the very last straw was Jen's attitude. I don't like her, John. I'm sorry, but I don't. And I think the feeling is mutual. And that's fine. Not everyone in this world has to like me. I'm not that conceited to think that everyone will be okay with what I look like and want to be my friend, but when I'm forced to sit there and be polite and listen to insults…that's not okay."

"You're right, it's not."

Quinn couldn't stop the tears from forming in her eyes and spilling down her cheeks. She'd thought she was all cried out. She'd cried until she'd almost made herself sick the night before, but apparently she still had some tears in her. "You hurt my feelings, John," she said softly.

John didn't apologize again. Instead, he moved until he was lying behind her. He was on top of the covers, but he wrapped his body around hers and held her tight.

"I just needed some space last night. It was all just too much. I don't want to break up with you or anything, and I'm sure I'll learn to trust you again, but everything had been so good between us that you letting me down kinda took me by surprise. That's all."

"You *will* trust me again," John said after she'd finally fallen silent. "I hate that all that happened to you yesterday, Emmy, but you have to talk to me. I'm not a mind reader. I told you before that I'd screw up, and assuming you wouldn't have any issues in going over to Taco's was a mistake. But next time something like that happens, speak up. Telling me you've had a hard day and just want to stay home won't upset me. I could've called Taco and told him we couldn't go, or I could've gone by myself."

"But you said Taco specifically invited us because he wanted Jen to feel more comfortable."

"I did. But that still doesn't mean you have to do something you're not in the mood to do. So please, next time I assume something or speak for you, *tell* me."

"I will."

"Good. Now, about what Jen said and what I *didn't* say...I'm so sorry, Quinn."

"I know."

"The more I thought about it last night, the more I realized what she'd said was just as bad as someone coming right up and telling you to your face that you're a freak, which you *aren't*. Jen was just more subtle and sneaky about it. I know you don't believe me, but you're beautiful."

Quinn scoffed.

John ignored her. "I wouldn't want you to wear a bunch of makeup, because then I wouldn't be able to see your cheek turn pink when you blush. I wouldn't be able to nuzzle your neck because I'd get your makeup all over myself. The first thing I noticed about you was your eyes. They're extraordinary. Then it was your smile. It truly lights up your face. And I don't care what all the close-minded assholes in the world say, you are unique and beautiful. And nothing you say or do will ever change my mind about that."

He moved his hand then and put it over her heart. "And most importantly, I love what's inside here. I've never met a more compassionate and loving woman than you."

Quinn stilled.

Did he...? No, he didn't.

"I love you, Quinn. From the top of your head to the bottom of your toes."

He *did*.

"I'm broken, John. It's almost impossible for me to trust anyone. I don't like most people, and I'd rather hide in my bed than face anyone when life gets too overwhelming."

"And? We're all broken in one way or another, Emmy. Some of us just hide it better."

"You aren't," she accused.

"When I was seven...I was abused," he said quietly.

Quinn gasped and turned over until she was facing him. "*What?*"

"By a babysitter. He was fifteen, and the son of my parents' friends. He did it twice but I never told anyone. Not my parents, not a doctor, not the pastor at our church...no one. Not until five seconds ago."

Quinn palmed his cheek with her hand. "What happened to him?"

John shrugged. "Nothing that I know of. But I still think about it. Remember how helpless I felt and how confusing it was. He hurt me, and I was too embarrassed to tell my mom or dad anything about it."

"God, John, that sucks."

"It took me a long time to be able to be alone with a guy again. Even the boys in my class. There are still times today when I'm alone with one of the guys and I feel uneasy. Even though I know they'd *never* do anything like that, the same feelings I had when I was seven come back."

"Give me his name," Quinn demanded. "I'm going to talk to Beth. I won't tell her why, but I'll have her track him down and make his life a living hell. She can cancel all his credit cards and make sure his credit is ruined. Ooh, I know, I'll have her make an anonymous report to his boss. I don't care where he works, no one will want a child molester on their payroll! Then I'll—"

"No," John interrupted gently. "I've moved on, Quinn. He's in my past, or as much in my past as I can put him. Don't you see? We've all got shit that we struggle to deal with. All of us. Whether it's a death in our family, someone abusing our trust, a disability, being picked on and bullied as a kid. It's how we deal with that shit that defines us. And Emmy, you are one of the strongest people I've ever met. I don't see you as broken. You're bent. There's a huge difference."

Quinn stared at him, trying to gauge if he was telling the truth or not. To see if he was really okay. It was hard to think about anyone ever overpowering the strong man in front of her.

John went on. "I won't let you down again, Quinn. At least not when it comes to not speaking up when someone is being a douche. I know I'll have to figure out when it's appropriate to put them in their place and when a glare will do, but I promise that I'll never give you a reason not to trust me again."

"Okay," Quinn said. There really was no other answer. She was adult enough to know that she was as much at fault for what happened last night as John was. She should've said she didn't want to go out to eat. She should've spoken up for herself and not let Jen bully her. It was long past time for her to start sticking up for herself instead of ignoring people when they were rude or relying on others to say something on her behalf. She shouldn't have gotten as upset as she had and refused to go back to John's house.

Burying her face against his chest, she mumbled, "I don't want you to regret loving me."

"I won't," he vowed.

"John?"

"Yeah, Emmy?"

"I'm hungry."

She felt him smiling into her hair. "Then it's a good thing I bought two dozen doughnuts."

"Two dozen?" she asked, not picking up her head.

"Yup."

"I think I might love you back," she whispered.

"I'll stick around until you're sure," he told her.

CHAPTER THIRTEEN

*T*hat evening, after Quinn ate her share of doughnuts, showered, did some laundry, and picked up her place, they headed back to Driftwood's house. Keeping a tight hold on Quinn's hand, as if she might somehow disappear if he let go of her, Driftwood led her out of the building to the parking lot.

When they got close to his truck, Driftwood stopped in his tracks and stared.

Willard was standing in the parking lot with a stack of bright blue papers in his hand. But it was Driftwood's truck that really snagged his attention. It had the same blue pieces of paper stuck under his windshield wipers. They were also stuffed into the grill and one was shoved under the passenger-side door handle as well.

The sight of Quinn's neighbor with the fliers in his hand made him see red.

He dropped her hand and started to charge after Willard, but Quinn grabbed hold of his shirt and held on. "No, John!"

"He isn't getting away with this shit again," Driftwood said. "Let go."

"No," Quinn said and held on more firmly.

He tried jerking his shirt out of her grip, but she tenaciously held on. They watched as Quinn's neighbor finally saw them and ran back toward the lobby of the apartment. Once he was out of sight, Driftwood sighed and turned to Quinn.

"He can't keep doing this shit."

"I know, but he hasn't really done anything illegal."

"Quinn, he scratched 'repent' into my truck!"

"We don't know it was him. Does he even drive? I've never seen him get into a car. He's always here."

She had a point, but he wasn't ready to concede. "He just covered my car with more religious pamphlets." He leaned down and picked up one of the bright blue pieces of paper blowing around the parking lot. On the bottom of the page were flames, with a devil-like caricature grinning from within them. There was another Bible verse across the top that said:

James 4:7
Resist the devil, and he will flee from you.

. . .

"I have to say, I almost miss the simple messages about bringing God into your life," Quinn quipped.

"This isn't funny," Driftwood said between clenched teeth.

"I know. But John, he was putting them on everyone's vehicle. Not just yours."

Driftwood looked around and, sure enough, most of the cars around his also had the blue papers under their wipers. "I don't like your neighbor," he said after a moment.

"Neither do I. So can we go? Get away from him?"

"Yeah, Emmy. We can go." Driftwood walked her over to his truck and ripped off the flier on the handle before opening the door for her. He wanted to throw the paper on the ground, but he couldn't bring himself to litter. After shutting the door, Driftwood walked around his truck and picked up as many of the blue pieces of paper as he could. He threw them on the floor of his backseat and put the vehicle into reverse.

Right before he backed out of the parking space, he happened to look up.

There, on the second floor, in the apartment at the end of the building, a man stood in a window, staring down at the parking lot. Driftwood could tell even from this distance that it was Willard. The bastard was watching—and he had a perfect vantage point to see everyone who came and went from the complex.

Not wanting to alarm Quinn, he didn't acknowledge that he'd seen the man, but he did make a mental note to talk to Beth. It was about time they found out more about Willard. And, if possible, do what needed to be done to evict the man. Even though Driftwood hoped Quinn wouldn't be living at the complex much longer, Willard was a threat to anyone who lived there. It was in everyone's best interest to get him to move on.

As it turned out, Driftwood didn't get a chance to call Beth that night. The second they entered his house, Quinn had backed him against the wall and kissed him. One thing led to another, and they left a trail of clothes on the floor that led from the front door to the bedroom.

The next morning, both he and Quinn had to go to work and, after an intense lovemaking session in the shower, they had to rush around to make it to the lab and fire station on time.

Then work was crazy for Driftwood. From the second he arrived at the station they were on the go. They hadn't even been able to sit down for lunch, they were so busy.

It wasn't until Driftwood was lying in bed at the station, after talking to Quinn and making sure her day had gone all right, that he remembered. But by then, it was close to eleven o'clock and he was exhausted. Telling himself he'd call Beth first thing in the morning, Driftwood closed his eyes and was immediately out.

As luck would have it, however, the tones went off

at four the next morning, and everyone was sent to a huge warehouse three-alarm fire. They were on scene until three in the afternoon, making sure the fire was completely out and wouldn't rekindle the second they left. The good news was that no one was injured or killed, the bad news was that the building was a complete loss.

Fires were a weird thing. They were devastating and destructive, but they were also exciting and exhilarating for the men and women who fought them. Each one was different, no two fires acted the same way. The science and physics behind them were the same, but the adrenaline rush from entering a burning building or from trying to figure out how best to put out the fire was a high Driftwood couldn't explain to someone who wasn't a firefighter.

Medical calls and vehicle accidents were exciting, but in a completely different way.

They'd battled the massive warehouse fire for almost twelve hours straight. The community had come through in a big way by donating water, pizza, and even an air-conditioned truck so the firefighters could get a small break from the fire as they refueled their bodies.

As they made their way back to the station, exhausted and dirty, Driftwood pulled out his phone. He had a few texts from Quinn. Work was going fine, she felt pretty good about the progress she was making on the destroyed samples from earlier. She hoped he was safe and she looked forward to hearing from him.

The second he walked into the fire station and could get some privacy, Driftwood took out his phone and clicked on Quinn's name.

"Hey, Emmy."

"John! Are you okay? Is the fire out?"

"I'm fine, and yes, it's out. We're back at the station now."

"Good. Was anyone hurt?"

"Nothing serious."

"I'm glad. Are you getting off work at your usual time?"

"We should be. It depends on if we get a call right before shift change, but here's to hoping not."

"Want me to make something for dinner?" Quinn asked.

"That would be awesome."

"Want anything in particular?"

"No. Whatever we've got in the house is fine. Don't go to the store. I'll take care of that tomorrow when I'm off." Driftwood never thought having this kind of conversation would be one of the highlights of his day. Talking about what to have for dinner and who would do chores.

"I can stop by the store on my way home. It won't take very long," she told him.

Remembering the difficult day she'd had the last time she'd gone to the store, to get the stupid potato salad for Taco's dinner party that they hadn't even eaten, Driftwood immediately said, "No. It's fine. We've got some hamburger in the fridge and lots of pasta. You can just make a quick and dirty spaghetti or something."

"You sure? I don't think we have any salad. The last time I looked in the drawer, there was black stuff growing on that bag we bought."

"I'm sure. All I need is a bunch of carbs…and you."

"Well, I think I can help you with both those things," she said coyly.

Loving their banter, Driftwood smiled. "I know you can," he told her.

"Okay, Sophie is rolling her eyes at me," Quinn said. "I need to go. I'm finishing up here, then I'm going to stop by my place and grab my big stockpot."

"Quinn, I've got a pot," Driftwood told her.

"I know, but it's not like mine."

"I don't think the pasta cares what kind of pot it's cooked in," Driftwood said.

"Whatever. Besides, I need to grab some more clothes."

"I don't think that's a good idea. At least not by yourself. I'm not comfortable with you going over there with Willard living right next door." Thinking about Willard made him remember that he needed to call Beth, to have her look into Quinn's neighbor and see what she could find out about him.

"I'm just going to run in, grab some stuff, and leave. I'll lock my door the second I get inside and I'll carry my cat-shaped brass knuckles. Will that make you feel better?"

"I'd feel better if you waited until I was with you to go over there," Driftwood told her.

"I'll be fine, John. Promise," she said. "I know to be careful, and I can't live my entire life locked in your house."

"All right, but please be careful."

"I will." Then she chuckled. "I didn't think you'd complain this much about me moving more of my shit in."

"Emmy, if I had my way, you'd be giving your landlord your notice and moving *all* your stuff over to my house."

She was quiet for a beat after his pronouncement. Then she said, "I'm not ready yet, John. I'm trying, but..." Her voice trailed off.

"You don't trust me fully yet," Driftwood finished for her.

"It's not that, it's just—"

"It's fine. I understand," he interrupted her. "I get it, I do, Quinn. I fucked up, and it'll take time for you to feel like you don't need your own space to hole up in and hide from the world...from me. I had a long talk with Taco about Jen. He wasn't happy with what she'd said either. I think that was actually the last straw for him. He called her last night and told her that he didn't think things were working out between them. You aren't going to have to see her again."

Driftwood heard Quinn let out a small sigh of relief, and he hated that she'd bottled up her feelings about the other woman and hadn't shared them earlier.

"From here on out," he said sternly, "you tell me if you don't click with someone and I'll make sure you don't have to spend time with them."

"That's not fair," she protested.

"*You* are what's most important to me," Driftwood told her. "And if someone does something to make my girlfriend uncomfortable, then I don't want to be around them."

"You'd pick me over your friends?" she asked quietly.

"*Yes*, Quinn. I love you. I want to give you a life filled with happiness and love, not uncertainty and insecurity. You've had enough of that shit to last you a lifetime."

"I… No one has ever picked me over their other friends before."

"Well, I am."

Driftwood heard her clear her throat before she said, "Tell Taco I'm sorry. I know he was hoping Jen would be more than a short-term girlfriend."

"He's okay," Driftwood said. "Disappointed, yeah, but honestly, he said there was always something about her that made him hold back. Her body was banging, and she was pretty, but he said sometimes she said and did things that were just…off."

"Maybe we could have him over sometime for dinner and a movie?" Quinn asked.

Driftwood would never get tired of her generous spirit. "Yeah, Emmy, that sounds good. Now, I need to get going. If I don't hurry up and snag a shower, the others will hog all the hot water, and the last thing I want is to get home and still be smelly and gross."

"I appreciate that," she said with a laugh.

"I thought you might. Be careful when you go to your apartment."

"I will. Have you talked to Beth yet?"

"No, but as soon as I'm out of the shower, I'm going to call her."

"I'm sure it's fine. I mean, aren't there background checks done on people when they sign a lease? I can't remember all the papers I signed when I rented my apartment, but if Willard was a serial killer or an over-the-top religious nut who kidnaps people and forces them to listen to him preach for hours on end... wouldn't that've come up when he rented his apartment?"

Driftwood didn't even crack a smile. The image she put in his brain of the overweight older man tying someone to a chair and trying to save their soul wasn't funny in the least. Especially because he imagined *her* in that chair. "I'm sure it would've. Just be safe all the same. I'll talk to Beth and she'll find out what Willard's deal is in two point three seconds, I'm sure."

"Tell her I said hi," she told him.

"I will. I love you, Quinn."

She took a deep breath. "I love you too, John. Drive safe."

He hadn't meant to pressure her to say the words

back, but he couldn't deny that hearing them was the most memorable moment of his life.

He'd fucked up the night before last. He'd told her she could count on him and trust him to always have her back, and then he hadn't. She'd thought she was safe, surrounded by friends, and he'd let her get hurt. Never again.

"I will. I'll see you at home," he told her.

"Bye."

"Bye, Emmy."

Driftwood clicked off the phone and closed his eyes for a long moment. *Home*. It was crazy how much that word meant to him now. Before it was just a place where he kept his shit and where he slept when he wasn't at work. But now it was his connection to Quinn. He'd had no idea how much she would come to mean to him when he'd met her all those months ago, but now he couldn't imagine his life without her.

Sleeping without her next to him had been an eye-opener for him. He'd gotten used to holding her, to having her near. But when she'd slept at her apartment, deliberately putting space between them, he'd realized how much he'd come to need her.

He needed her to keep him grounded. To keep him from being too absorbed in his work. To give him balance.

Opening his eyes and putting his phone down on the little table next to the bed in the room he used when he was on shift, Driftwood pulled his sweat-soaked, nasty-smelling shirt off and headed for the showers.

* * *

Quinn smiled as she rummaged through her underwear drawer. She had a lot of ratty old cotton panties in there, but she wanted to find the newest ones to bring with her over to John's house. As she sorted through them, she thought back to their phone conversation.

It was crazy how low she could be one moment, and then the next she felt on top of the world. And if she was honest with herself, what John had done hadn't really been so awful, it had just felt like it at the time.

He'd apologized, brought her doughnuts, and gone out of his way to do whatever it took to try to reassure her that he'd do his best not to let her down again. Realistically, she knew he would. Just as she'd disappoint him too. But it was realizing your mistakes and apologizing that made the difference.

She loved John. Quinn had always worried about whether or not she even knew *how* to love. She hadn't had role models when she was growing up to show her how to love unconditionally. No one had taken her in their arms when she was upset after being bullied and told her she was beautiful and loved. She'd never had a safe place to go to lick her wounds.

But even as she'd lain in her bed in her apartment after John had driven off, she'd wished she was at *his* house. She hadn't wanted to be anywhere near him when he'd dropped her off, but as the night went on, she'd realized that she missed him. Yes, she'd been upset, but she still knew without a doubt that she was safe with him.

She could be angry, and he'd give her space but still be there.

She could be frustrated, and he'd give her an outlet.

She could be sad, and he'd be right there to give her a shoulder to cry on.

She'd been scared to tell him she loved him, as she'd never said the words to anyone before, but today on the phone, she realized that she couldn't imagine her life without him in it. She'd worried about him all day, knowing he was at the huge warehouse fire that had started early that morning. Her world was better because he was in it, and while they still had a lot to learn about each other, she wanted to spend the rest of her life by his side.

It was actually very freeing to say the words. To let him know she loved him. And now that the words were out there, she felt content. Relaxed. She couldn't wait to *show* him how much she loved him tonight, as well.

Shoving a bunch of panties into a large shoulder bag, Quinn went to her closet and pulled some more work blouses off hangers. She folded them and added them to the bag, along with two pairs of slacks, three pairs of jeans, a few T-shirts, and two more pairs of shoes. She still had a lot more clothes to bring to his place, but this would tide her over in the meantime.

Carrying the heavy bag to the living area, she put it down next to the kitchen counter and leaned down to open the cabinet next to the stove. She was pulling out the huge stockpot when there was a knock on her door.

Standing up, she hesitated for a beat. Could it be John? Had he gotten off work early and come over here to help her pack? She pulled out her phone and didn't see a text or a message from him. Smiling, Quinn put her phone down on the counter and headed for the door. It would be just like him to come over and help so she'd have *more* of her stuff at his house.

She peered through the peephole...and frowned in confusion. It wasn't John standing there. Hesitating for a beat, debating with herself on whether or not to answer the door, she finally undid the latch and opened it.

"Hey."

Before she could say or do anything else, a huge fist came flying toward her face.

Not able to dodge it, Quinn grunted in pain and fell backward to the floor, holding her cheek in her hand. Trying to get her bearings, she didn't move fast enough to keep from being kicked in the side.

She curled into a ball and felt her flip-flops come off, but her shoes were the least of her worries at the moment.

Looking up, she asked, "Why?"

But she got no answer. Instead, a needle was jammed into her thigh.

Screeching in pain, Quinn tried to kick out, to get away, but whatever drug had been inside the needle was quickly taking effect. Her head began to swim and her limbs felt heavy.

The last thing she heard was a deep voice saying, "Resist the devil, and he will flee from you."

CHAPTER FOURTEEN

*D*riftwood frowned when he opened his garage and didn't see Quinn's car inside. She should've been home way before now. They didn't have another call, but he and all the others did hang out for a while after their shift was over, talking to the next shift. A huge fire like the one they'd fought was rare, and everyone who hadn't participated wanted to know everything about it.

He'd finally left forty-five minutes after his shift was over. Quinn should've had plenty of time to go by her place and be at his house by now. Driftwood wondered if something had been wrong with her car and she'd gotten a ride from Sophie, Autumn, or Tory. Although if that was the case, he'd have to give her hell for not calling or texting him.

But the second he opened the door to his house, Driftwood knew Quinn wasn't there. Everything was quiet…too quiet. There were no delicious smells emanating from his kitchen, and she usually liked to have some sort of music playing while she was cooking.

Just to be sure, Driftwood did a quick walk-through of his house, and after finding it empty, headed back to his truck.

As he backed out of his garage, he pushed her contact info on his phone and waited impatiently as the call rang through his truck's speakers.

He frowned even harder when, after several rings, he got her voice mail.

"Quinn, it's John. I'm worried about you. Where are you? Call me."

He hung up and immediately dialed Beth's number. He probably could've called Dax, Quint, or any one of his law enforcement friends, but the only person he knew who could do anything immediately was Beth. The computer hacker had the skills to work under the radar, and if something was wrong with Quinn, Beth was the one he needed right now.

"Hey, you miss talking to me already?" she asked as she picked up the phone. "I don't have any info on the mysterious Willard yet. You *just* called me."

"I can't find Quinn," Driftwood said without preliminaries.

"What?"

"Quinn. She was supposed to be at my house cooking dinner, but when I got here, she wasn't."

"Take a deep breath," Beth ordered. "Did you call her?"

"Of course I did. I got her voice mail."

"Did it immediately go to her mailbox or did it ring a bunch beforehand?"

"It rang like six times," Driftwood said.

"Okay, so her phone is still on then, that's good," Beth said. "Have you checked her apartment?"

"I'm on my way there now."

There was silence on the other end of the line for a beat. Then Beth said, "Wait…it's been, what…two minutes that you haven't been able to ascertain where she is and you're already freaking out? Don't you think you're overreacting? What if she's in the bathroom? Maybe she has a stomach problem or something and didn't bring her phone in there with her. No one wants their boyfriend to hear them pooping while they're on the phone."

Driftwood wasn't in the mood for Beth's humor at the moment. "She should've been at my house at least an hour ago," he told her. "She's not there. She didn't call me to tell me she's running late. Something's wrong."

Beth's tone was much more serious when she responded, "What do you need me to do?"

"I don't know!" Driftwood said a bit frantically. "Find her. Do your thing. Hack into cameras…look at traffic cameras and find her car. Ping her cell phone. *Something.*"

"Okay, first, it's not that easy to just hack into traffic cameras to find a specific car. Do you know how long that shit takes?"

"Beth," Driftwood warned. "Please."

"Right. Fine, I'll track her cell phone. Hang on..."

Driftwood drummed his fingers on the steering wheel as he sat at a red light. He wanted to break every single traffic law to get to her apartment, but the last thing he needed was to be held up by a ticket.

"Okay, triangulating now. You do know that this is illegal, right?" Beth asked.

"If this was Sledge missing, would you be worrying about what's legal and illegal right about now?" Driftwood asked.

"Fuck no. Okay, it's almost done...hmmm."

"What?"

"She's at her apartment."

"She is?"

"Yeah. Well, at least her phone is."

Driftwood breathed out a sigh of relief. "She doesn't go anywhere without her phone," he told Beth.

"Where are you?"

"I'm about five minutes from her apartment complex. Why?"

"I don't think you should go into her apartment alone. Let me call Dax and get him to meet you there."

Driftwood's blood ran cold. "Why?"

"You know why," Beth said.

Pushing his foot harder on the accelerator, Driftwood didn't respond.

"Driftwood?"

"There's no way in hell I'm waiting. What if she's hurt and can't get to her phone?"

"Okay, okay. Are there cameras at her apartment?"

"Yeah. I've seen some on the outside of the building and in the lobby."

"I'm calling Dax and Quint. I know you know this, but I'm going to say it anyway—don't touch anything unnecessarily. If something's actually wrong, and there's evidence, you don't want to contaminate it."

Driftwood gritted his teeth and didn't respond.

"Did you hear me?" Beth asked impatiently.

"Yeah. I heard you." He heard, but didn't like the implications. Visions of Quinn lying hurt and unable to move wouldn't leave his head. He wished he'd left the station right at the end of his shift and hadn't stayed around shooting the shit.

"I'm going to hang up and call Quint and Dax now. Keep calm, Driftwood," Beth warned. "No matter what you find. The last thing Quinn needs is you losing it. If she's there and mad at you for some reason, don't freak out and say something you'll regret. If she's there and hurt, use your skills to help her, and if she's not there... well...just don't lose your shit. We'll find her. Okay?"

"Thanks, Beth," Driftwood managed. He couldn't imagine any of the scenarios she'd suggested, although he hoped like hell she was just mad at him for some reason and refusing to take his calls. He couldn't think of anything he'd done in the last couple hours since he'd last talked to her, but at the moment, that would be the best scenario.

Maybe she'd just lost her phone and hadn't left her place yet because she was looking for it. They'd laugh at how fast he'd panicked and go home and have the pasta dinner they'd planned.

"Call me once you have more information," Beth ordered.

"I will."

She clicked off the phone and Driftwood clenched his fists around the steering wheel as he pushed his luck by going fifteen over the speed limit down the street that led to her complex.

He pulled into the parking lot and his eyes scanned the cars even as he pulled into one of the visitor parking spaces.

There.

Her Toyota Corolla was sitting in her assigned parking space. Driftwood got out of his truck and jogged over to it. He peered inside and was somewhat relieved to find it empty. He walked around it and didn't see anything out of the ordinary. No scuff marks on the ground and no damage to the car itself.

Turning on his heel, Driftwood hurried over to the front doors, through the lobby, and up to Quinn's apartment. He turned the knob, only to find it locked. A pang of relief went through him. He knew it was premature, but he'd envisioned her door being broken down and her lying on the floor, hurt.

Driftwood banged his fist on the door. "Quinn? It's me. Open the door."

He waited, and she didn't answer.

Knocking once more, he called, "Quinn! Let me in!"

He tilted his head and didn't hear anything coming

from inside her apartment. He cursed his lack of fore-sight in not getting a key to her place. He'd given her keys to his house, but hadn't thought he'd need one to her apartment since they spent most nights together at his place. Driftwood debated his next move.

He could break down the door, but that would defi-nitely be destroying evidence, not to mention it would piss off the super, and probably Quinn too. But then again, if she was lying inside hurt and needing medical care, he'd be an idiot not to get to her as soon as possible.

Putting his ear to the door, Driftwood strained to hear any little sign that would tell him Quinn was inside.

Nothing.

Blowing out a frustrated breath, he ran back down the hall and stairs. He knocked as loud as he could on the door in the lobby labeled, "Manager."

Within thirty seconds, it opened.

"I need a key to apartment two twenty-seven," Driftwood said.

The older man wasn't so easily intimidated. He crossed his arms over his chest and frowned. "Why?"

Driftwood tried to calm himself. If he pissed this man off, it would take even longer to get inside Quinn's apartment. "My name is John Trettle. I'm a firefighter and paramedic for the city of San Antonio. Quinn Dixon is my girlfriend. I can't get ahold of her and I'm afraid she's hurt and can't come to the door. I tried calling but it just goes to voice mail. Her car is here, but she's not answering the door. You can stand there and watch me the entire time I'm in her apartment. I just need to make sure she's okay."

The man eyed Driftwood for a long time. What seemed like ages, before he said, "I've seen you around here before."

Sighing in relief, Driftwood nodded. "Yeah. We've been staying at my house for the most part. But she was stopping by here after work to grab some things before heading to my place. When I got home, she wasn't there. As I said, her car is here, but she's not answering. Can you please help me? All I want to do is make sure she's not hurt."

"Have you called the cops?"

Wanting to strangle the man, Driftwood forced himself to stay calm. "Yes. They're on their way, but if she's hurt, I can help her. I have medical training."

"You don't have no bag," the manager of the apartment building said logically.

Clenching his teeth, Driftwood said, "I know. I don't need it. I can find what I need in her apartment and I'll call 9-1-1 if necessary."

"Well, I'm not sure. This is highly unusual," the manager said, rubbing his chin.

"Please," Driftwood begged. "This isn't like her. I'm worried about her. I'm not up to no good. I swear."

"All right...but only because I've seen you with her before. I'm not the kind of manager who lets any ol' person off the street into my apartments."

"Thank you," Driftwood said in relief, making a

mental note to get a key made for Quinn's apartment as soon as possible.

"Wait here," the old man said as he turned around and went back inside his office/apartment.

Driftwood did his best not to scream in frustration as he waited for the man to return. After at least a minute, he reappeared with, honest to God, a huge circle keyring with about forty keys on it. It jingled as the man shuffled through the lobby.

"Those cameras work?" Driftwood asked as they headed for the elevator.

The manager looked up. "Yeah, why?"

"Just in case."

The old man shrugged.

"I'll meet you up there," Driftwood told him, knowing he wouldn't have the patience to take the elevator to the second floor. Not waiting for the man's answer, he headed for the stairwell.

It took several more minutes, but finally the manager was walking down the hall toward Quinn's apartment. The keys jingled as he walked and the sound grated on Driftwood's nerves.

"I've just got to find the right one," the man mumbled, fingering the keys as he stood in front of the door. Finally, after what seemed like hours but was really only a minute or two, he said, "Gotcha!"

The manager put a key in the lock and the knob turned with a click.

"Step back," Driftwood said, gently pulling the man back.

"Hey, wait. You said that I could watch you. Don't want you stealing nothin'."

"He isn't going to take anything," a low voice said from down the hall.

Turning in relief, Driftwood watched as Quint Axton and Daxton Chambers came toward them. The SAPD officer and Texas Ranger had impeccable timing. Beth must've gotten ahold of them immediately for them to already be here.

"As he said, please step back," Dax told the manager. "We appreciate you assisting, but please let us do our jobs."

The manager nodded and took a step to the side, but he didn't leave.

"Let me go in," Quint told Driftwood.

"No."

Dax put a hand on Driftwood's arm. "Let us do this."

"No. And we're wasting time. Move," Driftwood bit out.

He entered the apartment and called out, "Quinn? Are you here?"

The silence that greeted him was eerie. Driftwood tried to walk farther into the apartment, but Dax stopped him once more.

"Careful where you step."

Driftwood looked down—and felt his heart skip a beat at the small reddish stain on the hardwood floor. Stepping over the blood stain, he called out, "Emmy?"

When he got to the kitchen, he stopped in his tracks.

There on the counter was Quinn's cell phone.

He began to shake.

The stockpot she'd been so determined to bring back to his house was sitting on the floor next to an open cabinet, and there was a large bag full of what looked like clothes on the floor beneath the counter.

Driftwood heard Quint and Dax searching the apartment, but he couldn't move from his spot in the kitchen.

She'd been here. Right here. But now she was gone. The door was locked, it hadn't been broken into from what he'd seen. But that small stain on the floor told its own story.

"She's not here," Quint said, reentering the room.

Feeling as if he were moving in quicksand, Driftwood took his phone out of his pocket and clicked on Beth's name.

"So?" she asked in greeting.

"Check the cameras. She's not here. Her phone is, but Quinn's missing."

CHAPTER FIFTEEN

*Q*uinn's mouth was drier than she ever remembered it being in her life. But that wasn't her main concern. She was freezing. Literally shaking, she was so cold.

Prying her eyes open, she tried to figure out where she was and why in the world she was so bitterly cold. But when she did look around, nothing made sense.

She was in a small room with white walls and no windows. There was no furniture except the chair she was sitting on. Directly in front of her were three fans, all on high and pointed straight at her. Quinn could also feel air hitting her from behind as well.

The air conditioning in the room had to be cranked all the way down, and she was also wet. Her hair was dripping into her lap, making the air hitting her even colder. Her ankles were secured to the legs of the chair and her arms were tied behind her back.

But the most alarming thing was that she was

wearing only a bra and her panties. Quinn had no idea where her clothes had gone.

She grimaced, and realized her face was throbbing in pain as well.

Then it came back to her. Opening her apartment door and being hit in the face. Being jabbed in the leg with a needle and everything going black.

She jerked against her restraints, doing everything in her power to break free, but it was no use. The zip-ties holding her to the chair were too tight to break and she realized the chair itself was also secured to the floor.

"Hey!" she yelled. "Is anyone there? Let me go!"

Silence greeted her, and Quinn felt her breathing speed up as she began to panic. Had she been left here? Why? And why the big chill out? "Help!" she yelled. "Someone! I'm here! Help me!"

She heard noises at the door, and she continued to struggle. "Get me out of here! Please!"

The door opened—and Quinn wasn't surprised to see who entered, but it was the second person who entered the room who made her eyes widen in shock.

"You!" She breathed the word in disbelief.

* * *

Driftwood paced the hallway outside Quinn's apartment in agitation. He'd been kicked out to try to preserve evidence. Beth was already hacking into the security cameras in the building while they searched through Quinn's apartment, not bothering to wait for them to ask the manager for access. She was scouring them for anything that would be helpful, from footage inside the lobby as well as the parking lot. Quint and Dax had called in their crime scene investigators but in the meantime, they were trying to see what they could find in Quinn's apartment themselves, to figure out what had happened.

And Driftwood was left to pace. And worry.

A noise at the end of the hall made him turn his head—and he saw red. He was moving before he'd even thought about it.

Willard had come out of his apartment, and he was holding a pair of shoes.

Quinn's shoes.

He'd recognize the flip-flops anywhere. She carried them in her purse and changed into them as soon as she could after leaving work. She always said wearing closed-toe shoes and socks strangled her feet.

His hand was around Willard's throat and he had him up against the wall before the other man could escape back into his apartment.

Quinn's flip-flops fell to the ground as Willard grabbed hold of Driftwood's hands, trying to pry his fingers off his throat.

"Where is she, asshole? What'd you do with her? Is she inside your place?"

The other man didn't say anything, couldn't. His face was turning red as he tried to get air into his lungs.

"Whoa! Easy, Driftwood!" Quint yelled as he ran up and took hold of his arm.

"Let him go," Dax ordered as he came up on his other side.

"He's got her shoes," Driftwood bit out. "And the other day we caught him red-handed putting those freaky religious fliers on my truck. He's *always* staring at Quinn. He's got her. I know it!"

"Fine. But you strangling him won't do anything to help find her. Let go of him," Quint demanded.

Driftwood stared into Willard's eyes, wishing he was alone with the man. He'd force him to confess what he'd done with Quinn. Where he'd stashed her. But his friends were right. Killing him wouldn't make it any easier to find her, even if it would make Driftwood feel better.

He loosened his grip on the man's throat and watched in satisfaction as he wheezed in and out and brought his hands up to his throat to massage it.

"Where is she?" Driftwood bit out. "Tell me right now, asshole!"

Then Willard did something extremely odd. He lifted his chin, pointed to his throat with a finger, and shook his head.

"What are you trying to say? I don't understand," Driftwood responded. "Start talking and quit this pantomime bullshit."

Willard opened his mouth and pointed to it this time, while he shook his head again.

"Damn it," Driftwood swore. "Enough!" He reached

for the man again. This time to shake some sense into him. To hit him. To do anything to make him stop playing games and fucking tell him where Quinn was.

A voice coming from down the hall stopped him.

"He's mute."

Driftwood turned to stare at the manager. He hadn't left. He'd been standing in the hall watching everything unfold the entire time.

"What?" Quint asked.

"His name's Willard Whitley. He's mute. Lived here for eight and a half years and I've never heard him say a word. He works out of his apartment, pays his rent on time, and hasn't ever caused me any problems."

Dax turned to Willard. "You can't talk?"

Willard shook his head. Then took two fingers and pointed at his eyes before pointing them down the hall.

"You saw? You saw what?"

Willard used his pointer finger and jabbed it toward Quinn's door.

"Quint, search his apartment," Dax said, taking hold of Willard's upper arm.

Without pause, Quint slipped through the open door next to them. No one said a word as Quint did a sweep of Willard's apartment looking for Quinn. He reappeared again in less than thirty seconds. "She's not there. But I found these."

Quint was holding a stack of bright blue pieces of paper.

"Those are the fliers we saw him putting on my truck," Driftwood said.

"He wasn't putting them *on* your vehicle," the manager said. "He was taking them *off*. I thought the same thing and was pissed, but then I watched the security tapes. There were these two guys lurking around the parking lot and they were putting that shit on everyone's cars. I shooed them off, and then Willard came out and started to pick them up. He watches."

"Watches what?" Dax asked.

"The parking lot," the manager said. "As I said, he works from his apartment, so he knows what happens around here. His window overlooks the parking lot. He's almost as good as a security system. More than once he's given me information about what's going on. The drug dealers stopped using the lot as a place to pass along their wares because the cops always seemed to catch them in the act." He used his head to indicate Willard. "Thanks to him."

Driftwood turned to stare incredulously at the man he'd completely misjudged. "What does he do for a living?" he asked the manager while looking at Willard.

"He writes those captions that show up on them videos on the Internet."

Willard held out one hand flat and used his other to pantomime writing on a piece of paper.

"Get him something to write on," Driftwood ordered, still holding Willard's gaze.

Quint pulled a small pad of paper out of one of his many pockets, along with a pen, and handed them to Willard. Quinn's neighbor immediately began to write.

Driftwood read his note when he finished.

I'm also a ghostwriter. I write everything from romance novels to blog posts for people who don't have the time or inclination to write them on their own. I am not the bad guy here. I saw them though.

Driftwood looked up from the paper. "Who?"

Willard quickly began writing again. *There were three of them. A woman and two men. I've seen the men around before. In the parking lot. Leaving the fliers.*

"How'd you get her shoes?" Driftwood asked Willard.

He scribbled on his pad of paper. *They were outside her door. I'm guessing they came off in the scuffle at her door, and they either didn't notice or didn't care about them when they left with her.*

Just then, Driftwood's phone rang. His head was swimming.

Willard wasn't the bad guy.

If it wasn't him, who'd taken Quinn? And why?

He saw it was Beth calling. "Did you find her?" he asked as he answered.

"Yeah. Sort of. I'm sending the pertinent parts of the videos to your phone."

"Send it to Quint and Dax too. They're here with me."

"Already done," Beth told him quickly.

Driftwood opened the text he'd just received and clicked play. The lobby of the apartment complex came into view. The video was black and white and grainy, but within seconds, he saw the back of a woman's head come into frame. She was wearing high heels, jeans, and a dark blouse. Her hair came to the middle of her back, but he couldn't see her face. She was followed by two men, both wearing dark clothes, and one was pulling a large suitcase behind him. They waited for the elevator and disappeared when the doors shut.

"I can't see their faces," Driftwood told Beth.

"Continue watching," she said.

There was no sound to the video, and he knew Quint and Dax were watching it on their phones at the same time. The screen went black for a moment, then the lobby came into view once more. The same two men exited the elevator with the same suitcase being towed behind them.

But it was the woman who caught his attention.

"Is that...?" he gasped.

"Yeah," Beth said in a pissed-off tone. "It is. And if I had to guess, I'd say Quinn was inside that suitcase."

The video changed and now showed the parking lot. They all watched as the two men headed for a white panel van. They both leaned down and, working together, threw the large suitcase into the back of the van, shut the door, climbed in, and drove off.

The woman who'd been with them climbed into a familiar-looking tan four-door Mercedes and followed behind the van.

"Call Taco," Driftwood growled. "Tell him we need every scrap of information about his ex-girlfriend that he can give us."

"Already on it," Beth reassured him. "That bitch won't get away with this!"

"That's Jennifer Hale?" Dax asked.

"The one and only."

"What does she want with Quinn?" he asked.

"I have no idea," Driftwood said. "But she's not going to get away with this."

Willard shoved a piece of paper at Driftwood. It had a series of numbers and letters on it.

"License plate number?" he asked Quinn's neighbor.

Willard nodded and began to quickly write on the pad of paper once more.

I listened as they left Quinn's apartment. The woman asked if the compound was prepared.

"The compound?" Driftwood asked. "Are you sure?"

Willard nodded, then wrote some more. *She then said some sort of Bible verse. Something having to do with the devil prowling and a lion looking for someone to devour.*

"Any ideas?" Driftwood asked his friends. They shook their heads.

"Peter 5:8. 'Be alert and of sober mind. Your enemy the devil prowls around like a roaring lion looking for someone to devour.'"

All four men looked at the manager.

"You sure?" Dax asked.

"Of course. I'm a Christian man. Before my wife passed, we went to church every Sunday and even led a Bible study group."

"Did you overhear anything else?" Quint asked Willard. "Anything about where this compound is or why they were taking Quinn?"

He shook his head.

"You hear all that, Beth?" Dax asked.

"Yeah. It's not much. A compound and a quote about the devil. But that license plate is pure gold. I'm on it and will be in touch."

Driftwood clicked off his phone. As much as he wanted to storm out of the apartment and track down Quinn, one, he didn't know where she was. And two, he had an apology he needed to make. "I'm sorry," he told Willard. "When we saw you staring, we assumed you didn't have the best intentions."

Willard bent over his pad of paper. *I know. I should've tried harder to explain. To tell you about the men in the parking lot. But just like your woman doesn't like being stared at because of her birthmark, I don't like when people cringe away from me and think I'm a serial killer. It's why I keep to myself.*

Now Driftwood felt like shit. "When we find Quinn, we'd love to have you over for dinner sometime. Maybe we can't make up for the way we treated you or what we thought, but we'd like to try."

Willard shrugged, then pointed down the hall.

"Right. We're going. I'm going to find her," Driftwood vowed.

Willard nodded and pressed his lips together.

"Come on," Dax said. "The CSIs should be here soon, but I'm not sure they'll find anything that will be of any use to us. We need to talk to Taco."

Just then, something clicked in Driftwood's head. "Wait," he said, and turned his phone back on. He clicked on the video Beth had sent and zoomed in as it played. He watched the group get into the elevator and waited impatiently for the footage to continue. When the elevator opened and the men walked out and through the lobby, he concentrated on the man with the light hair and the beard.

"That's the guy from the bar!" he exclaimed.

"What guy at what bar?" Dax asked.

"The Sloppy Cow. Quinn and I were there with the Station 7 gang a couple months ago, and this guy was there. We almost ran into him as we entered and he was a jackass."

"You sure?"

"Positive," Driftwood said.

"So…they've been watching and following Quinn then. But why? Why her, and why wait so long to grab her?"

"Opportunity?" Quint asked.

Driftwood had no idea what Jen and her friends would want with Quinn. But whatever it was, it couldn't be good.

Turning on his heel, he walked past the manager, who was still hanging on every word, and headed toward the stairs. Quinn's life was in danger. Of that he had no doubt. He didn't know why, didn't know where she was, but he knew the who. That had to be enough to find her. It had to be.

CHAPTER SIXTEEN

Quinn wasn't surprised to see Jen the bitch enter the room. But she was completely shocked when she recognized the man who came into the room behind her.

The man from the bar. The asshole she'd confronted in the grocery store. Had he been following her even back then?

"You!" she hissed as Alaric leaned against the wall just inside the door. She'd been knocked out so fast she hadn't had time to recognize who'd done it. But seeing the man she hadn't really suspected at all was a shock.

Both Jen and the two men with her kept their distance, not giving Quinn any chance to try to head butt, bite, or otherwise hurt them. "Him," Jen agreed with a smug smile.

"What are you d-doing?" Quinn asked, her voice stuttering from the cold. "Let me go."

"I don't think so. You see, we're saving you."

"S-Saving me? From what?"

Jen pushed off the wall and sauntered toward her, but not close enough to touch. "The devil."

Quinn blinked. "What?"

"The devil, Quinn. You've been marked. I did what I could to save your soul, but it didn't work."

"Jen, I don't know what you're talking about. Please, l-let me go, give me my clothes, and we can t-talk about this."

She shook her head. "Oh, no, you're not going anywhere. We can't have you walking around and spreading the devil's word. We're going to save you... help you repent, purge the devil lurking within you."

Quinn could only stare at the woman in front of her. She was crazy. Seriously crazy. "Why would you think I've got the devil in me? I believe in God. I go to church when I can."

"Because you've been *marked*," she enunciated clearly. "Did you not hear me before?"

"Marked?" Quinn was genuinely confused.

Jen ran a hand down her own cheek and neck. "The devil's mark. It was placed on your body by Satan himself, as a seal of your pledge to obey and service him."

For a second, Quinn could only stare at her.

This was about her *birthmark*? Jen seriously thought that just because she was born with the mark, she was possessed by the devil? She was completely insane.

Shivering, she turned to the men behind Jen. "Please, untie me and let me go home."

"Alaric," Jen said, staring into Quinn's eyes. "Please tell the marked one how the Bible has given us the clues and how we know she is a minion of Satan."

"Gladly, sister," the man with the blond beard said.

Sister? Oh shit, the man she'd taunted in the grocery story was Jen's brother? This was not good. Not good at all.

"We know that red is the color of Satan. Revelation 17:4 says 'And the woman was arrayed in purple and scarlet color, and decked with gold and precious stones and pearls, having a golden cup in her hand full of abominations and filthiness of her fornication.' And we know the afflicted call their marks port-wine stains. Of course, on a ship, the port light is red and always on the left. Mark 10:40 says, 'But to sit on my right hand and on my left hand is not mine to give; but it shall be given to them for whom it is prepared.'"

"And for whom is the left hand of God reserved?" Jen asked her brother.

Quinn shook her head and tried to wake herself up. This had to be a bad dream. A very bad dream. But Alaric kept talking.

"Matthew 25:33. 'He shall set the sheep on His right hand, but the goats on the left. Mathew 25:41. Then shall He say also unto them on the left hand, depart from me, ye cursed, into everlasting fire, prepared for the devil and his angels.'"

"Exactly right," Jen praised. "So, there it is. The biblical prophecy that states those with red port-wine stains have the mark of the devil, and they should be cast into everlasting fire. You were marked because you are bad, Quinn. Plain and simple. You are a vessel of Satan, and we must cast him out!"

As Quinn listened to this woman, someone who she'd done her best to befriend and be nice to, use the name of the Lord to cast aspersions upon her character and judge her for something she had no control over, something snapped inside her.

She leaned forward in her chair as far as she could, reveling in the way Jen quickly stepped backward, and said, "You see my m-mark as something bad, but I see it as the opposite. I see it as being t-touched by God. I was a chosen one. I'm *proud* to have it! Only the very s-special and treasured get this mark. It's people like *you* who're treading on thin ice. You think God will approve of you judging me? I'm a test for you, Jen, and news f-flash—you're failing.

"Matthew 7:12, 'Do to others what you would have them do to you.' Also, Luke 6:37. 'Do not j-judge, and you will not be judged. Do not condemn, and you will not be condemned. Forgive and you will be forgiven.'"

Jen crossed her arms over her chest. "So we're going to have a battle of Bible verses? Fine. James 4:7. 'Submit yourselves, then, to God. Resist the devil, and he will flee from you.' Repent, Quinn. Our church is trying to help you! Your protestations are just proving you're on Satan's side instead of ours."

"Your *church*? You're all b-bigots! You've bastardized the good and true meaning of the Bible for your own twisted beliefs. I'm no more m-marked by the devil than *you*. Do you not have any blemishes on your skin, Jen? No moles, no unusual dark spots?"

"No."

"I d-don't believe you," Quinn said. "Corinthians 5:10. 'For we must all appear before the judgement seat of Christ, so that each of us may receive what is due us for the things done while in the body, whether good or b-bad.' When we finally stand before the Lord, which one of us do you think will be judged for the good and w-which do you think will be judged for the bad?"

Jen looked taken aback for a moment, then stubbornly shook her head. "I tried to *save* you!" she said. "When I first met you at that heathen bar, I gave you some of my special holy water, to try to make you see the light, to repent and repel the devil, but it didn't work."

"You spiked my drink?" Quinn asked, horrified.

Jen gave a nod. "But it wasn't enough, so when you came to Hudson's house, I gave you pure, undiluted holy water—and you *still* didn't see the light."

Quinn felt sick. She'd assumed her stomach hurting the morning after dinner was something simple. Stress from the way the night had ended up. Jen could've killed her. She could've put anything into her drink or food.

"I did my best to help you. Sharing the word of our Lord to get you to turn to Him to save you, but you ignored it all!"

"The f-fliers?" Quinn questioned.

"Yes. I *tried*, but you wouldn't listen! And those

other awful women weren't helping. They turned you against me! If you'd only turned to *me*, this could've gone a different way. We could've prayed together. I would've helped you remove the mark from your face by using bleach and prayer. And you were supposed to call my friend. This would've been so much easier if you had come to us willingly."

"You tried to lure me here?" Quinn asked in shock.

"Of course. But you looked at me with such contempt, I knew it was futile. That we would have to do things a different way. But make no mistake, we *will* eject Satan from your body, no matter the harm it does in trying."

"So if my b-birthmark d-doesn't go away, you're going to kill me?" Quinn asked.

"We will do everything in our power to remove the devil's mark before we resort to that," Jen said, eerily calm now.

Quinn knew she should be scared. She should be terrified of Jen and her minions and what they had planned.

But instead, she was pissed.

She'd been told over the years that her birthmark was a sign that she was evil, but she'd also been told that it was a mark from God, that she was a test for humankind. Those who were benevolent and compassionate toward her passed His test. Those who were judgmental and ugly weren't following His commands to love thy neighbor.

She hadn't believed any of it. The birthmark was

simply a discoloration caused by a capillary malformation in the skin. But sitting there, practically naked, freezing, and listening to Jen and her cronies tell her she was a minion of Satan, she had a revelation.

There wasn't anything wrong with her.

She was just fine; it was everyone *else* who was broken. The women at the convenience store who'd stared at her. The men at the grocery store who did the same. Everyone who told her she'd be pretty if she just covered up the mark on her face.

Quinn was perfectly happy with her face the way it was, and she didn't need her birthmark forcibly removed, thank you very much.

The people who were truly ugly were those like Jen. Like the boys at the softball game. Like the people who laughed at her and called her names. *Quinn* wasn't the ugly one—it was all the close-minded people who couldn't look beyond superficial imperfections.

And John loved her exactly how she was. She knew that down to the marrow of her being. She'd been around long enough to be able to tell when people were uncomfortable around her. When they were lying about not caring about the way she looked. John loved her. All of her.

Fuck these crazy assholes. They had to be in some sort of cult or something. There was no way normal, God-fearing people would be acting this insane.

"So, what's your p-plan?" Quinn asked, figuring the more information she had, the better.

"Well, first we must make sure we keep you cold.

Satan doesn't like the cold, so we're subduing him, making sure you can't use his powers by keeping your body temperature down. Then we'll see if we can't remove the devil's mark off your face."

Quinn shivered, and not from the cold this time. "D-Don't touch me, Jen. I mean it. You'll r-regret it if you do."

For just a second, Quinn saw fear cross the other woman's face. But she recovered quickly. "I'm worried you're already too far gone," Jen said sadly. "That I found you too late."

"You f-found me?" Quinn asked.

"Yes. Part of our mission is to find lost ones who need our help."

"Our?"

"My church. Right now, we've only got a few dozen members, but we're gaining momentum and fighting against the evils in this world."

Quinn stared at Jen in disbelief. *Her* church? "You run this church?"

"Yes."

"How do you find these lost ones?" Quinn asked, thinking that the more information she had, the better the chance she could talk her way out of this.

"We look for them. In grocery stores. At parks. On the streets. We even infiltrate other heathen churches."

"And who are the lost ones, exactly?"

"People like you. Who have the mark of Satan. Or who have been led down the path of destruction… drugs, fornication…that sort of thing."

"And how do *you* help them?"

"Just like I'm helping you," Jen said without a shred of emotion.

Thinking about someone else being in the same position she was right now was horrifying. "What if they can't be helped?"

Jen smiled then—and finally, Quinn was absolutely terrified.

"We send them to Hell where they belong."

Oh shit. Shit, shit, shit.

If Quinn thought she could escape by telling Jen what she wanted to hear, she'd do it. But Jen wanted her birthmark gone. And since Quinn couldn't control that, simply declaring that she'd expelled the devil, or whatever it was Jen wanted, wasn't going to work.

She was screwed.

Jen turned to the man next to Alaric and nodded. He stepped outside the small room and returned seconds later—with a bucket in his hands.

Before Quinn could react, he'd thrown the contents of the bucket in her face.

Sputtering and gasping for air as the cold water dripped down her nose and into her lap, she stared at Jen in disbelief as renewed shivers racked her body.

The water, along with the air conditioning and the fans blowing on her, made the room seem twice as cold as it probably was.

"Come on," Jen said. "We've spent enough time in her company. We need to go and pray for her soul..."

and to make sure Satan hasn't somehow gotten his claws into us simply by being in her presence."

The trio turned to leave and Quinn panicked. "You can't leave me here!"

The men left the room, and Jen turned. "Why not?"

"Because! I'll freeze to death. Let me go, Jen. You never have to see me again. *Please.*"

She tilted her head as if considering Quinn's plea.

Then she said, "No," and turned and left.

The door closing behind her sounded loud even with the fans blowing.

An image of a coffin closing flashed through Quinn's head before she closed her eyes. She renewed her struggle to escape her bonds, but they were too tight.

Her body shivering nonstop now, Quinn kept her eyes closed and thought of John. Where was he? What was he doing? Had he realized that something was wrong?

"Please," she whispered. "I'm here, wherever here is. Please find me. I'm not ready to die."

The only answer to her plea was the sound of the fan motors.

* * *

Driftwood hadn't slept at all. His house had been set up as a sort of mission central. He paced back and forth next to his dining room table. All of his friends from

Station 7 were there, as well as most of his law enforcement friends. Dax, Cruz, Quint, Wes, TJ, and Hayden.

Cruz had called in an FBI specialist on cults, and Dax and Wes had called a colleague in the Texas Rangers who had extensively studied cults as well, specifically religious ones. A SWAT team was on standby and Beth was feverishly working with her friend, Tex, to find out as much information as possible about Jennifer Hale.

He couldn't stop thinking about what Quinn might be going through. Beth had done a quick search on Jen and said she belonged to a church called The Edge Community Church. They had a website, but Beth said that it was a barebones thing with hardly any information. One thing it did say was that they didn't have a building where they worshiped because they believed that God was everywhere, and they didn't feel the need to limit themselves.

Which made finding Quinn all the more difficult.

"I'm sorry, man," Taco said quietly, coming up to Driftwood.

"For what?"

"For bringing that bitch into our fold."

"This is not your fault," Driftwood told his friend. "I don't know a lot about what's going on, but I do know that."

"Jen helped kidnap your girlfriend," Taco said in anguish. "How could I not have seen the fact that she was bat-shit crazy?"

"Because you're a good person who doesn't go looking for the evil in people," Driftwood told him.

"Well, maybe I should start from now on." Taco shook his head. "If anything happens to Quinn, I'll never forgive myself."

"Stop it," Driftwood told him.

"How? I can't stop thinking about the fact that I was the one who introduced her to Jen!"

"You know as well as I do that there's evil everywhere. And if we concentrated on that, we'd never see the good in the world."

Taco laughed, but it wasn't a happy sound. "I'm done."

"With what?"

"Women. You and the rest of the guys might've all found someone, but I'm out."

"You can't give up on women just because of one bad apple," Driftwood said.

"Watch me. I was so desperate to have someone in my life, I picked a bat-shit crazy cult member!" He shook his head. "When we get Quinn home safe and sound, I'll just concentrate on making sure she and all our other friends' women are happy. I don't need a chick."

Driftwood wasn't sure what to say. He understood that Taco was a bit shell-shocked after hearing that Jen had been involved in Quinn's kidnapping, but perhaps after some time went by, he'd change his mind.

He looked at his watch. Six in the morning. Driftwood was more than aware that time was ticking away.

Kidnap victims rarely lived longer than twenty-four hours after they were taken.

Cruz's phone rang.

Every single person in the room turned to look at him as he answered.

"Hello? Yeah. Okay...what? Oh shit. Hang on." He held his cell phone against his chest and told Quint. "Tell SWAT they're going to get an address any second. But they absolutely are *not* to move out until you say." Then he turned to TJ. "Got your rifle?"

Driftwood instantly felt sick. TJ used to be a sniper when he was a Delta Force soldier, and as far as he knew, the man had only used his keenly honed skills once since he'd been out. And that was to save his fiancée, Milena, from the insane man who'd been about to kill her and take her son out of the country.

"Yes," TJ said without hesitation.

Cruz put his cell back up to his ear. "Okay. Give it all to me." He listened for several minutes as Driftwood got more and more impatient. Whoever was on the other end of the line obviously had more information about Quinn and possibly where she was. They should be moving out right now. Not sitting around staring at Cruz while he was on the phone. Not only that, but the FBI agent should've put the call on speaker.

Just when he thought he was going to burst, Cruz said, "Got it. Thanks. I'll be in touch." Then he clicked off the phone and turned to the group waiting impatiently for information.

"That was Beth," he said. "Tex uncovered details

about Jennifer. She was born Mary Magdalene Hale. She was raised in a commune in California and changed her name to Jennifer when she moved to Texas. Information is sketchy on why she left. We've got the address to her house, and Quint will lead the SWAT team on a raid there."

"I want to be there," Driftwood said immediately.

"No," Cruz said flatly.

Driftwood opened his mouth to complain, but Cruz continued.

"Tex found out where Jen lives, but *Beth* discovered that The Edge Community website has a secret back-door. Apparently, the members have a special login they use to find out when and where meetings will be held." Cruz paused.

"And?" Taco asked.

"There's been a special meeting called for tonight. An exorcism."

"*Fuck*," Driftwood swore.

"Where?" Moose asked.

"What time?" Chief growled.

He heard his friends, but Driftwood couldn't look away from Cruz. He needed this information. Needed to be there. Needed this to be done and for Quinn to be back in his arms.

"Beth doesn't know where yet," Cruz informed the group.

Driftwood turned away and put his hands on the counter and dropped his head.

He felt a large hand on his back, supporting him,

but he couldn't think. Couldn't appreciate the friends who were by his side at that moment.

"She's working on it though. The location is in code. It's taking her some time to crack it. But hopefully, Jen'll be at her house and the SWAT team will get her to talk."

"Jen's smart," Taco said. "I never went to her house, and she never really told me anything super personal. I don't know anything about her family, she wouldn't talk about her friends."

"Well, maybe if she thinks her friends are in danger, she *will* talk," Cruz says. "Tex is working on tracing the people who have logged into the site in the hopes of finding out who they are and where they live. If Jen won't talk, then maybe the others in the congregation will."

"And Quinn?" Driftwood asked, still looking at his countertop. "Where is she? What's happening to her?"

No one had an answer for him.

An hour later, the San Antonio Police Department's SWAT team made entry into Jennifer Hale's residence. The house was completely empty...except for a back room with a boarded-up window, some chains on the floor, half a dozen electric fans, and a puddle on the floor.

CHAPTER SEVENTEEN

Quinn was confused. She had no idea how much time had passed since she'd seen Jen. One hour? Three? Twelve? A week? She knew she'd been going in and out of consciousness. She'd pass out from the cold, then be shocked back into wakefulness when a bucket of water was poured over her head. Then she'd pass back out until the next time.

She remembered someone coming in and holding a knife to her neck as someone else took a pair of scissors to her hair. Quinn had the vague thought that she should be upset about her hair being cut off, as she'd had long hair her entire life—better to hide her birthmark—but she was more offended by the fact that the women sent in to do the deed had been wearing gloves so they didn't have any skin-on-skin contact with her.

Every single person she'd come into contact with was wacked. Every encounter just hammered home even more that it wasn't *her* who was possessed by the devil. It was Jen and all of her crazy followers.

The one time a couple of the crazies had come near her with a bottle of bleach, Quinn had lost her mind. She'd fought against her restraints so hard, she'd felt blood dripping from her wrists and ankles. Her frantic actions had scared the crap out of the women who'd been sent in to attempt to remove the "devil's mark," and they'd left without trying to bleach her skin.

But the cold had finally done its job. Quinn was lethargic, and it was extremely difficult to summon an ounce of energy to fight when three men, including Alaric, came into the room and unattached the chair from the floor. They picked her up, chair and all, and carried her out.

She vaguely remembered Jen warning the men to make sure Satan didn't touch them. They put her into a vehicle and drove off. It could've been hours or minutes, but when they stopped, all Quinn could think about was how glorious the warm air felt on her frozen body. Being out of the torture chamber with the fans and water felt outstanding.

She heard people talking around her, but couldn't make out the words. It felt as if she were floating, and she was so exhausted. Quinn closed her eyes and let the darkness take her.

* * *

The number of people in his house had drastically

reduced from earlier that morning. After the SWAT team had made the raid on Jennifer's house, and hadn't found Quinn, all of the firefighters had hung around with him until he'd finally kicked them out. Hanging around his house wasn't going to do anything to bring Quinn home and Driftwood knew the others were worried about their own women. The cops had also all left, except for TJ and Cruz. Taco was also still there as he was convinced it was his fault Quinn had been taken, and he wasn't leaving until she was found.

Driftwood appreciated the support, but he still couldn't think about anyone but Quinn. It was lunchtime. Had she been fed? She hadn't eaten since lunch yesterday. Had the assholes from The Edge Community Church given her anything to drink?

He knew Beth and Cruz were keeping information from him, but at the moment, he didn't think he could handle hearing anything if it was bad news.

They had the time for the supposed exorcism that was going to happen in around four hours, but still no location. Beth had been working nonstop to try to crack the code. Apparently, it had something to do with the Bible, but so far, she hadn't figured it out.

The most disturbing piece of information hadn't come from Beth, however. It came from Cruz's FBI contact. There had been a string of disappearances in the area recently. Enough that it raised questions at several local police departments, and they'd contacted the FBI to investigate.

A sixteen-year-old boy with a bad case of acne.

A three-year-old with a cleft lip.

A forty-seven-year-old man with neurofibromatosis.

Every case had involved some sort of facial disfigurement.

And the scarier part was that none of the missing people had been found.

Not one.

Driftwood refused to think about that.

No, they'd find Quinn. There were no less than five different law enforcement agencies actively looking for her. Word had also gotten around to the fire stations in the city, and every available search and rescue team was also on the lookout, not to mention the men and women searching on foot.

Quinn would be found. And she'd be fine. She had to be.

It took another three hours, but Cruz's phone finally rang once more. This time he put it on speaker.

"Tell me you found the location," Cruz said in lieu of a greeting.

"Done. It took Tex, me, two pastors, and a local priest to crack the code though." She rattled off an address. "I looked it up on one of the government's satellites. There isn't a building on the premises, it's just a patch of land in the middle of nowhere. It hadn't drawn much attention because it's located next to one of the city dumps. No one's interested in buying and developing it because of the stench from the trash."

"Holy shit. The dump? That's a perfect place to hide a dead body," Cruz said.

Driftwood stood up so fast, his chair crashed to the floor behind him. He clenched his fists, his fingernails digging into his palms.

"Sorry, Driftwood," Cruz muttered.

"Exactly," Beth said. "If The Edge Community Church is responsible for the disappearance of all those other people, they could've easily done their 'exorcisms' on this property and, when they didn't work," her voice hitched, as if she didn't want to say the rest, "just buried the bodies in all the trash next door. If they did, no one would smell anything off because of the dump. It's almost the perfect location...if you're torturing and killing people."

That was it. Driftwood was done. He stalked over to his front closet and pulled out the shotgun he kept there.

As soon as he had it in his hands, TJ grabbed it and tore it away.

"Give it back," Driftwood said in a low, controlled tone.

"No. I'm not going to let you do anything that will get you put in jail. Quinn needs you, man. Here. With her."

Driftwood knew he was on the verge of exploding. He'd been calm for over twelve hours now. He'd been patient. Let Beth do her thing. But he was done with that. No one was going to fucking burn Quinn's body. No fucking way.

"Besides," TJ continued, "this shotgun isn't going to do you any good. I've got this, Driftwood. Trust me."

Driftwood looked into TJ's eyes—and saw what he was looking for.

Steadfast confidence with a touch of anger.

He needed to know that his friends were just as pissed as he was when it came to Quinn's situation. Whatever it was.

"Promise me you'll make sure that bitch doesn't get near her."

"I promise," TJ vowed.

Taking a deep breath, Driftwood nodded.

"Driftwood?" He heard Beth calling from the phone.

He turned to the table, where Cruz was now standing and holding his phone.

"What?"

"You've got fifteen minutes to meet Dax, Wes, and the rest of the task force and SWAT team. They're gathering at Station 7 to come up with a plan before heading out. They agreed to let you and Taco go with them...for medical backup, just in case. There will be a ton of other ambulances on standby, but I knew you needed to be there."

"Thank you," Driftwood choked out. He *did* need to be there.

"There was talk about seeing if we could sneak someone in undercover, but with the small number of people in the congregation, that would be almost impossible. Not to mention, Jen has seen literally all of us because she was at the softball game," Cruz said.

Driftwood nodded. He'd thought about that too. If they had more time, Cruz could've infiltrated the church group to try to see what was really going on and who was involved, but because of the situation, their time was up.

"I offered to call her and try to get back together with her," Taco said. "But no one thought she'd go for it. Speculation is that she was just dating me to get to Quinn."

Driftwood heard the pain in his friend's voice, but didn't have time to reassure him.

"So now the plan is to surround the main meeting space and go in all at once. From what Beth was able to see through the trees and using the satellites, there's only one road in and out. We'll block that and surround the clearing they usually use for their sermons or whatever. We'll use smoke bombs and flash bangs to confuse and subdue everyone. We're gonna get Quinn out of there," Cruz said.

Driftwood nodded. He couldn't speak. His throat was tight and even though he hadn't eaten anything, he felt like throwing up. He could charge into a burning building without a second thought, put a tourniquet on a leg that had been severed without wanting to barf, but the thought of Quinn being in the middle of what was obviously going to be a huge tactical takedown was making him physically ill.

"Thirteen minutes, guys," Beth warned. "Get a move on."

Without a word, everyone headed for the door.

They had very little time. *Quinn* had very little time. Every second counted.

* * *

Quinn felt warmer than she had in what seemed like forever. She still couldn't move her arms or legs, but the warmth she felt on her face was like bliss.

She forced her eyes open—her eyelids felt like they were held down with lead—and had to close them again when a bright light sent shooting pains into her skull.

Squinting this time, she tried again.

Fire.

A nice, big fire crackled in front of her. The heat from the flames felt delicious after being cold for so long.

She closed her eyes and reveled in the warmth seeping into her skin.

"She's coming around!" a voice yelled.

Groggily, Quinn squinted her eyes open once more and turned her head toward the voice. It took a minute for things to fall into place, but as soon as they did, the terror Quinn had felt earlier, however long ago that was, returned tenfold.

Jen was standing in a clearing wearing a long white robe. There were about twenty or so people standing around her, each wearing the same robe. Men, women, and even a couple of children.

Jen was preaching. She was talking about the devil

taking root and how she'd done her best to cast out Satan, but it had been no use. That the devil had too firm of a grip and must be destroyed.

She talked about how it wasn't a sin, because God was good and just, and was supportive of any deeds done in His name and in the name of destroying evil.

Quinn tried to open her mouth to protest, but realized she couldn't. Something was covering her mouth, preventing her from saying a word.

The heat from the fire was quickly growing uncomfortable. What had felt good moments earlier now almost burned.

Figures I work with burned skin for a living and now I'm going to be on the other side of my research, Quinn thought bitterly.

Jen turned to face her, and Quinn could barely keep her eyes open, even squinting. The heat felt as if it were melting her face.

"In the name of Jesus, we denounce you, evil one! We gave you a chance to leave this body and go back to your own realm, but you didn't. You've given us no choice but to send you back to Hell. Light it!"

Light it? Quinn was confused. The fire was already lit.

She heard a whoosh behind her. Then to her right and left.

Whipping her head around, she saw Alaric, then another man she'd never seen before, both stepping away from piles of burning sticks and wood.

Realization hit.

She was still strapped to the same chair she'd been stuck on since Jen had grabbed and drugged her, but it was now sitting in the middle of a massive pile of debris. Sticks, paper, straw, firewood, and cardboard. There were four other fires set to the north, east, south, and west of her. A line of flammable materials led from each of the burning piles—straight to the one she was sitting in the middle of.

Jen was burning her alive.

Quinn tried to scream, but with her mouth taped, all that came out was a muffled screech.

The heat was unbearable, but now it was hitting her from all sides. Crazily, Quinn longed for the cold she'd experienced not too long ago.

Throwing her head back, Quinn let out another muffled shriek. It was supposed to be John's name, but instead it just sounded like a pathetic moan.

By the time Driftwood and the other arrived at the abandoned property, most of the SWAT team had already surrounded the area. FBI agents as well as Texas Rangers had also gotten into position. There was absolutely no way anyone would be escaping from law enforcement.

But Driftwood didn't care about that. All he cared about was Quinn. Was she here? Was she all right? He had no idea what was happening since he wasn't wearing a radio. He couldn't talk to or hear the communications between the different teams.

He and Taco were standing at the edge of the parking area...waiting. They could see smoke from a small fire, and hear voices, but not what they were saying. The hardest thing he'd ever done in his life was stand there.

"Fuck this!" he muttered. "I'm going in."

Taco put his hand on Driftwood's arm. They were both wearing their bunker gear, as it was almost second nature to put it on when they got to the station. "Careful," was all he said.

Driftwood nodded. Both men walked silently through the parked cars toward ground zero, as the SWAT team had named the area where the group had their meetings. He had every intention of staying back and watching everyone get taken down, and being there for Quinn...

But what he saw from the surrounding trees had every good intention flying from his head.

Jen was standing in front of a small group of people. They were all wearing white robes and she was gesturing wildly. But it was the woman sitting in a chair behind her that drew Driftwood's attention.

Quinn.

He was relieved to see her for a split second, but then the scene sank in. Jen yelled something, and four men holding torches each leaned over and lit small bonfires at their feet. That might not have been so bad

—until streaks of flame shot from each small bonfire toward Quinn.

Driftwood was moving before he'd even thought about it.

About the same time he started running, all hell broke loose. Flash bangs went off all around the area, deafening Driftwood, but he didn't stop. His eyes were locked on Quinn. Smoke filled the air, both from the fires and from the devices the task forces had thrown.

Flames shot up from the debris around the chair Quinn was sitting in, and he heard a muffled sound coming from her.

Faster. He had to run faster.

Ignoring the screams of terror and forceful commands from the officers all around him, Driftwood's eyes stayed on the woman he loved.

He wasn't going to make it to her in time. He almost couldn't see her because of the flames surrounding her now.

As if in slow motion, Driftwood leaped over the smaller fire to Quinn's left and barreled toward her. Without slowing down, and not feeling the heat through his bunker gear, Driftwood grabbed Quinn around the waist, chair and all, and continued running.

In the back of his mind, he heard sounds coming from her, but all he could think of was getting her out of the flames. The yelling continued but Driftwood didn't stop. He plunged into the cool shade of the trees. Breathing heavily—from stress, not exertion—he finally stopped and put the chair down on the dusty ground underneath a grove of trees.

He barely noticed Taco at his side, beating at his shoulders and back.

"You're on fire, man," his friend said.

Driftwood ignored him, trying to figure out how to free Quinn.

"I need a knife!" he cried desperately.

"Here."

Driftwood took the box cutter Taco held out to him and attempted to cut the zip-ties holding Quinn to the chair. They were so tight, her hands and feet were blue. But when he put his hand on her, he wasn't so sure that was why they were discolored.

Despite being almost burned to death, her skin was strangely chilled.

Driftwood's hands were shaking so badly, he knew if he got the knife anywhere near her, he'd slice her to ribbons. "I can't," he said, and handed the box cutter back to Taco.

"I got this. Be ready to catch her," Taco warned.

For the first time, Driftwood looked at Quinn's face. He barely noticed that her hair had been hacked off. He was more concerned at the dazed look in her beautiful emerald eyes. A piece of duct tape had been slapped over her mouth and her birthmark was an angry purple instead of the dark pink it had always been before.

"What'd they do to you, Emmy?" he whispered before trying to pry the tape off her mouth.

She whimpered in pain and he groaned in commiseration. "I know it hurts, Em, but we need to get this off so you can breathe better."

Taco freed one of her hands and it fell limply to her side. She didn't lift it to touch him or to take the tape off herself. She just sat there, in shock. Before he could finish removing the tape, her second arm was freed and she fell into him. Her head landed on his shoulder and she was dead weight in his arms.

"Hurry, Taco," Driftwood urged.

In thirty more seconds, she was completely free of the chair. Driftwood stood, taking Quinn with him. Her head lolled on his shoulder and, for a second, he was terrified he'd been too late. That she'd literally died in his arms.

Taco put his fingers on her throat and, after a moment, said, "Passed out. We need to get her to the truck."

Nodding, Driftwood turned to head back the way they came, but a loud shot ringing out made them both freeze. Then Driftwood dropped to his knees and covered Quinn's unconscious body as well as he could. There were more screams from the cult members and more yelling from the SWAT team and Texas Rangers.

Concentrating on the feel of Quinn's warm breath against his neck, Driftwood stayed stock still. Seconds seemed like minutes, but finally they heard Cruz's voice above all the crying and yelling.

"Driftwood?"

"Here!" Taco yelled.

They heard branches breaking as Cruz moved toward them. He exploded through the trees and stopped suddenly at seeing them.

"Is she…" His voice trailed off.

"She's alive," Taco answered for Driftwood. "But she needs to get to the hospital. We heard the shot. Is the scene secure?"

"TJ," was all Cruz said. "Come on, we'll go around."

Taco helped Driftwood get to his feet with Quinn still in his arms, and they followed Cruz.

By the time they got back to where they'd left the Station 7 truck, there were two ambulances parked behind it. Driftwood walked straight to one of them and Taco opened the back doors. He helped his friend up into the back of the ambulance and Driftwood placed his precious burden on the gurney.

Within seconds, the paramedics were there, assessing and starting treatment. They got the tape off her mouth, leaving behind a large red mark, but the ninety-nine percent grade alcohol they'd used had done its job, allowing them to remove the tape with minimal damage to the skin on her face other than the red mark. Driftwood kept out of their way as much as possible, which was hard in the small space, but he wasn't leaving. No way in hell.

He ignored what they were doing and saying, and put his hands on Quinn's cheeks.

Several moments later, Quinn's eyes opened a crack.

"Hey, Emmy," Driftwood said softly.

He hadn't been sure what her reaction to seeing him, and knowing she was safe, might be...but it wasn't what he got.

She opened her mouth and let out the most bone-chilling sound he'd ever heard.

Her limbs went rigid, and it seemed as if she screamed with her entire body. Her eyes widened in horror, her fists clenched, and the sound that escaped was a mixture of panic, hysteria bordering on disbelief, and terror.

The paramedics froze and stared at her incredulously.

The sound was distressing and intense, but Driftwood didn't try to stop her. She needed to get it out. She'd been through hell and needed the outlet. He was used to seeing people in pain, saw it on every shift. Broken bones, cuts, bruises...but this was the kind of scream that put every thought on hold. It rooted everyone in place as they experienced the same agony that Quinn obviously had.

The sound stopped as abruptly as it had started. Driftwood ran his thumbs over her cheeks and made sure to stay in her line of vision. "You're safe now, Quinn. I've got you."

She mouthed his name, then her eyes closed as she fell unconscious once more.

"Holy shit," one of the paramedics said after a moment. "What the hell happened to her?"

"I don't know," Driftwood said, "but she's okay now."

"Damn straight she is," the second paramedic said. "You got this, Rob?"

"Yeah. I'm sure…" He looked at Driftwood with one brow raised.

"John."

"I'm sure John can help me if needed. Let's get her to the hospital."

Driftwood never introduced himself with his given name. He was Driftwood, plain and simple. But if Quinn could hear what was going on around her, he wanted her to know he was there. Her John. Maybe hearing the name she called him would help soothe her.

The other paramedic climbed out of the back of the ambulance and Driftwood felt and heard the engine starting up.

The drive to the hospital was long. Quinn's body temperature was a bit low, which was strange after almost being burned alive. Driftwood couldn't imagine how in the world it had gotten so low, especially since it was in the lower eighties outside right now. Her wrists and ankles were shredded from the zip-ties that had held her to the chair. Her birthmark was an alarming purple color and she was definitely dehydrated.

But she was alive. That was all Driftwood cared about. They could deal with the mental and other physical aspects of what she'd been through. As they pulled into the hospital, Driftwood leaned over and kissed Quinn's forehead. Then he leaned down and kissed her birthmark and whispered in her ear, "I'm here, Emmy. I'm not leaving you. You're safe. Do you hear me? You're safe."

She didn't open her eyes and she didn't answer him verbally. But the long sigh that escaped and the way her shoulders visibly relaxed spoke volumes.

CHAPTER EIGHTEEN

A month later, Driftwood stood in the dugout and watched as Quinn was dragged by Moose from second base to third. She and Penelope had latched on to his legs to try to keep him from crossing the bases, but they were laughing so hard they weren't being very effective, and Moose being so much bigger and stronger than they were wasn't helping their cause.

Driftwood couldn't remember whose idea it was to have a guys-against-girls kickball game. Although he hadn't been thrilled with the idea at first, he could see it was just what everyone had needed.

He hadn't seen Quinn this happy since before she'd been kidnapped. It had taken a while for her to rediscover her normal persona, but he thought that she was finally mostly back to being herself.

One thing Driftwood had been glad to see was that, while she had nightmares about the kidnapping, she hadn't seemed upset about what had been behind it all…her birthmark. They'd had a talk late one night while she'd still been in the hospital. He'd climbed into her bed, ignoring the hospital rules against it, and held her while they'd talked.

"Are you upset about your hair?"

"No."

"Emmy, it'll grow back. We can get you a wig in the meantime if you need one, to make you feel more like yourself."

"I don't want one, John. I realized something when Jen was spouting all that crap about me having a devil's mark."

"What's that?"

"That my birthmark wasn't the problem. I didn't have anything to do with this. I didn't ask for it. And yes, it has affected my life and made me who I am today, but if someone has a problem with it, that's on them."

"Yeah, it is."

"And you know what else?"

"What?"

"I'm glad my mom gave me up at birth. I'm glad she didn't want anything to do with me. I saw those kids there, John. They were being brainwashed to think exactly the same way Jen did, and all the other adults around them. If I had been born with perfect skin, I might've ended up being just as prejudiced as my mother. I might've grown up to be just like Jen. Seeing imperfections as signs from God that the person wasn't good enough or worthy."

John wasn't sure what to say.

"I'm going to do my best to stop hiding. I am who I am, and that's that. I'm going to call Doctor Ballard and get the laser treatments. Not because I want to look like everyone else, but because if I don't, I'll most likely have more complications later in life. I'm going to stop hiding behind my hair. Cowering in my apartment instead of going out and having fun. If someone stares, let them. If they want to call me names or gasp in horror, that's on them, not me."

"I love you, Quinn Dixon," John said. "I'm so proud of you, you have no clue."

"I do. Because I love you back, and I'm just as proud of you. Taco visited me today, and he told me what happened. That you ran straight through two full-blown fires without even slowing down. That when he got to us, you were literally on fire."

"I'd walk through a million fires if it meant protecting you from the heat," he said, emotion making his words wobble.

"Thank you," Quinn whispered. "Thank you for finding me. For having friends with connections who could track me down in time. Just...thank you."

"Thank you for hanging on," John answered.

Watching Quinn shriek with laughter as Moose reached down and hauled Penelope over his shoulder, even while gently disengaging himself from Quinn, made Driftwood realize exactly how lucky he'd been.

The doctors had said Quinn had a fifty-fifty chance of brain damage from being hypothermic for so long.

Jen might've been crazy, but she was smart enough to know how to torture someone. The room she'd put Quinn in, how she'd kept her wet, and with the fans and AC on…it would've killed her eventually.

Quinn's doctor said the only reason she'd survived being in the middle of that bonfire was because her bodily functions were already so repressed from being cold that she hadn't breathed in much of the hyper-heated gases and her skin had been partially frozen.

She was literally a walking, talking, laughing miracle.

His miracle

"You're up, Driftwood!" Chief yelled. "Show 'em how it's done!"

Quinn picked herself up out of the dirt where she'd been sitting, laughing so hard she'd been clutching her stomach. She gestured to the other women to get closer to home plate. "Come on in, ladies. Easy out!"

Driftwood chuckled. Easy out, huh? He'd show her. He'd kick that ball all the way to Chicago.

Mackenzie smiled as she took a couple giant steps toward him. She was the pitcher, and Driftwood didn't like the evil grin on her face. She brought her arm back and lobbed the kickball toward him.

He prepared to kick it as hard as he could—until Quinn dashed forward and stood right in front of him.

His brain immediately stopped his leg from moving so fast, and Driftwood gave the ball a weak side swipe, to make sure he didn't kick it right in Quinn's face. He watched in disbelief as it bounced right toward Sophie.

She ran forward and grabbed it before running back and jumping on top of first base.

"Out!" Penelope yelled in glee.

He hadn't even taken one step toward first base.

Driftwood put his hands on his hips and mock-glared at Quinn. "That wasn't cool! I could've hurt you!"

She walked right up to him and put her arms around his neck and gave a little hop. Driftwood immediately put his hands under her butt to help her. She clung to him like a little monkey. He felt her lips brush against his ear. "I knew you wouldn't hit me."

"I could've," he grumbled, walking with her off to the side so Quint could take his turn. He had a feeling their team was doomed. None of them would do one damn thing that might hurt their women. They never should've agreed to play against them.

Quinn pulled back. "I've got something for you," she said with a sly gleam in her eye. "Reach into my front right pocket."

It was an awkward angle, but Driftwood finally got his fingers into her pocket. He teased her by caressing her as much as possible despite the odd angle. She shifted in his grip, and he tensed when his teasing backfired. She pressed right against his dick, and he felt himself getting hard.

Grabbing the small object he found in her pocket, and ending his own torture, Driftwood pulled his hand out. The second it cleared her jeans, she grabbed the small black bag and dropped her legs.

Driftwood let her go...and stared in confusion as she went down on one knee in the dirt on the softball field.

She looked up at him with love in her eyes—and held up a shiny ring.

"I've waited my whole life for a man like you. Will you marry me, John Trettle?"

He vaguely heard the catcalls around him, but he ignored them. He must've paused a little too long, because Quinn rushed to fill the silence.

"I know, I know, this is weird. But I vowed to myself that I refused to hide anymore. From my feelings and from the reactions of others. So I decided, what the hell? I love you. You said you loved me. I've practically moved in. We might as well get married. That is...if you want to."

"Yes," Driftwood growled. "A million times yes!" Then he leaned down and grabbed her around the waist. He twirled her in a circle until she was laughing hysterically and yelling at him to put her down.

When he did, he loved seeing the smile on her face. "I love you, Emmy."

"I wasn't sure what kind of ring you wanted, but I thought I couldn't go wrong with platinum. We can get one of the rubber ones too. Maybe they aren't rubber. Silicone? Anyway, the ones that you can wear when you're on shift."

Driftwood smiled back at her and let her push the ring over his knuckle. It felt right there. He knew men didn't wear engagement rings, but he didn't give a fuck. He wasn't ever taking his ring off.

"What are you smiling at?" she asked him.

"Can't I just be happy?" he returned.

"Well, yeah, but that isn't your 'just happy' smile. It's your 'I'm up to something' smile."

He loved that she knew him so well.

He'd planned to do this later, but this was the perfect time. Surrounded by their friends, by love.

Reaching into his own pocket, Driftwood pulled out a small black bag that looked suspiciously a lot like the one she'd had in her own pocket.

Then it was *his* turn to drop to one knee in the dirt. "Quinn Dixon. I've loved you almost from the first time I saw you. You made me work harder than I have in my life to get a girl to even look twice at me, but I wouldn't have had it any other way. Will you do me the pleasure of being my wife?"

"Just remember who asked first," she quipped before adding, "and of course I will!"

He took her left hand in his and kissed her ring finger before slipping the modest princess-cut diamond onto her finger. He stood and took her into his arms and kissed her, bending her backward over his arm. She grabbed hold of his arms and kissed him back. He loved that she trusted him enough to know he wouldn't drop her.

Then they were surrounded by their friends. Everyone was laughing and clapping.

"I got it all on video!" Beth exclaimed.

"Me too!" Mickie chimed in.

"Me three!" Blythe called out from the stands.

"Party's at my place!" Sledge announced. "Caterers are there setting up now."

Driftwood looked down at Quinn and laughed. "Let me guess, you told Sophie what you were planning."

"Yup," she said with a huge smile. "And I'm sure she told the others, including Beth."

"And I told Sledge. So I suppose it's only natural they decided to throw us an engagement party."

Beth sidled up to them then. Driftwood reluctantly dropped his arms from around Quinn and let her have some girl time.

Soon, she was surrounded by her girl posse. Sophie, Adeline, Beth, Penelope, Hayden, Laine, Mickie, and Mackenzie were all there. Corrie was too, but she was sitting in the stands with Erin, Milena, Hope, and Blythe, who were all pregnant and sitting out the game so they wouldn't get hurt.

"We ordered a doughnut cake." Driftwood heard Beth tell Quinn. "And I got that caramel sauce recipe from Driftwood and we have one of those fondue fountains filled with the stuff."

Quinn groaned and put a hand on her belly. "My stomach hurts just thinking about it. But I can't wait!"

Everyone laughed.

Driftwood felt a hand land on his back. He turned to see Squirrel standing there. "Happy for you."

"Thanks. And hey…I'm sorry I almost beat you up that one time."

Squirrel laughed. "No you're not, but that's okay."

"Come on, everyone. I never thought Driftwood was gonna ask. Let's go party!" Sophie said.

Everyone quickly headed for their cars, leaving Quinn and Driftwood alone on the softball field.

"We should go," Quinn said softly.

"Yeah. I know." Driftwood ran his eyes from the top of her pixie haircut down the side of her cheek. The birthmark was slightly less red. She'd had her first treatment a week ago and was scheduled to fly back to California in two weeks for her second. "You feeling okay?"

"I'm fine," she reassured him. "Great, in fact."

"I love you," Driftwood told her.

"I love you back," Quinn assured him. "Now, come on. I'm hungry, and I hear caramel-dipped doughnuts calling my name."

They walked off the field arm in arm, and when they sauntered by the stands next to an adjacent field to get to his truck in the parking lot, both ignored the way a man stared at them as they passed. After what they'd been through, stares and the occasional comment didn't bother either of them anymore. As Quinn said, other people's attitudes and prejudices weren't their problem.

EPILOGUE

One month later

Driftwood sat stock still in the courtroom as he listened to Quinn recount exactly what she'd been through at the hands of Jennifer Hale.

Every single one of the firefighters who weren't working were there as well, supporting them. Their women would've been too, but Quinn had asked them not to come. They knew what had happened to her, but she'd admitted that she was afraid if they heard all the details, it would somehow change their view of her.

Sophie had argued the most, but Quinn had finally broken down in her friend's arms and begged her not to come. Of course Sophie had agreed...but Driftwood knew the women would grill their men for details about what had gone on in the courtroom.

Not only were the firefighters there supporting Quinn, but so were Dax, Cruz, Quint, Wes, Hayden, Conor, TJ, and even Calder Stonewall, one of the MEs for the city. Some, like Cruz and Dax, had to testify, but the others came to simply support their friends.

Driftwood and Quinn, of course, had attended every day of her preliminary trial, and even though he'd already known most of what had happened to her, Driftwood *still* could hardly believe Jennifer had turned out to be as evil as she was.

Apparently, she was the ringleader or priestess or...*whatever* of their little sect. She wasn't attending the local community college to be a nurse, that was just one of the many places she trolled for people who she thought might be possessed by the devil. Her followers did the same, stalking coffeehouses, libraries, and grocery stores, among other places. When they found someone who they thought was impure, or had a devil's mark, they would stalk them. Leave religious pamphlets everywhere the person went.

Then, one of the "congregation" would befriend the person. Secretly give them holy water to try to cleanse them. When that didn't work, they'd eventually ramp up to kidnapping. Once people were in Jen's clutches, she would use various techniques to try to "remove" the devil from their bodies. When it didn't work—and it never worked, because of course the victims weren't possessed—the congregation would meet at the abandoned lot next to the dump and burn them alive.

Then, just like Beth had hypothesized, the group

would simply throw their victims' bodies in the trash dump conveniently next to their killing field.

Everyone who had been present at Quinn's attempted murder had been arrested—except for Alaric, who'd been shot by TJ when he'd pulled a gun and started to run into the trees where Driftwood had taken Quinn. The members' trials were mostly still pending, and most were undergoing psychological treatment to try to decide if they were competent enough to even stand trial. They'd been so brainwashed that many believed Jen was actually Jesus Christ reborn.

Driftwood had never been prouder of Quinn. She'd recently had her hair styled, now that it had grown out a bit more from the hack job Jen had done on it. Her birthmark was considerably lighter than it had been even two months ago, but it was still clearly visible. Probably always would be.

But Quinn held her head up and didn't shy away from looking the judge or Jen in the eyes as she spoke. She recounted how she'd seen Jen at her apartment door and had opened it, thinking something was wrong.

She told the courtroom how Alaric, Jen's brother, had hidden from view until she'd opened the door, and how he'd hit her in the face. Then how someone had jabbed a needle into her thigh and knocked her out.

But it was the way Quinn talked about being tortured that almost did him in. Reading the words on the police report was one thing. Hearing Quinn recount the way she'd felt, how cold she'd been, and how scared she was that she'd never get out of that room, was chilling.

Driftwood had known Jen was crazy...but he hadn't known just how much.

Taco shifted uncomfortably in the chair next to him, and Driftwood had a feeling if *he* was feeling stupid and naïve that he hadn't seen through Jen's crazy, then Taco was feeling ten times worse.

Instinctively, he did something he never would've thought about doing before this moment. He reached over and grabbed Taco's hand.

He didn't turn his head to look at his friend, he just held on, feeling Taco's hand gripping his back...hard.

Jen's attorney stood up and started his cross examination. Quinn never faltered. She answered every single one of his questions calmly and intelligently. The only time she got emotional was when she recalled how Jen had instructed her followers and brother to make sure they didn't touch her without gloves on, so they wouldn't be "contaminated."

The lawyer stopped his questioning way earlier than the prosecuting attorney had. Then Quinn was done. She stepped down from the witness stand and headed back toward him and the seat she'd vacated when she was called to testify.

When she passed the table where Jen was sitting, she purposely walked as close to it as possible. Driftwood—and every single person in the courtroom—saw

Jen loudly scoot her chair away from the aisle and look at Quinn in horror as she passed.

Smiling, Quinn calmly opened the small wooden door separating the courtroom area from the spectator gallery.

Expecting Quinn to sit in the open space next to him, she instead gestured for Taco to scoot over. He did, and she sat between them. Then she reached a hand toward each of them. Both men laced their fingers with hers.

Driftwood knew by the way she gripped him that she wasn't as calm as she appeared on the outside. Her engagement ring dug into his hand, but he didn't bother to readjust his grip. The reminder that she would soon officially be his was enough to calm him. Leaning over, he kissed her temple reverently. There would be time for words later.

For now, it was enough that she was safe, happy, and healthy…and his.

* * *

That night, Quinn lay in bed with John. They were naked, and she was lying on top of him. They both needed the full-body contact after the long and emotional day they'd had.

Quinn's head rested on his shoulder, and she'd stuffed her hands under his back. He was warm…so warm. An odd side effect of nearly being frozen to death was that now she always felt cold. The doctors said it was more a psychological side effect, and that her body was actually at a normal ninety-eight-point-six body temperature.

But bless John, he never complained and always had a blanket for her to snuggle under whether they were on the couch, in the car, or lying in bed. And he was always so warm. It was one of the million things she loved about him.

"Are you really okay, Emmy?" he asked softly.

"Surprisingly, yeah. I'm not saying that was fun or that I want to do it every weekend, but it felt good standing up to her. Telling everyone what a crazy bitch she is."

"I'm very proud of you."

"I'm proud of myself," she returned. "John?"

"Yeah?"

"Do you think Taco is all right?"

"Honestly? I don't know. On the outside, he's fine, but I have a feeling inside...he's a mess."

"I saw you grab his hand. That was awesome."

"Firefighters aren't known to be the most demonstrative group of people, but he's one of my best friends. I'd die for him, just as I know he would for me. He wanted to be there for you today, but he was struggling hearing just how awful Jen was."

"I hate her," Quinn whispered. "Not only because of what she did to me, but because of what she did to those other people she tried to 'save.' They weren't as lucky as me. They died probably scared out of their minds. But I also hate her because of what she did to

Taco. He deserves to have an amazing woman at his side. Someone who loves him as much as I love you. I hate that Jen only pretended to like him to get close to me. I hate that he's even more closed off than before. And I hate that I have a feeling it'll take a really long time for him to open himself up to trying again."

"He'll be okay," John murmured as he ran his hands up and down her back.

"How can you be so sure?" Quinn asked.

"Because he's got you. And me. And everyone else. We won't *let* him give up. There's someone out there who's perfect for him. He just has to be receptive to opening himself up when he finds her."

"I love you," Quinn said, shifting on top of her man. "The first time you told me that you thought I was pretty, I thought you were making fun of me. The second time, I figured you were just throwing the poor ugly woman a bone. The third time, I was actually irritated. And the fourth, I ignored you altogether. But somewhere along the line, I realized that you were serious. That you honestly thought I was beautiful. It took a while, a really long while, but you know what?"

"What, Emmy?"

"I believe you." The words came out as a whisper. "I might not ever win any beauty pageants, and there will always be people eager to tell me so, but being around you makes me believe it."

"Good. Because you *are* beautiful. And you're all mine," he added after a beat.

"I'm yours," she reassured him. "And you're mine."

"Yup," he agreed. "Yours."

Quinn was suddenly aware of his erection between her legs. They'd made love a few times since she'd gotten out of the hospital, but it had always been initiated by him. For the first time in her life, Quinn wanted to be the aggressor. She wasn't afraid of being turned down, not with John.

She began to move her hips, the tip of his cock brushing against her pussy as she rubbed against him.

"Quinn," he warned, grabbing her hips to try to hold her still.

"Yes?" she asked with a gleam in her eye. Moving a hand down her body, she reached between them and grabbed hold of his cock. He went from semi-hard to ready to fuck in seconds.

When she moved and pressed her folds against him, he halted her with a strong grip on her thighs. "Wait, Emmy."

"Why?"

"It's been a difficult day for you."

"It has," she agreed. "And now I need my man to make it better." She squeezed his cock again, and a groan escaped him. Sitting up, the blanket falling around their hips, she came up on her knees and positioned John right where she wanted him.

Before he could move, she was sliding down.

Quinn shifted her hand to her clit and began to stroke herself, loving the feel of his hot, hard shaft inside her. John stayed frozen under her, waiting for her to let him know when she was ready for him to move.

She looked at him and stilled. The look on his face was so beautiful, Quinn wished she had a camera so she could capture it and look at it anytime she was feeling down or wondering how on earth he could love *her*.

He wasn't looking at where they were joined together. He wasn't staring at her tits or even her birthmark. John's eyes were glued to hers. And the love and tenderness she could see there was absolutely beautiful.

Her. John was looking at *her* that way.

"Move," she whispered.

"This is gonna be fast," he warned.

"Good."

"Stay right there, just like that, and hold on," he ordered.

Quinn loved it when he got bossy. "Yes, sir," she quipped, then leaned over and braced herself on his shoulders.

His first thrust made her squirm.

His second made a moan escape her throat.

His third had her biting her lip.

The fourth and fifth made her arch her back.

She lost count after that, concentrating on the feel of him, hot and hard inside her. Then, even as he continued to pound into her from below, one hand moved between them and roughly tweaked her clit.

"That's it, my beautiful Emmy. Come for me. Come on my dick. I want to feel it."

It took another couple of thrusts, but then she was there. Her entire body shook as she exploded in orgasm. She would've fallen if John hadn't grabbed hold of her hips and held her above him as he pushed inside her one more time and stayed there.

And throughout it all, his gaze never left hers.

"I love you," he said when he could speak again.

"Love you too," she mumbled.

He chuckled. "Stretch out, Em."

She straightened her legs but didn't move off him. She felt John pull the blanket back up and over her, once again enclosing them in a cocoon. They were both a bit sweaty and she could still feel him inside her.

A minute or two went by, and she finally said, "I didn't give you a chance to put on a condom."

"Nope."

"I'm not on anything."

"Hmmmm."

When he didn't comment further, she lifted her head. "Did you hear me? I could get pregnant. It's not really the right time of the month, but still."

"I heard you," he said, then brought his hand to her head, pushing it back onto his chest.

"I can practically feel you beating your chest in a 'me Tarzan, you Jane' kind of way," she complained.

"Do I want kids? Absolutely. Do I want them in nine months? I'd kinda hoped to have you to myself for a little longer. But I wouldn't be upset about you being pregnant with my child, Emmy. I love you. I'll love you forever, and I'll love any kids we happen to make together. But I just had one of the best orgasms in my life. My cock is still inside you. I've got my woman naked and sated on top of me. I refuse to freak out about anything right now."

"Well…all right then," Quinn said with a small chuckle.

"All right then," John agreed.

John fell asleep not too much later, his cock finally slipping out of her body, and Quinn could feel how wet she was between her legs. She smiled.

Her life definitely hadn't been all sunshine and roses. She would never be miss social and would always prefer to hang out at home rather than go out. But she had more than a handful of good friends and protectors who would always have her back.

And she had John.

She couldn't ask for anything more.

In fact, if she had to live her life all over again, every second of pain and humiliation she'd felt, even the torture she'd endured at the hands of The Edge Community Church's members…she would without hesitation…if it led to this moment right here.

Closing her eyes, Quinn fell asleep with her head on John's chest, the sound of his heart beating in her ear.

* * *

A week later, while Driftwood and Quinn were in California for another laser treatment, Station 7 received a call for a fire in progress.

Taco, Squirrel, Chief, Crash, Sledge, Moose, and Penelope flew into the trucks and raced to the scene.

The second Taco jumped out of the pumper, a man ran up to him.

"There's a kid inside! My neighbor. At least I think he is. A teenager. He's only thirteen!"

"We'll get him," Taco assured the man.

He and Squirrel immediately began prepping for going inside. Without discussion, they entered the house. They'd been working together for so long, they knew each other's strengths and weaknesses. If anyone was going to find this kid, it would be them.

The house was pitch black with smoke. It was already hot enough that Taco dropped to his knees and began to crawl forward. He felt Squirrel close on his heels.

Feeling his way around the room, Taco was surprised when he almost immediately ran into something large and bulky. A body.

Signaling to Squirrel, Taco grabbed the boy under his arms and began dragging him back toward the door. Three minutes after they'd entered the fully engulfed house, they exited.

The second Taco saw the boy when they got outside, he knew they'd been too late. The paramedics would do their best, but he'd seen enough victims of smoke inhalation to know that the kid had been inside too long. Had inhaled too many of the deadly gases.

He rushed the teenager farther away from the burning house and placed him on the ground. "He's gone," he told the paramedics who rushed up. "We were too late." They immediately starting giving the boy oxygen and doing CPR.

Shaking his head, Taco turned to find Sledge and see where he was needed next.

Before he could take more than a cursory glance around, a woman was in his face, screaming.

"You killed my baby!"

Taco took a step back, but the woman didn't retreat. She pushed against his chest and yelled, "You should've been faster! You took too long to get to him! He's dead because of *you!*"

"Whoa," Taco said quietly, holding his hands up. "Stand back, ma'am."

"No! *You* did this! It's *your* fault!"

Finally, a sheriff's deputy reached them and took hold of the hysterical woman by the arm. "You need to step back for your own safety."

"He killed my son!" the lady yelled, completely ignoring the officer.

"Don't listen to her," another officer told Taco. "She's plastered. We saw her pull into the driveway next door." He pointed to a dark green Volvo parked half on the lawn and half off it. There was a mailbox lying on its side in front of the car, obviously having been run over.

The woman was still screaming at him, even while being dragged away by three officers.

"Neighbors said she leaves her kid alone all the

time," the first officer said. "She goes off to buy drugs, apparently. This isn't your fault."

Taco nodded. He knew it wasn't, but it didn't make the situation any better. A child was still dead.

"You're going to regret this!" the woman called out. She was resisting being put in the back of one of the deputies' cars. "Mark my words! *You. Will. Regret. Killing. My. Son!*"

Taco turned away from the hysterical woman. The fire still raged behind him, and there was a lot of work to be done.

Two weeks later, on a Saturday, Taco and Driftwood were grocery shopping to stock the fire station's pantry. Quinn had decided to accompany them, just so she could spend more time with her fiancé. They were having her former neighbor, Willard, over for dinner again the next night, and she was buying the ingredients for veal parmigiana.

Taco was impressed that Driftwood had made good on his dinner invitation to the man. Willard had truly been innocent of everything that had happened, and Taco knew his friend felt bad for thinking *he* was the one behind Quinn's kidnapping.

And, surprisingly, Quinn and Willard had hit it off extremely well. Beth and Sledge had eaten with them one night, and had rigged up a computer program that could talk as Willard typed. Taco had heard all about how hilarious Willard apparently was, and how the girls had laughed all night.

Taco was glad for his friends. They'd been through hell, and it was nice to see them both so happy now.

They were all laughing and chatting their way through the grocery store when they turned a corner—and Taco's cart slammed into another.

"Oh!" the woman pushing the cart said in surprise.

"I'm so sorry," Taco apologized immediately.

"It's my fault," the woman said. "I should've been paying attention."

"Koren?" Quinn asked.

"Quinn?"

"The one and the same!"

"I almost didn't recognize you with short hair!" Koren said.

Quinn laughed. "Because my birthmark was so hard to miss?"

"It actually looks like it's faded," Koren said with a little forehead wrinkle.

"Well, it has. I've been getting laser treatments," Quinn explained.

"Cool!"

"Oh, Koren, this is my fiancé, John, and this is his friend, Taco. They're both firefighters."

Koren gave them a little wave. "It's good to meet you." Then she stared at Taco for a beat longer. "Were you on the news recently?"

Taco immediately felt uncomfortable around Koren. For one, she had long blonde hair, like Jen had.

And any reminder of *that* colossal mistake he'd made wasn't good. But he also felt uneasy for another reason. He couldn't put his finger on why…just that she made him nervous.

"Yeah, he was the firefighter who found that poor kid the other week," Quinn told Koren.

"Oh my God. That was terrible. I'm so sorry. That had to be really hard on you."

Her words were sympathetic and polite, but Taco was already tired of being in the spotlight for that unfortunate event.

Though, for some reason, *Koren* recognizing him didn't irritate Taco.

But then, *not* being pissed off about it actually pissed him off.

Internally shaking his head at how ridiculous he was, Taco merely nodded at her.

Koren stared at him for a moment longer, as if she were trying to read his mind, before turning back to Quinn. "Well, it was good to see you again. I was sorry to hear about what happened to you too. Man, how crazy."

"You can say that again," Quinn agreed.

"I'm glad you're okay," Koren said, directing her words at both Quinn and Taco. "I need to get going. I'll see you later."

The second she was out of earshot, Quinn smacked Taco on the arm.

"Ow!" he yelped, grabbing the spot she'd hit. "What was that for?"

"For being rude to my friend."

"I wasn't rude!" he protested.

"You *were*. I wasn't setting you up for *90 Day Fiancé* or something. Jeez."

"What's that?"

"A reality show. Anyway, you didn't have to be so mean to her."

"I wasn't *mean*. At least, I wasn't trying to be."

Quinn looked around before stepping up to him and saying quietly, "I know she kinda looks like Jen, but the blonde hair is where the similarity ends. I don't really know Koren, but she was nice to me. She's not a psycho. Stop beating yourself up about what happened. It's done and over with."

"I know."

Quinn sighed, then nodded. "Good. Now, we still need breadcrumbs. Did we pass them already?"

Driftwood had been watching the interaction, but hadn't spoken, which Taco appreciated. He'd already gotten the third degree about not giving up on women or dating from the crew. He didn't need it again.

As they continued down the aisle and turned to head to the next one, Taco glanced over at the checkout lanes. Koren was standing in line, waiting for her turn to check out. She wore a pair of jeans that hugged her ass and thighs, and a tank top that showed off her curvy frame. Her hair might've been like Jen's, but their bodies were as different as night and day. Jen had been stick-thin, while Koren had curves in all the right places.

She was tapping her foot to an unknown beat. She was also staring down at her phone, probably doing what everyone else did when they were bored... scrolling through Facebook or something. She looked perfectly happy to be standing in line. Not irritated or impatient. It looked like she could stand there all night.

Unlike Jen. She was always irritated about something. And she hated waiting. Now he knew it was because she thought she was above everyone else, and should get preferential treatment. And when she didn't, she'd turned ugly.

Shaking his head again, Taco turned his attention back to what he was doing...namely, shopping for the station. He had to stop thinking about Jen. And he definitely wasn't ready to start dating again. Nope. He might not be ready for another ten years or so. If ever. Women were trouble. If he was going to start dating again, he needed a woman with no baggage, a good relationship with her family, no threat of homelessness...no drama, period.

Right. As if. He knew women like that were few and far between. Which meant he was safe.

Taking one last look at Koren, he swallowed hard. She had bent over her cart, resting her forearms on the handle. He couldn't help but look at her ass. It was at the perfect height for him to grab hold of her hips and—

He stopped his thoughts right there.

No. He wouldn't think about sex. The last time he got too desperate, he'd ended up dating a psycho cult leader. It didn't matter that they'd never actually gotten to the point of having sex…he'd been loyal to her and had done his best to help her fit in with his friends.

Turning his back on Koren and her delectable ass, he tried to convince himself that she was probably a bitch.

Regardless, and apparently unable to help himself, he turned his head yet again, and saw Koren smiling at an older lady holding a loaf of bread and a ham. She was gesturing for her to go ahead of her in line.

Sighing, Taco hurried to catch up with Driftwood and Quinn.

So what if Koren was pretty. Nice. Down to earth. Already friendly with Quinn…

She still wasn't for him. Nope. No way. No how.

* * *

Poor Taco. Look for his book, *Shelter for Koren* to come out SOON!

JOIN my Newsletter and find out about sales, free books, contests and new releases before anyone else!! Click HERE

Want to know when my books go on sale? Follow me on Bookbub HERE!

Also by Susan Stoker

Badge of Honor: Texas Heroes Series

Justice for Mackenzie
Justice for Mickie
Justice for Corrie
Justice for Laine (novella)
Shelter for Elizabeth
Justice for Boone
Shelter for Adeline
Shelter for Sophie
Justice for Erin
Justice for Milena
Shelter for Blythe
Justice for Hope
Shelter for Quinn
Shelter for Koren
Shelter for Penelope

Delta Team Two Series

Shielding Gillian
Shielding Kinley (Aug 2020)
Shielding Aspen (Oct 2020)
Shielding Riley (Jan 2021)
Shielding Devyn (TBA)
Shielding Ember (TBA)
Shielding Sierra (TBA)

Delta Force Heroes Series

Defending Allye
Defending Chloe
Defending Morgan
Defending Harlow
Defending Everly
Defending Zara
Defending Raven (June 2020)

Silverstone Series

Trusting Skylar (Dec 2020)
Trusting Taylor (TBA)
Trusting Molly (TBA)
Trusting Cassidy (TBA)

SEAL of Protection Series

Protecting Caroline
Protecting Alabama
Protecting Fiona
Marrying Caroline (novella)
Protecting Summer
Protecting Cheyenne
Protecting Jessyka
Protecting Julie (novella)
Protecting Melody
Protecting the Future
Protecting Kiera (novella)
Protecting Alabama's Kids (novella)
Protecting Dakota

Stand Alone

The Guardian Mist
Nature's Rift
A Princess for Cale
A Moment in Time- A Collection of Short Stories
Lambert's Lady

Special Operations Fan Fiction
http://www.AcesPress.com

Beyond Reality Series

Outback Hearts
Flaming Hearts
Frozen Hearts

Writing as Annie George:

Stepbrother Virgin (erotic novella)

ABOUT THE AUTHOR

New York Times, *USA Today* and *Wall Street Journal* Bestselling Author Susan Stoker has a heart as big as the state of Tennessee where she lives, but this all American girl has also spent the last twenty years living in Missouri, California, Colorado, Indiana, and Texas. She's married to a retired Army man who now gets to follow *her* around the country.

She debuted her first series in 2014 and quickly followed that up with the SEAL of Protection Series, which solidified her love of writing and creating stories readers can get lost in.

If you enjoyed this book, or any book, please consider leaving a review. It's appreciated by authors more than you'll know.

www.stokeraces.com
susan@stokeraces.com

Made in the USA
Columbia, SC
03 May 2022

59853269R00176